Adventuring

with Extreme

Prejudice

Alex Rollings

For Alison.

She knows why.

iv

Chapter 1

Percy winced as he was jostled in the saddle again. These roads had not been kind to his rear, and positively evil to his front. The horse, which Percy had affectionately named 'Big Smelly Bandit', really wasn't that big in reality, his shoulders standing no further from the ground than Percy's chest. It was this diminutive stature that caused Percy to rise and fall with the violent erratic-ness that would be more expected from atop a charger, storming into a vanguard.

"You're mocking me." He growled through gritted teeth. A cheerful whinny answered him. He sighed, fixing his eyes on the figure just ahead. Looking tremendously regal atop his beautiful black stallion, Marc had not paused for some hours. Nor had he spoken. In all that time not one murmur had betrayed the man.

"You said you'd teach me."

Percy wasn't sure if he had whispered or yelled that. In the eerie silence of the trail they followed, both were essentially the same. The silence reigned supreme for at least five minutes, with only the clippity-clop of hooves competing with it.

"Well, you're doing a grand job. Already, I've learned how to twiddle my thumbs with some skill. They rarely touch anymore. Do you think I should write home about this?" His words were filled with spite now, though he doubted Marc would notice. Early into their journey, he had seen the man's uncaring nature. That didn't bother Percy. What irritated him was that the warrior didn't even notice his anger, a lack of care was one thing, but observational skills were somewhat necessary for his supposed line of work.

'How can I learn how to spot danger from a man who cannot even tell the difference between anger and indifference?' He thought bitterly. He was unsure if his bitterness spawned from Marc's apparent ineptitude or whether it had more to do with the bruise on his behind causing him to spend every night sleeping on his front.

Percy nearly toppled from his saddle when the remarkably statuesque mentor broke his vow of silence. "If you're bored. List everything you see. And I expect my *apprentice* to appreciate silence." Said Marc. There was a tinge of annoyance to his words, but the emphasis on *apprentice* helped reassure Percy that he was not just a glorified and unpaid scribe.

It was with a defeated sigh that he began scribbling in his notebook:

1 x Boulder. Mossy. Looks like Marc's head.

3 x Pile of dung. Someone likes berries. Also looks like Marc's head.

Many x trees. Bark missing from few, deep gauges in many.

1 x dead deer. Head missing. No doubt it looked like Marc.

Percy's eyes were drawn back to the headless corpse; flies performed a drunken aerial dance above it as two foxes took it in turns to gradually diminish the cadaver. In these thick forests, teeming with life, all that would remain by the morning would be bones and the stench of natural selection.

He screwed up his face in distaste. As the child of academics, he had been sheltered from the ugliness of life, including trivial matters like death and that whole 'circle of life' thing. 'Survival of the fittest' was a saying that was simply out-dated and no longer relevant, at least in the mind of Percy. After all, his ancestral line of balding, overweight individuals who rarely exceeded the height of five foot extended back into the 'times of yore' when dragons roamed the land and gods still had a say in the lives of men.

Marc, however – thought Percy – certainly did live by this principle. The sword strapped across his back was the length of Percy's leg, and just as broad.

"I need a sword, don't you think I should have a sword? I mean, I would have thought that would be somewhat of a requirement." He said with a superior air, sure in his irrefutable logic.

"Somewhat," Marc replied.

"Then why do I not?"

"Because you did not bring one."

Percy opened his mouth to provide Marc with a witty retort, but he failed. So instead he mouthed the air as a fish would water before closing it and folding his arms childishly. He retreated into the blurred confines of his mind and began painting pictures there.

And they were grand pictures.

Daunting scenes flitted through his mind, battlefields which an armoured Percy dominated, where he could heft a claymore like it were a butter knife. The orcs that litter the field may as well be butter for how easily they were cut down. New images came into view, Percy walked hand-in-hand with a beautiful maiden who gazed up at him adoringly – as he was now seven feet of pure handsome and had a jaw like stone -. The sun was setting in the background, casting fiery light across the landscape and painting long shadows on a canvas of green and red. He would often surround himself in these fantasies when boredom took hold, or when his parents wanted to talk about his 'future in academia'.

Academia was not a future to Percy. It was a trap. Men and women surrounded themselves with walls of books, tomes and scrolls to ensure that they could not see what was advancing on them. Books would provide them with no defence when society eventually crumbles, and the walls built out of fear are destroyed by the fearless. Only a sharp edge would save Percy then. It was an exciting future to be sure.

His eyes fell to Marc's sword, confined within its plain scabbard and strapped across his back using a leather harness of sorts. The hilt was plain; cheap leather comprised the grip and the pommel was blunt and silver. Percy had yet to see the blade, but if it was anything like the rest of Marc, it would be bland and unimpressive. All in all, this was a far cry from what Percy had had in mind when Marc had described himself as an adventuring knight. There were no jewelled blades, swooning princesses and nary a dragon in sight: just the road and his trusty if somewhat foul-tempered steed.

A howl sounded through the dense forest, and a sense of primordial dread filled Percy, he turned to look in the general direction of the sound but could see no shadows in the eternal dusk of the forest.

"Just the wind," Marc said, never taking his eyes from the road. "The wind?" Percy snorted. "Did the wind grow claws and teeth? No, no, that was a wolf." He gazed between the trees, convincing himself that he could see furred forms moving about under the full canopy. "I've heard stories from this part; people go missing." He insisted, panic rising.

"People go missing from every part," Marc replied in an even tone. "The shadows eat them."

The image of a vast shadow filled his mind, gaping maw swallowing him whole. "Can… Can that happen?"

He asked gingerly. The only reply he got was a resigned sigh.

Percy kept a constant vigil, head snapping from one side to the other at the hint of a twig breaking or leaves rustling. Once again the silence was shattered by a hellish howl, closer this time and on the other side of the road.

"There! You cannot say that wasn't a wolf!" He almost shrieked.

"Of course, I can." Marc retorted. Percy took a deep breath, ready to release a torrent of complaints.

"Because that was a warg" Marc Continued.

A chill ran up Percy's spine. Wargs were common in children's stories. Nearly four times the size of a wolf and with a mean temperament they were said to attack travellers on the roads indiscriminately.

"That is no better!" He tried to say, but all that came out was a strangled squeak. He leaned to one side and began going through his pack, searching for anything he could use as a weapon. Quills, ink and parchment would do him no good. He attempted to devise a weapon comprised of a twig and sewing needles, all held together with pink thread. What he ended up with looked like a pin cushion that had sprouted a stem. He shook his head and stashed the abomination as deep in his bag as he could.

The only thing that had the slightest chance of stopping a warg would be Marc's sword. Its owner still seemed unconcerned by the tide of furry carnage that would no doubt be upon them at any moment.

"Almost there." His master said, raising a gloved hand and pointing toward a shape rising above the trees, obscured by the darkness but casting a stark silhouette against the night sky nonetheless. He could pick out the hazy silhouette of a manor house with battlements ringing its slanted roof, more for the aesthetic appeal over any protective function. As a cloud shifted from the moons face, its light allowed him to study it in more detail.

It was huge. Grander than any house Percy had seen in his home town, twice the size of Lord Lowry's house. Large, roughly-cut bricks had been used, and the windows were excessively big and lavish with bent metal spokes acting as patterns across them. The house was dark and lifeless; no light could be seen in any of the windows, not even that of a flickering candle.

"Is it abandoned?" Percy asked, his gaze fixed on the grand building.

"For nearly fifty years, aye. Owned by a Lord Landry, he owned this forest and the villages it hides. Not a nice guy though, met a gruesome end when the peasants

8

revolted against him and awarded him the rope necklace."
Marc steered his horse onto the gravel path leading to the
front gate set into a colossal wall.

Chains and a heavy iron padlock barred their way.
Percy snorted.

"It's locked? Are you certain it's abandoned?" he
asked.

"Quite," Marc replied as he slid down from his
saddle.

A rustling caused Perry to peer once again into the
darkness of the forest, searching for flickers of movement.
His heart was pounding now, and the constant threat was
wearing on him, whether that threat was real or not. A
metallic clash drew his eyes back to Marc. He had drawn
his sword, and the chain lay on the ground. As he pushed,
the gates slowly swung open with a horrible grating noise
that set Percy's teeth vibrating.

Marc lead his horse forwards down the drive, Percy
followed. The gardens surrounding the house were now
overgrown with weeds. A great fountain was covered in a
mass of vines and dead leaves. Percy could only imagine
how beautiful this garden must have been when the house
was still occupied.

One of the front doors hung open.

With great difficulty, Percy dismounted his horse at Marc's request. Marc took the reins.

"There's the stables. Wait here. Scream if you see a warg." Marc said as he led the horses towards the decrepit stables. Percy was confident he could hear mirth in the voice and proceeded to give the back of Marc's head a potent death-stare.

Through the open door, Percy could see nothing, only perfect darkness that seemed to swirl and flow as the wind stirred up dust.

Suddenly, the idea of camping with the wargs appeared to be the smart option. The darkness didn't scare Percy like the beasts of the forest; it made him feel uncomfortable, agitated and profoundly unwanted. Yet he felt drawn to it. The darkness didn't want him, but something in the gloom certainly did.

Marc's return startled him. "After you." He said.

Percy hesitated, looking at the doors like they were the gate to the underworld. He slowly approached the portal, pushing the door all the way open. He'd expected this to allow more light into the hallway beyond the door, but the darkness remained absolute. Summoning his courage, he stepped through onto the wooden floor. It creaked alarmingly.

Suddenly, he was thrown forward by a hand on his back which grasped him by the coat. He heard the door slam shut and turned to protest; Marc's voice cut him off.

"They're here." the warrior said in little more than a whisper.

Percy went silent and still while his heart did its best to be heard. In the blackness, he could just see the outline of Marc. He was crouched and had his ear pressed against the wood of the door. Percy frowned as he looked at what could only have been Marc's arm, it was extended and ended in a point. It took a moment to realise it was the sword, luckily the darkness hid his embarrassment at the mistake.

A deep, throaty growl cut through the silence like a rusty knife. Every hair on Percy's body stood on end as the monster investigated the door. He could hear it sniffing at the base and the occasional curious scratching as it probed the entrance for weaknesses.

Percy groped for anything that might pass as a weapon, the choice was between a candlestick and a chair-leg. He opted for the chair-leg and brandished it as though it was a broadsword.

Marc had one hand on the door-knob while the other clasped the grip of his sword. His plan was clear, he was going to open the door and impale the warg. A quick, easy kill. Percy silently willed him not to act.

Luckily, the noises became fainter, and they could hear the soft thuds as the warg retreated. They waited a further two minutes in silence before relaxing.

"The stables!" Percy whispered, panicking. "They'll kill the horses!"

"No. It's old but secure. Regardless, in a fight between a warg and that pony of yours, I know who I'd put my money on." He chuckled to himself.

Percy visibly relaxed. Marc had a point, he'd rather face the fury of a warg than the foul-tempered nag, and he doubted even a warg could best Marc's charger.

"We should have stayed in the stables with them!" He exclaimed after a moment's contemplation.

Marc shrugged in the gloom. "Too late now. See if you can find some candles. I'm going to barricade this door." He said as he began shuffling in search of furniture.

Percy turned his attention to the hallway, he couldn't see very far down it, so he rested his hand on the wall as he progressed down it. He felt his finger brush against the frames of what he assumed were portraits before touching the canvas. There were ragged tears in the majority of the paintings. 'Those peasants must have torn this place apart… Makes sense,' he thought as his hand finally plunged into emptiness. He felt for the frame of the door and stepped into the room. A window allowed the moonlight to faintly illuminate the room. He could make out several couches and tables, each was either on its side or reduced to firewood.

On the wall directly opposite the door, above an impressive marble fireplace was a family portrait. Lord Landry was about what Percy expected; tall, with fierce features and a mean look in his eyes. He had an unruly mane of jet-black hair streaked with silver. His hand rested on the back of the chair that his wife sat in. She was the opposite of her husband, with a round, soft face and a genuine smile. 'Must have made for an odd marriage' Percy observed.

On the other side of the chair was a girl, around Percy's age. Luckily, she had taken after her mother, though she had her father's hair. She looked afraid. Percy couldn't help but stare at the girl before laughing softly and shaking his head. 'Why would the painter catch her looking sad? It's your imagination, Percy.'

He dragged his eyes from the painting and set about his task. It didn't take long before he found another candlestick. This time it actually had candles in it.

Percy struck a match and lit the candles, illuminating the room in a flickering orange glow. He turned to appraise the painting in the new light.

Percy went cold.

The faces of the family had been slashed and torn to shreds. From the dust that had settled on the ragged etches and strips that dangled from the canvas, it hadn't happened recently.

Percy backed away from the painting.

"You found a light then," Marc said from the doorway, causing Percy to jump.

After a moment, he replied in a shaky voice. "Ah… Y-yes. Candles."

Marc looked Percy over. He was trembling.

"Did you see something?" He asked, his brow creasing with slight concern.

"Well…" Percy turned back to the painting "I saw the family. Their faces… Like the portrait was new and not all… Torn up."

"Hmm…" Marc pondered as he approached the painting. He crossed his arms and was silent for nearly a minute. "Blow out the candles." He demanded.

Percy frowned. He did not want to give up this source of light, it was the only comfort Percy had left.

14

"Do it." Marc commanded, looking over his shoulder at the boy. Percy obeyed.

At once, darkness flooded the room. It took a moment before moonlight crept up the walls and washed over the portrait. As it did so, the strips began taking their rightful places and fragments reappeared. It took roughly half a minute before the painting had restored itself to its former glory. Percy stared in shock.

Marc nodded to himself, stepping back until he was beside Percy. "It's the moonlight." He said aloud, Percy couldn't take his eyes away from the portrait.

"Lord Landry was rumoured to be practising magic. Pale magic to be specific."

Percy frowned, finally turning his eyes to Marc. "Pale magic?"

Marc nodded, deep in thought. "Well, while I'm no expert in magic… You see, Mages must take their power from somewhere… Witches take their power from nature generally, the trees, plants and animals. Mages stretch further, usually to the stars. Though, rarely, one will be adept at wielding the strange, cold magic that comes from the moon itself. When a great deal of Pale magic is cast in one place… This house, for example, it leaves traces behind. This painting is one such trace. The candlelight shows it as it is, the moonlight shows it as it was."

Marc caught a glance of Percy's confused face in the moonlight. He sighed.

"The moonlight will change things. Re-light the candles."

Chapter 2

The hours passed slowly.

Percy stared at the ceiling. They had fashioned two small beds from cushions and blankets. They were remarkably free of insects and almost clean.

Marc slept a foot or so to his left, with his sheathed sword beside him. Percy hugged his own. They had found a small armoury while exploring the house. The walls were covered with a variety of weapons, ranging from halberds to crossbows. Most were, according to Marc, purely ornamental, made from inferior metals. Upon inspection, Percy discovered that the crossbows didn't even have firing mechanisms.

Hidden away in a corner, however, was a small, painfully dull shortsword. Percy recognised it immediately as being the same sword used by the Triman legions over two centuries ago. Though it was nowhere near as impressive or devastating as the broadsword Marc wielded, it was light and fast and would do the job sufficiently. Plus, Percy had once attempted an ill-conceived swing with a broadsword and found himself being launched forward face-first into a tree. The short-sword was more than adequate. There were two words scratched crudely into the pommel of the blade, written in Triman. They translated as 'Honour Lost'. Percy briefly wondered if this was a bad omen. He dismissed it.

His eyes explored the room. It hadn't changed any more in the candlelight, the portrait was currently in tatters.

'Pale magic' Percy pondered 'how is it strange? I mean. Surely all magic is strange?'

He recalled an incident when a passing mage had gotten drunk and decided to demonstrate his awesome power. He claimed to have given a pigeon superior intellect. However, since the pigeon couldn't communicate this intellect, the townspeople had no choice but to call him a liar. Though, those who stared into the eyes of the pigeon did say they found it profoundly inspiring.

'So, in comparison to that… Pale magic is the *strange* one… How *fascinating*'

As he lay there, he rummaged through memories, compiling his knowledge of magic. Anecdotes heard from travellers, snippets of information and diagrams from old books all formed a relatively rudimentary understanding of the arcane arts. He didn't know much. He had always been more concerned with becoming the courageous warrior than the sickly mage. He had considered it far too scholarly and much too alike what his parents had planned for him.

'But *Pale* magic? Mysterious, cold and *strange*.'

He had to learn more. There had to be more knowledge in this house. Someplace where Lord Landry practised his *strange* magic. A sanctum of sorts.

'I mean.' He thought to himself, assuring himself that he was correct. 'It's not really something you do in the kitchen, is it?'

Slowly, he rose from the makeshift bed, careful not to wake Marc. He pondered whether he should take the candlestick or not. Marc was asleep, the lack of light wouldn't bother him, surely. Though he didn't want to leave his mentor bereft of any light in this place, he wasn't entirely sure why.

He plucked one candle from the stick and crept towards the door. Sneaking was impossible in this house;

19

the floor had become dry and warped and creaked alarmingly with every step. Marc didn't stir. For a survivalist, he slept heavily.

Once in the hallway, he gingerly pulled shut the living-room door. There was no click, and it slowly crept open until it was ajar. But it would do. Lifting the candle, he could appreciate the barricade that Marc built around the front door. Percy was still doubtful that it would stop the wargs if they really wanted to get in. When they explored the house, they found another entrance to the rear. However, it was locked. A chair was put in front of it just in case.

There was a door directly opposite the living room, which was the small armoury where they had found the sword. Towards the end of the hallway were two more doors and the staircase leading to the second floor of the house. One of those doors led into the kitchen, the other…

Well, they hadn't checked that one.

Why didn't they check that one?

'That wasn't there before' he realised with a jolt. Excitement wrestled with fear. For the first time in Percy's life, excitement won out, and he approached the door. He reached out with trembling fingers. The handle was cold.

Freezing cold. He pulled back his hand and clenched it a couple of times to let the blood flow through his fingers, warming them. On the second try, he opened it quickly and silently.

He held the candle through the opening to see beyond.

A staircase led downwards, at the end of the stairs was a white wooden door.

'A basement? Really?' Percy rethought his position 'I'm *really* going to go down to the basement of this old, abandoned, most likely haunted house?' he scoffed at the thought.

'Yes, I am. I *really* am.'

He wasn't certain that last thought was his own. But who else's could it be? Anyway, down the stairs we go. Before he could reassess the situation, he was standing before the white door. On closer inspection, he could see that it wasn't wooden, but more likely stone. He reached out and put the palm of his hand against it. It was cold and smooth like marble.

There was no handle, so he merely pushed. It gave little resistance before swinging open silently.

As the barrier gave way, air rushed into the room beyond, catching the flame of the candle and killing it. It took a moment to realise that while the fire was dead, the light remained.

There were several holes in the ceiling of this room, and mirrors were positioned under these holes, reflecting the white light of the moon towards what appeared to be a font in the centre of the room. The holes were not to the outside, but instead to tubes of mirrors, funnelling the light from outside and directing it at the font.

Slowly, Percy proceeded into the room. Besides the font and the mirrors, the room was bare of any decorations. The walls themselves had been painted black, and the floor had been paved with what looked like black marble. The font seemed to sprout seamlessly from the floor, as though it had grown from the stone.

As he drew nearer to the font, he could see that it was filled with water. Just ordinary water, illuminated by the light from the mirrors.

'It's only water' he thought to himself. 'Just water.'

He stared into the water. He could see something.

There was something in the water, a sliver of pure silver seemed to swim and twirl beneath the surface, and then it would disperse into a cloud before taking new shapes. Sometimes it was people, a family of three, then it would shift into an animal, then a pack of animals. He frowned and leaned closer to the surface to try and make out the features of the animal.

"A warg" he informed the empty room.

The wargs prowled through the small pool before in unison they turned to stare back at him. One by one, they dispersed and merged into one cloud. Again, it took form.

Percy almost laughed as he found himself staring into his own eyes, if his eyes were silver, that is.

He raised his hand, slowly lowering it to extend a finger into the water.

"It's called a Pale Fountain." Came a voice from the door, which was now shut.

Percy spun on his heels, grasping the grip of his shortsword and attempting to draw it. After a moment of fumbling with the clasp that secured it into the scabbard, he pulled it free and pointed it at the newcomer.

In front of the door stood a girl around Percy's age. Luckily, she had taken after her mother, though she had her father's hair. She didn't look afraid.

"I knew it was haunted." Percy blurted out.

The girl giggled, a smile tugging at the corners of her mouth.

'What, ghosts don't giggle, do they? That's not very threatening!' He thought frantically as his eyes moved up and down her. Her feet were very firmly on the ground, and there was no ethereal glow emanating from her. No chains dangled from her wrists, only a gold bracelet made from a chain of small fish. She wore a simple black dress with an embroidered collar and cuffs, it wasn't torn and didn't look particularly moth-eaten. If she were a ghost, then Percy would need to re-evaluate his perception of what ghosts are.

"I'm not a ghost" she said, as though she had read his mind. The smile had advanced to a grin, and she looked genuinely amused by the boy.

"No?" he replied, still pointing the tip of the blade at her "Then what are you exactly? You look just like the girl in the painting, but that was made fifty years ago!"

Her grin didn't falter, her eyes moved from him to the Pale Fountain.

"This entire house was built around it, you see. They're very rare, of course. Pale magic is *strange*." She said as she took a step towards it.

"It was you." Percy exclaimed with a creased brow "I shouldn't be down here… You were in my mind!"

The girl's grin grew again, and she suddenly looked very pleased with herself.

"Yup!" she said happily "I've never done that before, I wasn't certain it would work, you see. But I simply thought to myself 'Caitlin, if you don't try, you'll never know!', So I tried, and I succeeded! And now you're here!"

Percy didn't like that he had been manipulated, but she was currently blocking the door, and he wasn't certain he could best a gho-... *whatever* she was, with or without the shortsword.

"Why?" he asked.

"The fountain asked me to."

"Th-the fountain asked you too?" he asked, dubious.

She stepped forward until she was in front of the fountain, Percy circled around her until he was by the door, he let the tip of the sword lower slightly now that he was more certain he could escape if necessary.

As he watched, she dipped her fingers into the waters of the font, making lazy patterns before she cupped both hands and raised them out of the font, a small pool of water in her cupped hands. She turned and slowly walked to him, as she came closer, he let his hands fall until the sword hung uselessly from them.

She beamed as she looked up at him.

"Not just anyone can use Pale magic, you know. When the unworthy attempt to, they're inflicted with the curse. A terrible curse… But when a worthy candidate comes along… Well, they can do great things. It's said that a Pale Mage only comes along once every century or so." She said as she searched his eyes, she could see his fear, confusion and fascination, all fighting for dominance over the situation.

She looked back to the water, her expression growing solemn as she did so.

"My father… He thought he was worthy. It seemed to be true for a while, he did wonderful things. But it was all a trick, a cruel joke designed so that not only he would succumb to the curse. My mother and I were also affected. The townspeople came, tried to hang us. But the damned can't die that way, you know."

Percy couldn't tear his eyes from the small pool in her cupped hands, it was glowing a silver more vibrant than anything he had seen before. It was as though she held the moon in her hands. There was a terrible ringing in his ears, and her words had become distant, lost in the white haze that seemed to encircle his mind and ensnare his senses.

"But now, someone with the affinity has come. Drink deep of these waters, worthy one."

She lifted her hands to his lips and tipped them, Percy drank the water without hesitation. It was cold and delicious, fresher than any water he had drunk before. He felt the water spread out through his veins, along his limbs until the tips of his fingers and toes tingled slightly. After a moment, the coldness was gone, and warmth spread to every part of his body once again.

As the haze lifted, he could see Caitlin clearly. The sound of her voice came closer until he could hear her again, the veil over the world was raised once again.

"Now that my job has been done… I should be free…" she stared at her hands in confusion. "But I'm still here… Father said…"

Her eyes turned cold, and she snapped her head back towards the fountain like she was listening intently. Her face creased into confusion. She shook her head vigorously.

"No!" She screamed at the fountain. The ferocity of the voice caused Percy to take a step backwards and raise the sword. His senses were bright now, and he could see the immediate danger he was in.

"He lied! *It* lied!" She screamed as she turned her head back to him. His blood went cold. Her eyes had changed. Her pupils seemed to leak their darkness until her entire eyeball was black. She panted heavily.

She was transforming, Percy realised. He had read a chapter on transformations in the 'Monster Manual', and from what he knew, they weren't pretty. He wanted to run, to get away from whatever she was becoming. He couldn't run, he was transfixed by the spectacle unfurling before him.

As he stared in horror, she dropped to her hands and knees. Her limbs began to extend and expand with dense, wiry muscle. Her clothes seemed to dissolve as fur took their place. Her fingernails morphed into sharp, yellowed claws and her maw began extruding from her face. She opened her mouth, and a tortured squeal filled the air, as it did so, her teeth lengthened and sharpened until she had a mouth full of formidable fangs. She had tripled in size.

It took a moment for the realisation to hit Percy that he was now shut in a room with an angry warg. The newly transformed beast watched him with black eyes. Her jowls lifted into a snarl and saliva dripped from her maw.

Murder had manifested itself, and Percy was the object of its anger.

The sword would be useless, he knew.

'I'm going to die here. In the basement of a haunted house.' He thought to himself in resignation. 'That... Actually seems quite fitting'.

In the blink of an eye, the warg focused all the energy in its body into one explosive leap, and it dived towards him, its mouth was gaping open, ready to close on his throat. Percy instinctively leapt to the side, and at the same time, the door flew open.

The stone door connected with the warg's head with a sickening crack and it flopped back onto the ground limply.

Slowly, Percy turned to face the newcomer at the door.

Marc still had his boot raised. He lowered it to the floor and sighed deeply.

"When I say 'stay put and get some sleep', I did not, in fact, mean 'go investigate the basement and nearly get yourself mauled to death by a rabid warg'" he said in a weary voice.

Percy stared at him in shock.

"We need to move. More are coming." He said as he helped Percy to his feet. As though waiting for a cue, a cacophony of howls erupted. They ran up the stairs, swords drawn. The front door was rhythmically thumping inwards against the barricade. As it inched open, a snout pushed its way through the gap and sniffed the air, it then retreated, and the thumping began again.

The sound of claws being raked along wood came from the rear of the house, informing them that the back door was also under attack.

They were trapped between two beasts cursed by the moon itself.

This had not been what Percy had had in mind.

Percival

A week before

Percy let out an exasperated groan as he let his head rest on the back of the chair. He rubbed his eyes. The desk was covered in books. Old, dusty books that he suspected hadn't been opened in a great many years. He had found every book the library had on the warrior arts. Two volumes of weapons, their origins and proper methods of use were open to his right. On his left were several instruction manuals that detailed many of the fighting styles that were popular in the central kingdoms. Mixed in among them the 'Little Book of Big Weapons', a handbook which detailed some of the largest and most unusual weapons that existed. While flicking through that particular book it had occurred to Percy that if people put as much effort into creating medical devices as they did into making innovative killing machines, the arms race between killing people and saving people might never end.

The books directly in front of him were mostly history books that told the stories of several wars, detailing battle plans and the lives of the warriors made famous by them.

There was Bhoran the Berserker, leader of the alliance of mountain clans that challenged the Triman Legions. After a ten year campaign, he was eventually defeated and beheaded, but not before he had embarrassed the entire Triman Empire. After that, Rykus the Bold dominated the battle of Norran against the Morkan army. There was a painting that portrayed Rykus wading into the sea of Morkans, sweeping his battle-axe from side to side, decimating foes as he went. He later died to an unnamed soldier, but his name lives on through time as a legend. Another story told of the Wandering Prince, the elder brother of King George the Hungry, the current monarch. As the story goes, this prince revoked his birth rite to become king, in favour of wandering the land and finding his own source of fame.

Percy had smirked at that tale, everyone in the central kingdoms knew that King George had killed his brother and usurped his throne, 'The Wandering Prince' was just a story that the palace concocted to make the king seem innocent of any wrongdoing.

He rubbed his eyes before looking to the clock on the wall, it was well into the early hours of the morning. He had spent the day and night studying for tomorrow.

Tomorrow was going to be a very important day for Percy, perhaps the most significant day in his life so far. Tomorrow was the apprentice fair. The fair is a gathering where young men and women try to secure an apprenticeship with a master or mentor. It was split into three areas, the Tradesmen, the Scholars, and the Warriors.

His parents were expecting him to set up in the Scholars area to begin his exciting career with a professor or a historian. For the children of scholars, it was a cheaper option to enrolling in a university. He would learn from the professor while acting as an unpaid servant.

"More like a slave" Percy had commented when first researching his options.

Becoming a tradesman was roughly the same deal, the novice would aid the master in his work while learning the trade themselves, eventually taking over the masters art.

However, it was neither of these that Percy was interested in.

Percy wanted to be a warrior.

Percy the Brave had a nice ring to it. Perhaps Percy the Devastator. Though Percy was not a very warrior-sounding name. He would have to change it to something like Bruce or Jock, something suitably manly.

He would be attempting to secure the position of squire to a passing hedge knight. This would give him the chance to explore as well as to learn from the knight as he travels from place to place, slaying dragons and saving damsels.

He grinned as he contemplated what his future would now surely hold. One day he could be a fully-fledged knight with a suit of shining armour. King George himself would award him the knighthood for his heroic deeds. Perhaps he'll be the one that slays the dragons, though, he was fully aware that the dragons were gone. Even with the scores of knights and hunters that trailed them through the kingdoms, these were not their greatest enemy. In the end, time wore them down. They stopped laying eggs and allowed their species to just die out.

The death of the dragons was one of the greatest mysteries still to be solved. They were great, armoured monsters with enormous leather wings. Their claws were harder than steel, and their flames would turn whole legions to ash with no effort. They were nearly invincible and lived longer than any other creature. The most ancient of dragons had watched the kingdoms and empires of man rise and fall, but still, they let their kind become extinct. Just one of the many mysteries that Percy would uncover while creating his own legend.

"I should sleep...," he said out loud.

After rising from his seat he put his hands on his hips and leaned back, there were several loud clicks, a testament to how long he had been studying.

His room was small, there was his desk, a chair, and a bed. The rest of the room consisted of bookshelves. There was also a wardrobe, but he had long ago cleared his clothes out of it – which had been banished to a pile on the floor – to make way for more books. When he had run out of space on the shelves he had begun to pile the books on the floor, the tallest of these piles had reached his waist some time ago.

Percy had a meagre income which he gained from doing 'odd jobs' around town and every harvest he would help, this gave him some extra coin with which to buy as many books as he pleased. The majority were reprints, he was a frequent visitor at the printing presses where he would purchase rejects and miss-prints cheaply. Using this technique he had amassed an impressive collection of mostly legible books.

The pride of his collection was a rare first edition of the 'Monster Manual', a large tome which had a page dedicated to each of the known monsters and beasts inhabiting Urn. A new version was released every year as new creatures were discovered every year, so while Percy's version was not particularly up-to-date, it was more valuable and had more detail on some of the more classic monsters.

He fell face-first onto his bed, burying his face into his pillow. Once again, he allowed himself to slip into his fantasies, creating a scenario in which he was staring up at a dark tower, above it, angry clouds broiled and lightning streaked through the sky, casting erratic shadows over the landscape.

Wielding a sword roughly the size of an ironing board, he charged the tower, screaming a war cry at the top of his lungs. As he neared the tower, he fell into a deep sleep.

A knock at his door roused Percy from his slumber. He grumbled to himself, this always seemed to happen just after he had saved the princess and before he could collect his reward. Typical.

"Percival" the voice called, slightly muffled by the door. "It's time you woke, the fair opens soon. Up and at 'em sweetheart."

Percy grunted a reply at the door, and his mother left. He rolled onto his back and rubbed his eyes to get rid of the sleep. He let out an irritated groan, he'd barely had half a night's sleep.

Slowly, he sat up and lowered his feet to the floor. He could see out of the window from this height, and he could just see the sun peeking over the roofs of his neighbour's house. Not too far beyond that was the town square and the fair.

A smile spread across his face as a realisation dawned on him. If today went well, this could be his last day in this town and the first step in his journey to become a legend.

He washed quickly before dressing. His mother had already laid out clothes for him, they consisted of an embroidered vest and plain cotton trousers, as well as a pair of soft-soled shoes. This was perfectly suitable attire for a young man aiming to be taken on by a scholar, they communicated how humble he was.

However, it would not do for a warrior-in-training. Percy had hidden a pair of heavy boots, a cloak and a leather jerkin in his bag and intended to change somewhere between his house and the town square. He had even padded the jerkin slightly to make himself appear less scrawny, though in truth it only made him look odd and disproportionate.

Once he had changed into the outfit that would impress the scholars, he descended the stairs. He followed his nose to the kitchen.

"Ah, there you are." Percy's mother beamed as she looked him up and down. "You look so grown up!" she exclaimed, clapping her hands in excitement. Unlike the men of Percy's family, his mother was tall and fair-haired with a friendly face and a kind nature.

"I *am* all grown up, mother," Percy replied in the tone that by law all teenage boys have to address their mother with, a mixture of embarrassment and shame. Percy had turned seventeen a month prior, old for an apprentice of the trades and warriors, but perfect for that of the scholar who tended to take on older apprentices who have had a chance to gain a more 'overall' knowledge of the world before they specialise.

"Don't speak back to your mother," his father said automatically. He was sitting at the breakfast table with two books open before him and a plate heaped with toast beside them. He had a feather quill and was copying the contents of one book into the other. The invention of printing presses had mostly done away with hand-scribed books, but for old books for which plates had not yet been made, hand-scribing was still necessary. His father did this to supplement his wage as a teacher.

He was typical of the family line, short, overweight and balding. He largely ignored Percy and much preferred the company of his books to his own family.

"Good morning father," Percy said as he moved forwards, taking a plate from his mother. His breakfast was a special one, overflowing with sausages, eggs and half a loaf of bread saturated with a rich strawberry preserve. He looked at the plate, then his mother quizzically.

"This is enough to feed a horse, mother."

"Well… It's a big day! My little man's going to become an apprentice finally." She replied while shooing him over to the table. He took a seat and began to pick his way through the feast.

His mother took a seat next to Percy with a small breakfast of cheese and bread.

"You know…" his mother started, speaking between mouthfuls "Marcus Mertoni is rumoured to be attending today."

"The tax auditor?" Percy asked with a frown. Marcus Mertoni was a horrible little man who was hated throughout the town, primarily for his meticulous attention to detail. No resident had ever been able to cheat on how much they owed when Mertoni was around. This gained him begrudging respect from other scholars as well as mathematicians.

"The one and only. Perhaps if you get his attention, you could be the future auditor for this region! It pays well, and you get living quarters right by Lord Lowry's *estate*!" she exclaimed, putting a dramatic flair on 'estate'.

"And you'll only be hated by most of the town." Percy's father added from the end of the table, the corners of his mouth twitched into a smile before he caught his wife's eye. He propped a book up to make a barrier between himself and the rest of the table. "Never mind." He mumbled, "I'm sure being hated isn't *that* bad."

Percy's mother waved a dismissive hand at her husband. "Pay him no notice, Percival. This is *your* future you determine today, make the most of it. You're a well-educated, well-mannered, well-fed boy."

"-Man" Percy interrupted with a sour glance.

"…Man." His mother conceded with a sad smile. "The world is your oyster and all that… Oh, and pick up a loaf of bread while you're out."

Percival 2

As Percy left the house, he mulled over his mother's words. She'd had no idea how true they were. He felt a pang of guilt for the trick he was about to pull. But they had given him no choice, this was his only chance to separate himself from the life they had plotted for him, his only opportunity to forge himself a future that wasn't tedious, that would instead be filled with excitement and danger.

He attempted to console himself by insisting that before long they would congratulate him on the bold choice he would make today. It didn't work, so instead, he indulged in self-righteousness.

'Who are they to control my life anyway? Simply being my parents doesn't give them the right to stop me from fulfilling my destiny! I'm a grown man now, men should take up the sword and wander the world, creating the stories that will inspire the next generation to do the same!' He smiled to himself, convinced now that he was in the right, as usual, his parents were uninformed and nonsensical.

He ducked behind some bushes and changed into his 'warrior garb'. He checked his appearance in a shop window as he passed. He hadn't quite been able to catch the 'brave, capable warrior' appearance he had been looking for. Instead, he looked remarkably like a small child wearing his father's jerkin and boots. It would have to do, so he carried on.

He took his time to savour his surroundings, after all, it was important for a hero to remember his home, he had read many quotes that came from famous warriors who fought not for themselves, but to protect their homes. And others spoke of how they yearned for their home and sweetheart. Well, Percy had no sweetheart, he liked to believe the girls of his hometown were intimidated by his intellect, but in all likeliness, it had more to do with his short stature and how he exuded unease when approached by a member of the fairer sex. So he would have to settle for the other.

His town was fairly idyllic and wealthy. The homes and gardens were well-kept, and many were extravagant. Hedge-trimming had become a favorite pass-time recently and all around, hedges had been cut into strange shapes, depicting animals and symbols.

'Drat.' Thought Percy 'It would have made for a better tale if I came from some hell-hole.' He frowned lightly.

He was approaching the town square now and could see the tops of the large tents they had set up. Like in previous years, they had split the square into four segments, one for scholars, one for the tradesmen and one for the warriors. In the fourth segment, they had set up a small market to take advantage of the large number of attendants. This fair served not only this town but also the surrounding countryside and villages. It wasn't unusual for apprentices to have to relocate to other settlements after securing apprenticeships.

A crowd was already gathering. Percy recognised a number of his classmates from school. The majority were gathered outside the Scholar Tent, with a small huddle by the Tradesmen's tent.

Some of them looked excited, most looked nervous, and a few looked positively terrified. For a scholar who didn't gain an apprenticeship, there were few options. They could enrol in a costly university, or work in mind-numbing jobs for a year before the next fair. With every year, their chances of being taken on decreased, so the pressure to impress was immense.

Percy walked past these tents, drawing curious looks from his classmates. He enjoyed their surprise but didn't appreciate the doubting expressions.

The line for the warrior's tent was much shorter. In a relatively peaceful region like this, there wasn't much call for warriors, even though there was always work for a mercenary or a beast-hunter. However, for knights and the honourable, work was scarcer, often entailing tedious guard-duty or being a Lord's bodyguard.

Percy took the small number of candidates as a good sign, it meant there would be less competition. However, out of all the candidates, he certainly looked the least capable. At the front of the line, there was a group of boys, possibly a year or two younger than Percy, but they were twice his size, they had square jaws and heavy brows. Each wore some armour and had a sword at their hips, likely to be gifts from their parents. They were all polished to perfection, and their armour shone in the sunlight. They would be the first to be grabbed, Percy knew that he couldn't compete with them.

Behind these were the less obvious candidates, some were smaller with lean muscles, some were tall and well-built but had little in their heads. Only some of these were armoured, but all carried weapons.

At the end of the line, just in front of Percy were the undesirables. Small and sharp, these candidates came from the more impoverished families in town. Percy had been told that the majority of these would take the skills they learn and turn to banditry, it was unlikely any of them would be heroes. Percy scoffed and dismissed the thought that they were competition to him.

While Percy was physically less able than his competition, he had one thing many of the others didn't.

He had his brain.

Percy hadn't spent the night studying for nothing, he would dazzle his future mentor with his extensive knowledge of battle formations, proper warrior etiquette and the monsters of the wilds.

He let a grin spread across his face.

'These fools don't stand a chance!' he thought smugly.

Two guards stood at the entrance, wearing the tabard of Lord Lowry's household. Lord Lowry would not be at the fair, but his guards would make sure his presence was felt keenly.

The candidates filed into the tent. There were several stands where each candidate was supposed to lay out information about themselves, their experience and any awards they had won that would be relevant. Percy found a vacant stand and began laying out the paltry number of items he had brought.

His items included:

- His bronze and silver swimming awards.
- A copy of his school grades, with his results in History and Theoretical Battle Strategy, underlined and his mark from Practical Warrior Skills crossed out. This also had a list of the languages Percy spoke, or could at least recognise.
- A written recommendation from one of his teachers. Percy had tricked the teacher into thinking this recommendation was for the scholar's tent. With some clever alterations,

it looked like the teacher was praising Percy's strength and skill.

- A short statement he had written about himself, stating his aspirations and the benefits of taking him on as an apprentice.

He looked at the few items with a frown. It wasn't much compared to those around him, but it would have to do.

They were given a few minutes to set up before the masters began entering the tent. Percy inspected each closely. The first man through the door was tall, well-muscled and clad in the armour of a knight of House Lowry. He would most likely be looking for a squire. Percy wasn't interested in spending his life in the Lord's court, so he dismissed him and moved onto the second attendee. This man was a better option, he didn't wear any armour, and this most likely meant that he wasn't required to wear it at all times like the knight was. His clothes weren't overly fancy; instead, they were practical and looked somewhat worn, this hinted at the man being an adventurer.

Percy cleared his throat and spoke as the man passed. "Excuse me, sir!" the man turned and regarded Percy with a critical eye. Percy continued "Are you looking for a capable apprentice with more in his head that just a thick skull? Well, then look no further!"

Percy grinned as he repeated what he had written the night before. The man approached, clearly amused by the boy.

"Oh? Is that right?" He asked, looking over Percy's items. He picked up the letter of recommendation. "Oh my, high praise indeed."

Percy's heart leapt; this was going well!

"Oh yes, they've taken to calling me Percy the Magnificent around these parts you see. My skill is unmatched!" he exclaimed. He had passed 'bending the truth' long ago and was now in the territory of 'flat out lies', so he decided to enjoy himself.

"Oh yes, it's quite a strain having to fight every monster that comes within a ten-mile radius of the town, but I do it because I'm the only one who can. Of course, I don't have to tell you about the pressure placed on a warrior these days!"

"No, indeed you don't. Tell me, if you're already so adept then why do you require a mentor?" the man replied, scrutinising Percy's grade-sheet.

"Ah… Well…" Percy faltered, finding it challenging to come up with a suitable lie.

"Because the way that I see it, I can teach these other young 'uns, but I can't make you grow an extra foot." He said with a smile, placing the sheet back on the table.

The man walked away as Percy stood, shocked. His plan hadn't worked. The mentors weren't looking for someone as intelligent as he was, they were looking for someone mouldable and who they could teach. Otherwise, what would be the point of having an apprentice? He factored that into his next approach.

Time and time again he attempted to tempt mentors over to his stand. A few even approached to hear Percy spout lie after lie about himself and inspect his items. Each one had the same response. Percy was either too short, too smart or too scrawny. The majority of the mentors doubted whether or not Percy could withstand the trials put on a warrior. A number even mentioned that he might have more luck in the scholar tent.

Over time, the other candidates began to pack up their items, shaking hands with their new mentors. Contracts were signed. As he had expected, those who had been at the front of the line, those he had nicknamed the 'thick-skull parade' were all gone, having been picked mostly by knights. Many of the less obvious ones had also found an apprenticeship with a variety of mentors. Even a few of the 'undesirables' were gone, having been picked by men and even a few women who were obviously mercenaries.

Before he knew it, he was one of the only hopeful apprentices remaining. It had been some time since the last mentor had left.

'Well… That's that then' Percy thought, feeling a depression seizing him. 'What am I going to tell my parents? "Oh, well, worth a shot, right?"' He pictured their faces. His mother would be more shocked than angry, he could see his father's disappointment clearly. He could hear his voice 'Well… I guess we should have expected you to do something this stupid, Percival' he would say before he went back to his books.

His heart lifted slightly as a newcomer entered the tent. He wore a cloak, and his hood had been pushed back to reveal his face. He had a broad face and slightly flattened features, he seemed familiar to Percy. After a moment he put it down to the fact that several like him had come and gone throughout the day, probably looking for a seven-foot behemoth with arms like tree-trunks. Percy didn't hold much hope.

One by one the man visited each stand, asking several questions of each hopeful. Each failed to satisfy him. Percy took a little pleasure from seeing each being turned down, then it was his turn.

"Name?" He asked. His voice was gruff but carried well. It was the kind of voice that gave orders, but he couldn't imagine it saying 'Yes, sir'.

"Ah… Percy."

"Percy. Can you read?"

"Yes."

"Can you write?"

"Well… Yes."

"How well?"

"Well… I was top of my class in most subjects… My parents are scholars… But I can fight too! Don't you wo-"

"You speak several languages and can read Old Triman?"

"Well, strictly speaking-"

"You'll do."

Percy blinked, shocked by the suddenness of the decision.

"Uh…" He started "Wait… What exactly are you? What do you do?"

The man thought for a moment before replying with a slight shrug. "I'm an adventuring knight, I guess you could say." He replied cagily.

Percy glanced around, the other attendees were watching their exchange with evident surprise. One was slowly banging his head against his table in frustration. He then took a closer look at his possible mentor-to-be. He looked capable enough, there was clearly some armour under his cloak as he could see the outline of some pauldrons. He wore no surcoat.

He didn't look particularly dishonest, in fact, the man's calm grey eyes actually looked rather kind.

"And you'll take me with you on your adventures? Teach me to become a warrior?" He queried.

"I believe that's the typical arrangement. Yes."

"So… What will my duties be?"

The man frowned and thought on this for a moment.

"You will learn… You'll carry equipment as well as looking after the horses. Everything a knight might expect a squire to do."

Percy grimaced, he didn't want to be a squire.

"I'm sorry… I have no interest in sitting in a Lord's court for the rest of my life."

Percy screamed at himself internally 'what do you think you're doing!? This could be your only chance!'.

"I wouldn't worry too much. Like I said, I'm an adventurer. As will you be. I suppose you could say I'm an ex-knight."

Percy raised an eyebrow in surprise "You were banished by your Lord?"

The man smirked. "No, that's not quite right, think of it as voluntary suspension."

Percy frowned and took a moment to assess the situation. A man who called himself an 'adventuring knight', wishes for Percy to join him in his travels. So far, he had yet to give any information on what they will be doing during these adventures and seems to value intelligence and literacy over fighting ability. This was a strange case indeed and not one he had accounted for.

But this could be his only chance, it wasn't like there was a crowd jostling to give him an apprenticeship. He quickly weighed up the potential dangers and benefits of this particular partnership and finally came to the conclusion that he really had no choice in the matter.

"Well, then I accept your offer, Mister…"

"You can call me Marc."

Chapter 3

Present day

Percy looked around desperately, he was holding onto the grip of his sword so hard that his knuckles were turning white.

A sudden crash from the back of the house let them know that the back-door lock had not been designed to withstand the whirlwind of teeth and claws that the warg had subjected it to. There was no time left, they had to run. Marc had already started.

Percy hadn't noticed that the warrior had started up the stairs, taking them three at a time. He cursed under his breath and followed him. As he reached the second-floor landing, he saw Marc disappear into a room. He followed him, and Marc slammed the door shut. Ten seconds later, he had constructed a barricade.

Once he had finished, he scanned the room. It was the master bedroom and had a large, four-poster bed. There was also a huge wardrobe and a dressing table. The wide window had bars across it, barring their escape.

"The attic." He said suddenly.

Marc looked at him quizzically before his eyes flickered to the ceiling, a plan unfolding. He retrieved the chair sitting before the dressing table and stepped onto it. It creaked ominously but held regardless.

Percy held onto the back of the chair as Marc began to viciously attack the ceiling. Plaster rained down with every strike. Percy heard the front door barricade topple.

"So, the one that came in the back door helped the one at the front from the inside? They still retain some of their human intelligence then…" He said, curiosity replacing his fear momentarily.

"Not the time to analyse their behaviour, Percy" replied Marc. The hole in the ceiling was getting larger with every strike. He had reached the wooden planks covering the floor of the attic and was having to put more effort into each jab.

There was a loud thump as a furry body threw itself at the door to the bedroom, he saw the barricade jerk backwards with every strike.

"Eh… Marc…" He ventured, his breath was ragged, and he felt the panic rising. Marc didn't reply and instead continued his attack. There was another bang, and the barricade jolted. A furry head pushed its way through the gap it had made. He could see the insanity in its eyes.

"Marc!" He yelled as he felt the panic overtake him. Once the warg had created an opening wide enough, its colossal paw began clawing at the barricade, knocking some of the furniture over while tearing others apart.

"MARC!"

The air left his lungs as he was hoisted up through the hole. He grasped the edges of the wooden flooring above and added his own strength.

He found himself in the attic. It was a sparse room with no furniture, he had expected boxes full of children's toys and souvenirs from family holidays, wasn't that what was in every attic? This was just an empty room with a sloping ceiling and a window at the end. A window with thick metal bars protecting it.

Fingers grasped at the edges of the hole, he reached down and grabbed onto Marc's cuffs. However, he provided little aid as Marc was a large man in armour and there were toddlers stronger than Percy.

Marc grunted as he hauled himself up, he was halfway through the hole when the barricade crumbled. The door flung open, and two wargs fought to be the first through it, once the fight was settled the larger lunged upwards, attempting to close its jaws on Marc's leg. He narrowly missed, and Marc pulled himself into the attic.

He panted and watched through the hole as the beasts prowled through the room, the smaller one snarled, sending a chill through Percy's soul.

"They shouldn't be able to get up here…" Marc said between gasps "There's a trap door leading to the hall, we can drop down and make a run for it. Either that or we wait them out."

Percy sighed and turned his attention back to the wargs below, and his blood turned cold. One had begun nudging the pile that had formerly been the barricade towards the hole. The other watched what it was doing for a moment before helping. Their plan was evident. Percy felt a cold sweat coming on.

"I don't think that's really an option." He said, looking at Marc who had come to the same conclusion. He looked past him to the window. "Could we break those bars?" He asked.

Marc barely glanced at the bars before replying. "Unlikely. As you could probably tell from the huge, thick wall surrounding the entire estate, security here was pretty important."

Percy sighed and pondered their situation. A crazy, impossible thought found purchase in his mind.

"Do you have any more matches?"

Marc looked at him dubiously before he looked again at the window. Percy could see the realisation hit him. He chuckled before shrugging.

"Worth a shot I suppose."

He moved towards the window. The universe had sensed their dire situation and decided they were not worthy of a break, lightning illuminated the edges of the window and the landscape outside. Something was moving through the darkness, but the rain made it impossible to see clearly. The two wargs were in the room below, so unless the one in the basement had resurrected itself, it must be something new.

He produced a small box of matches and pulled one out. He struck it against the rough strip. The light hit the window, and at once, the glass disappeared, and the rain and wind hit his face. The bars broke and bent outwards. Something had been thrown out of this window with enough force to break the bars. He laughed and guarded the match with his hand.

Percy couldn't believe he was right. He thanked the gods for blind luck.

"It's not too far down! I think I could drop to the ground from here."

Marc looked doubtful. "There was something out there. Something moving."

Percy scanned the garden. Nothing.

"I thought there would only be three…" He said, beginning to wonder if Caitlin had actually died, or had merely been knocked unconscious. He silently scolded himself for not plunging the sword into her throat when he had the chance.

"We don't have much of a choice." He said.

He swung one leg up and over the edge of the window, time had removed the sharp corners of the broken glass. He pulled up the other leg and ducked his head through. The drop was more than enough to seriously injure him. He factored the soft, overgrown garden into the equation and surmised that the most damage he might do is a twisted ankle. This was an optimistic estimation, to say the least.

'Why am I doing this? And why am I first? Marc is the expert!' his inner voice screamed at him, baffled by his recent stupidity. He knew precisely why he had taken so many risks and why he was jumping first now. He wanted to impress Marc. Perhaps Marc had been waiting for a situation like this to test Percy. Maybe he had known all along what they would find in this house and the dangers they would face. Perhaps this was a test. Percy had never failed a test in his life – except those silly warrior arts tests which he didn't think would have prepared him for something like this anyway – and he wasn't about to start now.

He dropped like a stone. He closed his eyes so that he wouldn't see the ground rapidly advancing towards him. After a second, he felt a strange sensation, as though his descent was slowing. It was too brief to be sure of anything, and as he felt his feet hit the ground, he bent his knees as he had been taught. Rather than the horrific impact he had been expecting, it was light and pain-free.

'Well, of course, you weigh nothing!' he realised with a short laugh of victory.

If his landing was soft, Marc's was anything but. Marc hit the ground with the force of a war hammer and left a sizeable crater beneath him. He had done the same as Percy and bent his knees, but as he hit the ground, they buckled, and he fell forward. Rising from his undignified position on the ground was clearly difficult, and he grunted with the exertion.

From here, Percy could see the front door. He half-expected to see three pairs of black eyes. But the hallway was empty, and the racket still came from upstairs. The beasts had not discovered their escape yet.

"Come on," Marc commanded as he set off on a clumsy jog towards the stables. Percy noticed a pronounced limp in the man's gait but said nothing.

They arrived at the stables thoroughly soaked through. Percy shivered uncontrollably and had spent the journey glancing over his shoulder every other pace. Nothing followed them, but it was only a matter of time.

They entered the stables, relieved to be out of the rain, if only for a moment. 'Big Smelly Bandit' and Marc's charger – which Percy was reasonably sure had a name like Titan or Stomper – were in two separate stalls, quite happily staring into space. Titan turned his head to appraise his master, but Big Smelly Bandit found the wall directly in front of him more interesting.

Marc took the reins of each horse and began leading them towards the stables door. He stopped and swore creatively.

Caitlin's grin was crooked now, but it would seem the facial damage had only served to make it bigger. She had reverted back to her human form, but this made her no less terrifying.

"Oh, Percy." She said with a shake of her head "You're leaving already? But I've been dying to have you for dinner! I know I know, corny, but I've been waiting for years to say that!".

"Move, girl," Marc said in a frightening tone moulded by pain and necessity. Caitlin eyed the man warily.

"I was angry before… The fountain lied. Everyone lied. You can't really blame me when you think about it. But I've come to my senses! I understand why I wasn't freed, I understand everything! That door really 'knocked the sense' into me, you might say!" she continued. Her expressions were erratic, shifting from a maniacal grin to the very image of depression in a heartbeat.

Percy felt a pang of sympathy for her. For fifty years she had endured a curse due to the foolish actions of her father. She wasn't to blame in any of this. She was broken and betrayed. At the time his feelings seemed genuine and not alien.

"My redemption, my salvation will not be achieved by *killing* you! Well, that was simply foolish of me, wasn't it?" she continued, taking a step towards them. Marc raised his sword threateningly, and she stopped. "I'm supposed to *protect* you! The fountain has blessed you!"

Marc glanced at Percy, it occurred to Percy that while Marc may have figured out the curse, he didn't know anything else about what had transpired in the basement.

"Uh… I-I don't know what you're talking about" he said nervously. This could complicate his apprenticeship, he wanted to avoid it.

"Yes, you do! Don't worry though. I'll help you. I'm no expert, but I know a little…" she said desperately.

Taking her with them suddenly began to make sense. Percy was no fool, he knew that drinking the water had started something. He would need her. She was insane, but next time she tried to transform, he would be ready. He would kill her. He prayed he would have the strength.

"She's right." He said. Marc burst into a sudden bout of laughter. For about twenty seconds he was bent double, tears streaming down his face. Even Caitlin was looking at him like he was the insane one. He straightened up and wiped the tears from his eyes.

"Oh yes, of course, she's right. Let's take the homicidal, cursed shape-shifter, with all the sanity of a crazed lemur. That would make sense."

He eyed her and smirked.

"If you change, I'll kill you. I'm not like the boy, I won't hesitate. I don't have a heart." He said.

They believed him.

Caitlin

Fifty Years Before

Caitlin stood at the window of her bedroom with a curious frown etched on her face. There was a light advancing through the forest. First, it had been a trickle of little lights, like fireflies, increasing in brightness with every second. Then it became a steady river, the lights intermingling and merging into a single warm glow, then it stopped abruptly. Perhaps there was an army of fireflies marching through the forest. Probably on their way to face the Grasshopper clans of the mire, or the subterranean empire of the ants.

She smiled at the fantasy and filed the thought away for later. She lived for stories. Though not those boring

66

ones of men shaped like boulders clashing with other men shaped like boulders. She enjoyed the fantasy stories her father would tell her before she went to sleep each night. Fantastical tales of mythical creatures living in worlds brimming with magic and wonder, or the humorous stories of Bomm, the useless wizard who's every spell would go awry which always left her in fits of uncontrollable laughter.

She was free to indulge herself in childish fantasy, though she had become a woman almost a year ago, the isolation of her home allowed her to mature slowly, free from responsibilities and the pressures of having peers. She was lonely sometimes, but then she would play her games and forget that other humans even existed.

She leaned closer to the window and narrowed her eyes. She could make out the source of the light now that it had appeared from behind the thick cover of trees.

The flames of the torches flickered in the wind, their bearers had angry expressions, and those who were not carrying torches instead carried pitchforks, swords or axes. The sound of the mob reached her. For the most part, it sounded like senseless yelling, but a few words carried to her. *Monster* was one, *evil* was another.

"Well, there's no one like that here," she said out loud, shaking her head in disbelief, convinced that they had come to the wrong house.

Her mother and Lady of the house burst through the door. She crossed the room and grabbed her daughters' arm.

"Come, Caitlin. We must hide you." She hissed as she tugged frantically on Caitlin's arm. The girl resisted, looking at her mother with confused defiance.

"Hide me? Why ever should I hide?" she said with clear indignation. She had done nothing wrong, and neither had her family, yet here came the peasants with their torches and clubs. Well, she would give them a piece of her mind! "I'll march out there right now and explain to them very clearly that they have made a mistake, but that's alright, everyone makes mistakes. You just watch, we'll all be laughing and eating cakes within the hour." She insisted, but her mother would not relent, and she was pulled towards the door.

In the hallway, she could see the hatch to the attic, it was open, and a ladder led up to it, Lady Landry pushed her towards it.

"Up! Up!" she commanded. Caitlin obeyed, grumbling as she ascended the ladder, her mother pushed her from below.

Upon reaching the hatch, she hauled herself up and stood upon the uneven wooden floor. Her mother followed her up, shutting the hatch behind her and locking it. She hurried to Caitlin's side and wrapped her in a desperate embrace, squeezing her tight enough for Caitlin to gasp a little when she finally let go.

"Now, my sweetheart." She whispered. "You can't go down. Do you understand? You must remain here where it's safe." She smiled, but Caitlin could see the desperation and fear in it. Her bottom lip was trembling. Her eyes were less revealing, but the fear was present there also. Caitlin was beginning to understand the gravity of the situation.

"Daddy's magic…" she whispered.

Her mother nodded with a sad smile. Tears had begun to well in her eyes. "Daddy's magic." She echoed.

Caitlin may have been fanciful, but she was no fool, she was fully aware that her father's trips to the basement – to the strange black fountain she had glimpsed once – had something to do with the strange events that had been occurring in the forest.

The effects first began to manifest when large animals were found torn open in the forest. While this was not that strange in a forest full of capable predators, what was weird was that they were not eaten, like they had been killed for the sport. The second occurrence was when two known wolf packs abandoned their territories and travelled north, away from the house. This caused them to come into contact with the humans of several villages, ending in injuries and even a death.

Then the murders began. Reports came in of men and women found on the roads with wounds similar to those of the beasts.

At the epicentre of these events was the Landry household.

She had known something wasn't right. Her mind had used this fuel to concoct a story. Her father had created something, he had created a monster capable of committing these heinous acts. Perhaps it was caged in the basement?

A crashing came from outside, and both of them rushed to the window, looking between the bars to see what was going on below.

"Where are the guards? Where's Brian and the other boys?" Caitlin asked with a frown. Brian had gate duty today, father would not be pleased if he was slacking off.

"They ran." Lady Landry said with a shrug, more concerned that the gate had been forced open. The mob were moving down the driveway. She could see them more clearly now. The man at the head of the pack was called Henry Gottoer. Henry was a landowner, like her father. He had been attempting to convince the family to sell several of the smaller villages to him only a month before.

Her mother cursed. A fouler word than Caitlin had ever heard, the shock caused her to stare at her mother, forgetting the mob for a brief moment.

"He's using this to his own gain. This is simply business to him. What a beast of a man!" she explained, shaking her head. Anger had replaced fear and when Lady Landry was angry, she was a force to be reckoned with.

"Stay here, sweetheart, do not leave this attic, no matter what you hear. No matter what you see. You must promise me this." She said as she reached across and cupped her daughter's chin.

"Mother…" Caitlin began, intending to protest. She was certain there was something she could do. Surely the group outside were not wholly unreasonable, they had been the landowners here for decades, and they had never done them wrong. "No." her mother interjected, cutting her short. "Promise me."

"I promise…" she said, giving in.

Lady Landry smiled and nodded, lingering to run her eyes over Caitlin's face. She took note of every feature, and her smile grew. "Oh sweetheart, you have grown to be such a beauty." She said as a tear rolled down her cheek. She didn't indulge herself further, heading towards the hatch. Five seconds later and Caitlin was alone.

She watched through the window as the mob gathered its courage. Henry was yelling some words of encouragement at them.

"Here is a house of evil! A house that has borne forth creatures from the underworld. Lord Landry had signed contracts in blood, contracts with the demon that ravages your villages! It is your livestock who have perished at its vile claws, it is your loved ones that have suffered and your villages that have become tainted due to his evil sorcery!" she snorted and shook her head. They were all words with little meaning, intended only to rile up the mob and reassure them that they were in the right. From the looks on the faces of some of the larger men in the gathering, it would not be long before they would attack the house itself. She heard the front door open and pushed her face against the glass to see who was leaving the house.

Lord Landry strode down the drive with a commanding air. It was enough for some doubt to flicker across several of the faces. Caitlin smiled, confident in her father's ability to defuse the situation.

As he neared the crowd, Henry turned to face him, a scowl appeared on his lips.

"And here he is, the man who would sacrifice your children to the lord of the underworld himself. This servant of evil!" he yelled, raising an accusing finger.

"Oh, do shut up." Lord Landry said, bringing a smile to his daughter's face. He didn't seem afraid, not of the mob. Not of anything.

"I'm well aware that a rare beast has been roaming the forest. But this is not the first time this has occurred." He continued while scanning the crowd. "Or have you all suddenly forgotten the incident five years ago when the pack of giant rats surfaced in your cellars. Or two years before that when the great black snake appeared and snatched two children from the edge of Nierswood? These are the dangers we live with every day here in the deep forest. Every day a new creature appears, a new wolf pack

73

is formed, or a monster drags itself from the bog!" he shook his head in disbelief. "This is the price we pay to live here. This is the price we pay to call the deep forest our home. I am no monster, I have struck no deals with otherworldly powers, and this is not a demon that currently plagues our forest. It is a beast, a monster of flesh and blood, no different from the animals that we have grown accustomed to. You should be at home, ready to defend your families, not here harassing mine!"

He stopped and glared at the mob in defiance. Caitlin could not see his eyes, but she had felt the sting of his gaze enough times to know what was likely going through their heads now. Their expressions showed the shame of some while others were resolute in their persecution.

"Oh, come off it Aaron! You can't fool us anymore." Henry spat as he stepped closer. "You've been feeding us lies for years while you consorted with disgusting demons. There have always been rumours, Aaron. You tried to smother them, and now we see why. They were true all along." There was a general murmuring of assent throughout the crowd. "And now you will pay, Aaron, pay for your evil-doing. You have done your people wrong. Look at these people Aaron!" he raised a hand and gestured towards the mob. "These people are suffering, and it's all down to your own power grabbing!". Some of the crowd thrust their weapons and torches into the air and voiced their agreement.

"And now… You will pay. Take him!" he called as he backed away from Lord Landry. Several of the larger men advanced, grabbing him and restraining his arms. Lord Landry managed to land one blow before he succumbed. The struck man scarpered back towards the ranks of the mob like a kicked dog.

"Bring the rope!" Henry screamed, out of the crowd appeared a length of thick rope. The end had been tied into a noose. Caitlin's blood went cold as she saw it. They were serious, Henry wasn't going to back out as she had been expecting, he intended to see this through to the end.

She watched in horror as they forced her father towards a large oak tree. Tears rolled down her cheeks as they threw the rope over a sturdy branch. They slipped the noose over his head. One of the brutes was bitten in the process, and the sight of the blood sent an electric shock through Caitlin's mind.

She felt the change. The first indication was that her fear and desperation turned to a torrent of anger, boiling up within her until she thought it would warp the world around her. Her vision went dark, then red, then a whole myriad of colours. Her legs buckled beneath her as they morphed, becoming bigger, packed with powerful muscles. She wanted to be afraid, this had never happened before. She desperately wanted to fear what she was becoming. But the fear would not surface. Instead, the anger carried her through the agonising transformation.

She panted as she lay on the floor. Her vision changed and enhanced, she could see the smallest cracks in the wooden beams of the attic and the darkness that had surrounded her became brighter than day. As she reached out an arm to push herself up, she saw that her hand had become a paw, a giant paw as large as a bears and with claws more fearsome than daggers. She wasn't confused, the understanding was instinctive.

She turned to face the window. She braced herself and felt the building of energy in her legs as her muscles prepared themselves. Then she released it and rocketing towards the window. The glass shattered, the bars snapped and bent. The iron may as well have been wax.

Those below shrieked and stared upwards with faces that dripped delicious terror. Death flew towards them. Caitlin would have noticed the poetic nature of this if her every thought wasn't drowned in visions of blood.

76

The first to die was an ugly man who held a pitchfork. He didn't attempt to defend himself, and as Caitlin landed on him, she felt his ribcage collapse and his heart being pulverised. Such a horrific death would have shocked Caitlin, but the warg indulged itself as it charged through the crowd. Men and some of the women tried to stop her, swinging their weapons towards her or shoving their torches at her. They were futile gestures and were met with ferocious swipes and devastating bites. One by one they fell to the ground, and the thirsty soil drank up their blood, of which there was no shortage.

She heard the door burst open and a second warg joined her in the battle. Screams filled the air, and the mob turned to flee. Another beast halted their progress. Henry Gottooer was no more. A monster with a noose still about its neck had closed its jaws around the man's throat. Those holding the rope were still pulling, but they could not lift the incredible weight of the monster. The branch broke. The men turned and ran, but were caught before they reached the gate. As Lord Landry dispatched the two with relish, the mob streamed by him and ran in all directions, fleeing into the forest. Caitlin stopped at the gate, panting. The garden was more like a battlefield than anything else, peasants lay dead or dying all across it. Screams and agonised groans filled the air. They were music to Caitlin's ears. While somewhere inside this blood-crazed mind a young girl cried, sitting in the corner of a dark room.

The crying was drowned out by a howl. The monster sprinted through the gates, the other two following after a moment.

The hunt was on, and it was glorious.

Present day

Percy's mouth hung open, the story leaving him in a unique state of shock. Caitlin had recanted the tale at his request, but he had not known what he was asking for. Such a tale of tragedy and bloodshed was more than he had bargained for and wished Caitlin's origin had remained blissfully vague.

"Did it really require the sound effects?" Commented Marc. He had slowed his steed to walk alongside the other two to listen. While his mentor never ceased to amaze him in his ability to take anything in his stride, he had to agree with him on this. The noises Caitlin made somewhat detracted from the weight the story carried.

"Well, how would you know what things sounded like if I didn't make the sounds? It's just good story-telling." Caitlin replied. She rode with Percy, both of them perched on the foul-smelling pony.

"Why must she ride with me? You're the one with a charger!" he had complained. His mentor's answer was simply "Because you chose to bring her, and I don't fancy the thought of having my neck turned into a hound's chew".

This arrangement made the first few miles a terrifying experience. Every time he felt her breath and every time she spoke he would jump. She noticed this early on and delighted in scaring him often enough that he had become immune. Caitlin had begun the journey as a jittering mess, unable to control her emotions, swinging between despair and ecstatic happiness. As time went on; however, her mood became less erratic as she exerted more and more control over her mental state. The insanity had all but vanished from her eyes. The transformation was almost as dramatic as the one he had witnessed in the basement.

"What happened after that? Did… Did you kill them all?" he asked, not really wanting her to answer.

"Probably. The first few days were kind of a blur." She said.

"And then?"

"Well… I just lived really. For a while, I was able to become human again. We all could. We attempted to go on as normal which was impossible of course. As time went on, we began to spend more and more time as wargs until one day we found ourselves unable to become human again. We could still communicate and were mostly conscious, and so we didn't really see it as an inconvenience. After a decade or so though my parents stopped exhibiting any human tendencies…They gave in. I think I did the same not long after." She replied. She didn't sound sad, just slightly confused.

"But you're human now. I mean, not human… Human-shaped." Percy said awkwardly.

"Yes!" she said happily before she patted Percy's shoulder excitely "And it's all down to you!"

"Me?" he asked with a frown.

"You!" she confirmed, offering no more explanation.

Marc shook his head.

"Percy, the saviour of the damned. It has a certain ring to it, wouldn't you agree?" he smirked. Since Caitlin

80

had joined them his indifference had turned into an obvious irritation. He resented the idea of having her with them and the complications it would no doubt bring.

"And this whole 'blessed by the fountain thing', what can you tell us about that?" Marc asked.

Caitlin laughed and shook her head. "Oh, nothing really. I just said I could so you would bring me along."

"What?" Percy said, suddenly quite angry. "You lied to us? It's the only reason you're here!"

"Well… I just knew I needed to be close to you. To protect you."

"Protect me from what exactly?" he asked with a scoff.

"The world Percy, the world." She said quietly.

Chapter 4

The remainder of the journey through the forest had been uneventful. For some bizarre reason, all dangers had taken the trouble to avoid them. They had ridden for many days, mostly in silence. Emerging from the forest had been like walking from night into day. Percy shielded his eyes against the sun that hung lazily in the sky.

He heard a gasp from behind him, suddenly he felt Caitlin's hands on his shoulders as she pushed herself up to gain a better view. Behind them loomed forest, the wall of trees ran to the horizon, dark and ominous. Before them lay the plains. Fields of grass and wheat stretched as far as the eye could see, idyllic rolling hills completed the image.

"I've never been outside the forest" explained Caitlin, looking around with unconcealed joy. "You can see all the way to the horizon!"

Percy rolled his eyes. Clearly, Caitlin wasn't an accomplished traveller like he was. Though before Marc had found him at the apprentice fair, he had never stepped foot outside of his home town.

Marc glanced around before nodding and commenting brusquely. "Make the most of it, we're headed for Norda."

"The city?" said Percy with a frown. Norda was the largest city in Aellis and where King George's throne sat. It was supposed to be quite impressive.

"The city." Marc echoed.

"A city!" exclaimed Caitlin. "Well, this should be exciting!"

They passed through many villages and towns as they approached Norda, the epicentre of Aellis. They grew in wealth as they got nearer to the city.

The city itself was slightly underwhelming at first glance, an imposing wall hid the majority of the lower buildings, and the palace was too far away to peak over. Percy wished they had been able to observe the city from a higher vantage point, but the city had been built on a plateau, and the ground sloped downwards on all sides, starting about fifty feet from the city walls. Norda had been constructed during a time when war was never-ending, and therefore its defences were severe. The walls were said to be six feet thick, and atop them soldiers patrolled, their armour glinting in the unforgiving sun. Percy knew from plans he had seen of the city that at the rear was the port which served as the base of Norda's scant naval power on the Great Lake. If possible, he wanted to visit it and see the warships that moored there. He imagined them to be leviathans of wood and steel.

In Urn, the largest body of water was the Great Lake which pooled in the centre of Urn. From this, rivers led all the way to the titanic mountain range that ensured the inhabitants of Urn never left. As such the lake became the main staging ground for any naval warfare as this was the fastest way to travel to any of the other inner kingdoms and the outer nations via the rivers.

After the isolation of the forest, it felt strange to be part of a crowd again. Together they surged towards the main gate. Guards barred the way, interrogating all those wishing to enter.

"So… What do we tell them? I mean, you still haven't told us why we're here." Percy said as they neared the gate.

"You're here to gather supplies for the impending journey. I am here to meet a man about a dog. Just leave the talking to me," Marc said, dismissing any further questions with a warning glance.

One of the guards raised his face and eyed the group with unconcealed distaste.

"What's your business in Norda?" He asked, the words clearly tasted sour in his mouth, and he was forced to spit them out. His face was red, and Percy could see the man's hair was wet with sweat. He must have been on gate duty all day in the sun. 'Well, that'd put me in a foul mood as well I suppose.' Percy thought.

"We are soon to embark on a long journey. We wish to restock supplies at your famous market." Marc replied with a forced smile.

The guard regarded them suspiciously. "There are markets in the lower towns, perhaps you should try there?" he said.

"And miss out on being able to see Norda, the greatest city in the central kingdoms? My young apprentice back there-." he gestured back at Percy who smiled crookedly "has been prattling non-stop about visiting the Grand Arena. Fancies himself as somewhat of a gladiator you see."

The guard smirked as he took the measure of the boy. "'im? The gladiators would barely know they had hit 'im!" he shook his head and flashed a nasty smile. Whether it was a ploy or not, Percy wouldn't mind a trip to the arena, it was said that Triston the Devourer, the current champion stood at over seven feet tall and wielded a battle-axe that had once belonged to an ogre.

"Let's not dash the boy's hopes, eh? Now, may we enter my good sir?" Marc said, forcing his lips to curl into an awkward smile that made him look more nauseous than friendly.

"Aye, on you go." The guard said as he waved them by.

Norda was a city comprised of three rings. The inner circle was where the king's palace sat, and Norda's nobility resided. The second ring was where the well-off lived, this generally being merchants, master craftsmen and the insidious landlords. The outer ring was where the poorer citizens made their home. The outer ring was infamous for being home to the Nordan black market. People came from all over the central kingdoms to buy and sell goods that are typically considered to be illegal. The guards and nobles were well aware of its existence but after numerous failed attempts, realised that they would never be rid of it and that it brought a great deal of revenue to the city. Now and then they made a half-hearted effort to arrest some of the lower-ranking members of this organisation to maintain the pretence but largely left the market alone.

It was this ring that the odd party now meandered through. People were everywhere, going about their business at varying speeds. Guards patrolled the streets and children ran alongside them, taunting and tossing small pebbles before dashing into the many alleys that were hidden by the sprawling network of tall wooden buildings which housed countless families in their dark, cramped confines. Clotheslines crisscrossed above them, laden with rags that ranged from dark to light brown in colour.

There was a cacophony of sounds the likes of which Percy had never experienced. There was the laughter of the women high above, hanging out clothes, the drunken slurs of men stumbling in the gutter and the excited squeals of the children playing ridiculous little games.

Percy was in awe of the place. This place was really a thing of beauty, such a concentration of human life must breed the most interesting of tales.

Caitlin interrupted his reverie. "Something stinks." She said, raising a hand to cover her nose.

"It's a slurry of everything that comes out of a healthy human being," Marc said, nodding like a wise old man. "In the inner two rings they have a sewer network, but not here."

"So, they just throw it in the street?" she asked in shock. Percy resisted the urge to point out that she had spent the last fifty years defecating in a forest.

"No, they have outhouses. Below the outhouse, they have dug a big hole and placed a metal drum in it. The drums fill and overflow. A lack of flowing water or river means the only real place to wash is the lake, adding to this bouquet of aromas."

"Is this where you come from?" Percy asked, jumping at any opportunity to glean some information about the man.

"Yes and no," Marc answered before turning his horse to follow one of the roads that ran parallel to the inner wall, dissecting the outer ring.

After a minute or so he stopped his horse and Percy did the same. Elegantly, Marc dismounted and began leading Titan in the direction of an inn. The hanging sign announced it as being 'The Kings Privates', it looked run down, and the grime made peering in through the windows quite impossible. Percy shook his head slowly as he followed Marc's lead and dismounted – somewhat more clumsily than Marc -, he then helped Caitlin who patted Bandit's side. The pony had been genuinely affectionate to the girl despite her nature. Evidently he preferred a monster to Percy.

"We'll be staying here. Percy, there's a stable around the back. A stable-hand should be there to help you, arrange for the horses to be fed and watered then come inside." Marc ordered.

Percy walked forward, Bandit following. He took the reins of Titan from Marc and led both around the side of the inn.

After seeing to the horses, Percy rounded the inn again and entered via the front door.

He expected to find a raucous beer hall filled to bursting point with ruffians beating each other with wooden tankards and provocatively dressed maids weaving through the mayhem, serving drinks and food. What he actually found was a tavern void of human life. Or so he thought at first glance. After his eyes became more accustomed to the dim light, he could see that many of the tables were taken by solemn-looking men and haggard women who nursed their drinks. He had never witnessed such a depressing image, and there sat at a small table in the middle were Caitlin and Marc. Caitlin waved.

"I've ordered food," Marc said as he nodded towards the bar. "As well as a room upstairs. Eat, then wait upstairs. I should be back before nightfall." He rose and made for the door.

"Wait!" said Percy, spinning as his mentor passed him. "What do you mean? You're leaving us here?"

Marc turned and put on a face of feigned sympathy. "Oh, poor Percy. Don't want to be left alone with warg-girl?" his voice dripped with sarcasm. Percy straightened and spat "Don't mock me!"

Marc smirked before turning back to the door. "Then stop being so easy to mock." He said as he slipped through the door and disappeared.

Percy glared at the closed door, once again attempting to understand the warrior who seems so indifferent one minute, and so scathingly hostile the next.

He gave up when he noticed one of the unwashed patrons giving him weird looks.

Percy returned to the table in a huff. A plate of bread, cheese and meats appeared before them, as well as two tankards of ale. The woman who served them was far from provocatively dressed, and Percy was glad of it as she appeared to be sprinting towards the grave and was so large that her dress could be repurposed as a circus tent.

"There y'go my loveys." She said with a grin that showed off yellow teeth that would put Bandit to shame. She disappeared as suddenly as she appeared and left the two staring at the plates. Caitlin didn't wait for an invitation. 'The appetite of a warg, eh?' Percy thought with a frown. He took a sniff of the ale. It was well-known that ale was the drink of champions, so Percy had better get used to it. He lifted the tankard to his lips before he could change his mind and tipped it back. The bitter liquid filled his mouth, and just as quickly he let it slip down his throat, doing his best to avoid it touching his tongue. He slammed the mug down and forced himself to let out a contented sigh which felt like a betrayal to his sense of taste.

He attempted to take one of the larger chunks of bread from the plate, but a growl from Caitlin encouraged him instead to pick around what she had claimed.

"'Poor Percy' indeed." He fumed. "Poor Percy! Stay here. Pah, I think not! Finally, I'm FINALLY in Norda, and he expects me to remain in a smelly dark inn the whole time! I think not! Come on Caitlin!" he said as he stood up and began marching towards the door. He made it halfway before he noticed that he did so alone. He turned back to see Caitlin hadn't taken her attention from the meal.

Percy sighed. "Right, maybe after dinner then."

Marc navigated the dark alleys and winding roads of the outer ring expertly. He had put his hood up and his cloak covered the rest of him. In many environments a hooded man would appear to be suspicious, but in the outer ring a hooded man was more common than a non-hooded man and much of the outer ring operated a strict 'don't ask, don't tell' policy.

He passed by a butcher's shop and glanced in through the large glass window. Strings of sausages hung from hooks, and a large fat man was working at his chopping board, expertly dividing up a pig carcass into sellable portions. An old woman was using a mop to clean the floor. Next to this was a bakery and after that was a crumbling book shop. 'I'm sure Percy will sniff that out.'

He thought. He was no fool and was quite aware that Percy would not remain in the inn, his curiosity was his curse, and he would learn soon enough.

A pair of intoxicated guards stumbled out of a nearby tavern and laughing like madmen they ambled across the road. They had their helmets and swords and were therefore on duty, but in this part of Norda, guards were of little use.

Murderers could rest easy knowing that the vicious men paid to hunt them were busy protecting the homes of the rich and harassing the poor. Marc's face twisted with distaste. The city was in a sorry state.

He waited until the guards had continued on their drunken way before moving on. The labyrinthine maze of alleys and paths that made up much of the outer ring hadn't been planned. Instead, after the inner and middle rings had been constructed, the slums of the outer ring organically grew. Each new building was built on top of the previous, resulting in two rings. The upper ring that could be seen, and the lower ring, hidden from sight and the reach of the palace. While the entire city knew of this network of tunnels and cellars, and the criminal gangs that utilised them, they were allowed to go about their business provided suitable bribes were forthcoming.

The entrances to this underground were hidden around the outer ring but generally originated in the city's cellars. Marc read the sign of the building before him. *Theo's Threads*. The tailor's shop was small and dingy, with dirt-encrusted windows protected by thick iron bars. The door was heavy and made from thick oak. He knocked and waited.

About half a minute passed before he heard the deadbolts sliding open. The door creaked open about halfway. The old man that squinted up at him had a sour expression and a pair of glasses with lenses thicker than the bottom of a beer bottle.

"Yes? What is it?" he snapped, his face becoming more disapproving by the second.

"I'm here to see Merro. He's expecting me." Marc replied, refusing to wilt under the old timers withering glare.

"Merro? Nah, never 'eard of 'im. You must 'ave the wrong 'ouse." He said before attempting to slam the door shut. Marc's boot foiled his efforts.

"Just open the door. I've no time for secret handshakes and clandestine pass-phrases" Marc growled as he put a hand against the door and threw it open. The old man stumbled backwards and cursed at Marc with vulgarity that could only be found in an outer ring resident.

"Now you just march yerself back out that there door you laggard!" he ordered as he advanced on Marc, waving a finger that he believed more potent that Marc's sword. Marc held out an arm to hold the man at bay before pushing him aside and walking past. The man fumed but didn't follow as Marc crossed the room and approaching a door on the far end, behind the shops counter.

Behind the door was a set of stairs leading downward. At the bottom of the stairs, a large man sat on a fragile-looking chair reading a newspaper. The *Norda Evening Times* was the only newspaper in Norda and was rarely seen in the outer ring unless it was being used to transport a portion of chips. The man looked up as Marc descended the stairs.

His voice was surprisingly high and tinny considering his considerable bulk. "You Marc?" he said, looking Marc over with a calculating eye.

"You're Merro?" Marc replied as he descended the stairs. The other man smirked and shook his head. "Nah, my name ain't important. I'll be takin' you to Merro though." He said in his strange voice. Up close, he wasn't as large as he had initially believed, standing maybe half a foot shorter than Marc himself. Though, the man's build made him look taller. He was bald, a common trait in black-market types. It was a little-known fact that these men shaved their heads not to intimidate, but to protect themselves from the lice that infested the heads of those who brought goods from the tribes and clans of Jor and Sar.

After a moment of awkward silence, the unnamed man turned and opened the door behind him. Through it, a long, dark passage was just visible. Beyond the light of the staircase, there was only darkness.

"Take hold of the rope." The man said. "What ro-" Marc began before noticing the rope linked through one of the man's belt-loops. It was a short piece and had a knot at the end. "It's a maze in 'ere, and there's no light."

'I expect it also means I can't escape if things go belly-up' Marc thought with a frown. He didn't like the idea of being so completely at the man's mercy, but there was no other option, so he grabbed the rope, and they proceeded into the passage. He looked over his shoulder to see the old man closing the door behind them, a nasty grin on his face.

The journey was surprisingly uneventful, and Marc endeavoured to memorise every turn, but it soon became impossible as they seemed to double back on themselves several times. Many of the corridors were hallways from old dwellings, every now and then it opened out into cellars where there was some light. Light was able to filter through in certain rooms, and Marc could feel a gentle breeze and hear the cacophony of noises that could only have been from one of the many markets of the outer ring. The floor was rarely level, and at one point they were forced to climb a staircase that had become vertical. Most of this took place in complete darkness. Marc was thankful he still donned his armour as he crashed into yet another table or chair left behind when the building was abandoned.

As they neared the end of the ordeal, the passages became lighter, and they would emerge into fully lit rooms occupied by men and women going about their business, generally bartering or plotting. There were several small tavern-like areas with a dingy bar where a large tattooed man served frothy swill to quiet, destitute creatures that would quickly retreat to tables and silently stare into said swill.

Eventually, they reached a heavy wood door where two thugs acted as sentry's, each had a sword at their hip and a mean glint in their eye.

"Aye?" the smaller of the two grunted as they approached.

"'Ere to see Merro. He's expected." The guide replied, jutting a thumb back at Marc. The two sentries looked him over before one opened the door and passed through, shutting it behind him. The three stood in silence for around two minutes before the door opened again and the sentry waved them in. Marc looked around the new room with an amused smirk. Everywhere he looked people were revelling and drinking. They crowded around tables where games were played, either on boards or with cards, the losers would lament as their coin pouches were transferred to the winner, who would laugh and bathe in the short-lived glow of victory before it changed hands once again.

In amongst the gamblers were armed men and women, thugs from all over the central kingdoms who between them likely had more scars than the entire Aelissean Army. Marc was impressed, he'd been in the Hub before but when last he visited it was nearly empty, now it was bustling with activity. Norda's underground and black market were flourishing. As they made their way through the room, he glimpsed doors around the edge, as they opened and closed, he could see beyond. A crowd of people cheered around a sunken ring where two combatants fought. Marc sneered and turned his gaze from the barbaric scene. At the far end of the large room were two sets of stairs that led up to a second level overlooking the gambling hall. Under this was a long bar where several scantily clad barmaids served drinks that looked almost ingestible.

The guide led Marc up these stairs and through the mess of tables to the largest. It was occupied by a collection of individuals, their air of confidence informed Marc immediately that they were the 'higher-ups'. One of the men looked up at them as they arrived at the table, he stood and stretched out his arms in a welcoming gesture. His grin highlighted the scars that curved from the corners of his mouth and up his cheeks. Merro, or as he was often known, Grinning Merro.

"Well! You could be none other than Marc! Ladies and gentlemen, our esteemed guest has finally arrived!" Merro exclaimed. The others turned to face Marc. The majority were obviously Aellisians, though there were a few that had the skin-tone and features associated with other kingdoms, one even had the distinctive facial tattoos of the Sar Clans.

"I wasn't aware our dealings required such a crowd. You are Merro I assume?" Marc replied curtly, the guide had taken his place behind Merro.

"I am indeed. And quite right, quite right. My friends, if you would be so kind." He said with a nod, gesturing for his company to leave. They did so, giving Marc dubious looks as they went. Marc didn't wait for an invitation to take a seat opposite Merro. Merro took his own seat, not letting his characteristic grin drop for a moment.

"You have what I requested?" Marc asked. Cutting straight to the reason behind their meeting. Merro tilted his head slightly but did not answer, so Marc continued. "Your man in Ternustown assured me that you would have it upon my arrival in Norda. Did your man lie, or are you not worth your reputation?" It was unwise to insult an underground boss in his own territory, but time was of the essence.

Merro shook his head bemusedly as he leaned forward.

"I've heard of you, y'know. What you've been doing, where you've been going. I have what was promised you." From beneath the table he produced a package wrapped in brown parchment and secured with string. It was small and rectangular, like a thin book. Marc eyed it. A smile twitched at the edges of his mouth.

"For an item that is, for all intents and purposes, useless. It was strangely hard to procure." Merro continued. "The Great Library has an inner sanctum you see, guarded day and night. It's where they store books of power, books of importance. They have every edition of the Monster Manual in there y'know." He nodded, as though Marc should understand the importance. "Another thing they had in there, was this." He stabbed the package with his finger.

Marc frowned slightly, Merro was intelligent. Marc had known this from the start, but as he was the only man able to get the item it had been a necessary risk.

"Now, one of my men over there is a Triman. I say 'Vint, can you read this, my friend'. He replied 'I try, Mister Merro, I try.' I'm a naturally curious man, Marc. Very curious indeed. My curiosity only grew when he tells me that the language is old Triman. But, there are still words that he can recognise." If possible, his grin grew larger, taking on a wolfish quality as he leaned further still and lowered his voice.

"Cavorum Infinitatis. The Caves of Infinity to you or I."

Marc shook his head and smirked. "The Caves of Infinity? A familiar tale in old Triman texts. As I explained before, I am in the employ of a scholar with great funds and limited mobility. His interest is purely academic, and I'm only in this to get paid. He wouldn't dirty his hands by dealing directly with the underground, I have no such qualms." He said, adopting an air of smug superiority. His eyes scanned Merro's face, gauging his reaction. The grin gave nothing away, but he nodded and raised his hand's palms facing outward, a peaceful gesture.

"Of course, of course. I don't mean to pry into your business, my friend. As I said, my curiosity will be my downfall. However, due to the difficulty of this job, I was required to bring in an outside contractor. This cost me a considerable amount of coin and-" Marc cut in with a wave of his hand. "The deal was four hundred gold sovereigns for the Package and the... Equipment. You intend to transfer the cost incurred by your misjudgement onto me? That's simply bad business Merro, it wouldn't do to have the reputation of a man who ups the price at the last minute." Marc said, locking eyes with Merro.

"No, no. You're correct. That reputation would be a great disadvantage. However, I think we're both fully aware that you're not about to tell others of our little deal. In fact, I think you'd be willing to pay extra for my silence on this matter." Merro said, for once the grin dropped into a tight-lipped smile to illustrate his point.

Marc's eyes went stoney, and he crafted a mask of cold indifference to hide the rising anger that threatened to boil over and extend Merro's grin an inch or three. He'd underestimated Merro. In his haste to secure the deal, he hadn't properly weighed up the situation, and this was how he paid for his mistake.

"The new price is six hundred. For that, you get the book, the equipment… And my undying friendship."

"What's the price minus the undying friendship?"

"Unchanged, I'm afraid."

"Your friendship clearly isn't worth much then."

Marc could afford the new price, but they would be forced to go without luxuries such as beds or edible food for the rest of the journey.

"Five hundred." Marc said, determined to haggle.

Merro laughed and leaned back in his seat, shaking his head in disbelief. "You're here in my den, you've insulted me, and now you wish to haggle on the price?

Marc, they said you were insane, not stupid." He said in an amused tone. He wasn't angry. Clearly, he enjoyed the friction.

"Five hundred," Marc repeated.

Merro was silent for a moment before replying. "Five-eighty."

"Five-thirty."

"Five-fifty."

"Five-fifty."

Merro laughed and waved for a small, balding man to approach the table, he had the look of an accountant.

"Charles here will discuss payment methods with you. We accept all major currencies, even goods for goods transfers, providing you can guarantee quality. I gave the equipment to the men you requested, and they will be waiting at the Kings Purse Inn, I'm sure you'll have no issues locating an establishment of such esteem. After that, you can be on your way." Merro said as he stood and straightened his jacket, looking towards one of his companions he nodded. Marc frowned at Charles, he was a nasty-looking man with none of the charm or charisma of his boss. "Though, Marc. Few in the city can read Old Triman."

"Perhaps I'm acquainted with one of those few."

"The boy, or the girl?" Merro asked with a grin.

"You've been spying on me, then."

"I keep track of those lucky few I can profit from." He left the table, heading across the room towards a short woman with a crooked nose. He stopped, thought for a moment and span on his heels. "You might want to go find them. Your companions I mean. Who knows what bother they might have gotten themselves into?"

He winked and turned away.

Chapter 5

"Well?" Percy asked expectedly.

"Well…" Caitlin said, unsure. "It's certainly big. That's something."

Percy snorted in disbelief. "Big? It's magnificent!" he exclaimed as he raised his arms, attempting to embrace the entire scene. The Great Arena was more impressive than even he had imagined. It was colossal, bigger than any building bar the palace. It was oval-shaped and extended straight upwards. The walls were sheer stone, mostly white like the majority of Norda, but there were many patterns built into the walls using a black stone Percy couldn't recognise. The designs depicted warriors clashing and terrible beasts being overcome by the champions of the arena.

Ringing the top of the arena were a line of flags, the flag of Aellis and it's neighbours as well as the crests of prominent houses to indicate that they support the bloodshed, either through funds or through 'donating' slaves, beasts and even disgraced family members.

Several arches acted as entrances to the arena, and thuggish men stood guard at each. The area was relatively quiet as there were no big fights scheduled. Percy stood in silence for a moment, slowly shaking his head.

"This is it, Caitlin, this is where legends are born! Boris the boar, Henry the heavy… Even Clerra the cleaver fought in this stadium, to the roars of their adoring crowds. Can you imagine it? Steel clashing against steel, bones being shattered all the while you bask in the adoration of hundreds of people!" Percy exclaimed before turning to Caitlin and raising a finger. She had been gazing hungrily at a butchers shop at the edge of the square. "But be warned, for the crowd, or the 'mob' as they're often referred to are as fickle as they come! One week, you could be on top of the world, a lion's skull in one hand and a goblet of mead in the other. The next week, you're in the gutter, or worse!" He wagged his finger as though he was an authority on the matter.

Caitlin shrugged slightly. "It seems a little pointless." She said as her eyes drifted towards the butcher's shop again.

Percy let out a theatrical gasp, then waved his hand at Caitlin dismissively. "I shouldn't be surprised. A noblewoman raised in a stately home in the middle of a forest wouldn't know anything about combat."

"Combat?" Caitlin replied "No, not really… I know a little about killing though." Her grin was wolfish.

Percy flinched ever so slightly, it was too easy to forget what Caitlin was, her harmless appearance and cheerful demeanour were deceiving.

He waited a moment before speaking again. "Well… Yes. I imagine so… Let's see if they won't let us in then, shall we?" he said awkwardly, desperately trying to avoid the topic of his companion's more feral side, and by extension his own… Situation.

They crossed the square and approached one of the arches, the two thugs standing sentry eyed them with neutral expressions.

Percy forced a friendly smile as he attempted to step past. A meaty hand barred his way.

"No fights today, lad. Be on yer way." He rumbled, nodding back the way they had come.

"Oh… Well, that's fine. We only wish to see the arena, you see. Sight-seeing and all that." Percy replied, not letting his grin drop.

The guard raised an eyebrow and shared a look with his colleague who shrugged.

"Yeah alright, be out in five minutes, or I'll come lookin' for yer."

Percy nodded to the beefy gentlemen before proceeding into the stadium. As he emerged from the entrance tunnel he caught his breath and rushed forwards. The structure was genuinely overwhelming, all around him rows of steps extended up and out to accommodate the hundreds of spectators that swarm the stadium on fight days. The arena itself was huge, but simplistic, sunken into the stadium floor with several portcullises built into the walls. These would no doubt lead to the slave pens and gladiator halls that fed the arena. The floor was covered in sand, clean and white now but soon it would be stained red.

Percy took a seat upon the steps, after a moment Caitlin joined him.

"This… this has been my dream ever since I was a child. This place… It's like a temple. I mean… Don't get me wrong, a hero should travel, adventure and build their legend. But this arena is where they are truly tested."

Caitlin looked at Percy quizzically, but to him, she wasn't even there. Percy was lost in his fantasies. She didn't understand his feelings for this place, but she couldn't begrudge him them.

"Someday, they'll chant my name here, and I'll fell... a chimera or something! Right here." he said quietly, more to himself than anyone else.

He could see it clearly, the magnificent scene. He could see the light of the sun glint off his armour (immaculate and shiny despite the gruesome scene around him) facing off against a chimera, its lions head snarling as the snake-tail arced up and over it, hissing at Percy. He raised his sword, screamed a battle-cry and launched himself at the beast.

His reverie was interrupted as Caitlin dug a pointy elbow into his ribs. He hissed and gave her a quizzical look. Caitlin nodded to the archway at the opposite end of the arena. Two guards entered through it and looked around the steps. It didn't take them long to spot Percy and Caitlin. They immediately began circling the arena, moving towards them.

"Uh…" Percy said uncertainly "Perhaps… Perhaps we should leave."

Caitlin nodded enthusiastically, and they stood up and started walking down the steps towards the nearest tunnel.

They halted as two men appeared from the tunnel. They were guards, but they looked nothing like those who had greeted them at the city gates, or the thugs protecting the arena. Both wore full plate armour with a longsword at their hip. The symbol of the Aellisian royal family was engraved just below their throats. Percy felt a growing sense of dread as he came to the conclusion that these men must be the royal guard. There was no hint of emotion on their faces or in their eyes.

'The conditioning' Percy thought, excited despite the dread 'you can see it in their eyes!'

The Aellis royal guard was one of the most disciplined and ruthless fighting forces in the central kingdoms. They were not promoted through the ranks of the city guard, but instead chosen as children and raised by handlers in a distant keep. Around the age of thirteen, they were inserted into the army as fresh recruits. Those who excelled were then taken from the ranks when they turn eighteen and formally inducted into the royal guard, those who are merely 'satisfactory' remain in the army to make their own way. Those who are deemed 'unsatisfactory' are generally dead by that point anyway.

The closest guard nodded towards the two, he had dirty blonde hair slicked back with grease. He didn't look particularly kind, nor did he look cruel. Indifferent would be the word.

"You two. You will come with us." He said in a low, commanding voice.

"Uh… No, no, that's ok, we're quite happy here actually." Percy replied as he took a step backwards and spun on his heels only to be faced by two more guards, both with the same vacant expressions as the first two.

"It wasn't a request." The guard captain said, he made a hand signal, and the other three moved in to take Percy and Caitlin. An inhuman growl stopped them in their tracks, and he saw a hint of confusion crease their brows.

Percy regarded Caitlin with sudden cold fear, he let out a sigh of relief at the significant lack of fur and teeth. He had seen her transform into her cursed form before and he would sooner go blind than see the harmless-looking girl become a thing of nightmares once more. She met his eyes, and he slowly shook his head, if she changed here and now it would cause panic, and she would eventually be killed.

"Proceed." Commanded the captain in a level voice. It didn't take long for the guards to overcome their hesitance.

Both were projected forwards as two guards took up positions behind them, the captain led the way and the final guard walked beside Caitlin, clearly having decided that of the two, she was the most dangerous.

The captain led them through the city expertly, moving through alleys and side-streets with a navigational mind honed through years of stalking these streets during the night, hunting the city's most heinous villains, at least, all those who could be considered a threat to the royal family (which increased with every lousy harvest).

The buildings seemed to rise around Percy until they loomed over them like disapproving giants with glassy eyes and cold, grey skin. The shadows appeared to grow, extending beyond the bases of the buildings and stretching into the street, wandering into the domain of the light. Percy blinked in confusion and halted in his path, the following guard bumped into him and cursed softly.

Percy hadn't imagined it, the shadows were shifting and warping with no caster, they slid up the walls and across the cobbles like water on a rocking ship. At a bark from the guard captain, the others stepped in front of Caitlin and Percy, another bark and they drew their swords. Nearly three foot of gleaming, unmarred steel sent a shiver up Percy's spine and suddenly his own shortsword, smuggled within his pack back in the inn, looked minor, he couldn't imagine it ever being as intimidating, and he couldn't imagine holding it with the same confidence that the royal guard displayed.

With the four guards blocking his view, he could see very little. He couldn't see the shadows slithering to pool in the centre of the street. He didn't see a human form emerge from that pool. He certainly didn't see the form draw two daggers, both curved and vicious. He did, however, hear the guard captain give two quick orders. Percy knew very little of the code-speak that Aelissean guards used, however, he knew the second command was 'attack', the first was either 'Don't drink the ale', or 'take no prisoners'.

The guards launched themselves forwards, they moved expertly as a unit. The captain took centre-stage as two more flanked the figure. The final guard remained with Percy and Caitlin.

The guard captain, who Percy had named 'Grey', thrust his blade, attempting to pierce the figure just below his ribs. He timed his attack perfectly to coincide with two other attacks from his subordinates, the shadowy individual was trapped, no matter how he moved, he would be caught and skewered.

So he disappeared instead.

The guards gawped, their stony facades falling away, replaced by shocked expressions. Dumbfounded, they swung around, but the street was deserted.

A blade whipped across Grey's chest-plate, the sound of metal striking metal caused the others to whirl to watch Grey being catapulted across the street.

The other two sprang across the cobbles and swept their blades in wide arcs. Their steel met only air, and one guard was punched in the cheek, as he crumpled to the ground Percy was given his first real look at the attacker.

The knifeman wore simple clothes; dark grey loose trousers secured tight against his body here and there using lengths of string and a black vest with dulled bronze buttons made up most of his outfit. He wore a simple mask, moulded to resemble a face but with lifeless eyes (there were no eye-holes, so he had no idea how the knifeman saw), it was silver but tarnished by age. A symbol

115

was imprinted on the cheek of the mask, from this distance, Percy couldn't tell what it was, but it looked to be a crescent with a straight line passing through its centre, dissecting it.

'A bow?' Percy wondered to himself. His pondering was put on hold as the man was heading in his direction.

The last guard backed away, his blade steady, biding his time. As the knifeman drew closer, the guard chose his moment and charged forward, his sword sweeping upwards. He feigned to the left before striking from the right. The strike was parried with a curved dagger, and the knifeman bounced away, quickly circling the guard like a predator stalking its prey.

Percy leapt, and an all too familiar and embarrassing yelp jumped from his lips, he turned to find Caitlin frantically gesturing for him to follow.

'What a fool I am! I stand here gawping when I should be fleeing! The wolf-girl has more sense than me.' He chastised himself before following her. Together they fled down the street. Turning left, she led him back into the maze of alleys, back-streets and what Percy assumed were gutters.

Left. Right. Right. Left. Straight on. Another left.

Percy attempted to memorise the turns they took, he didn't really know why. He wouldn't be trying to find his way back.

He took another left and ran straight into Caitlin. She was surprisingly sturdy and he bounced off her, landing on his backside with a groan.

"You bloody, bleeding, smel-" his insults were sharply cut off as he saw the masked individual looming in the middle of the alley, daggers still drawn.

Percy nervously drew himself to his feet, Caitlin hadn't moved, having positioned herself between Percy and the stranger.

A long moment of silence passed.

"I have a message for you." The voice drifted towards them. It was soft, not villainous, but not compassionate either. He had an odd, melodious accent that Percy couldn't place. The stranger didn't speak again, he expected an answer.

"...Oh?" Percy replied, taking a small step back. If he retreated to the mouth of the alley, he could flee again and slip down one of the many lanes. 'Ridiculous' Percy thought 'He would catch me in a moment, he already did it once.'

"You travel with a man. Marc. I believe that is what you call him. You cannot trust him." Mask continued, stepping forward. A snarl stopped him as Caitlin's face began to deform. She caught herself just as her jaw began to stretch outwards, covering her face with her hand and turning away.

"Your Cursed One is well trained," Mask said in the constant, infuriatingly agreeable voice that Percy imagined would carry a thousand miles on a good day.

"Her... Her name is Caitlin." Percy retorted, he didn't know why, but it seemed important.

"Naming the Cursed does not make them human, it only makes them a pet." Mask waved a dismissive hand; his knives had vanished. "No matter, she will lose control again. Very soon. She is not my charge, you are." Mask locked his eyes on Percy's. Or rather, the silvery eyes of the mask found Percy's. It was profoundly disconcerting, and he couldn't stop himself from shivering under the dead gaze.

"You have no business with me, spectre," Percy said defiantly. He didn't know where he was drawing this courage from, but he hoped the well was deep enough to last until the end of the conversation.

"Spectre? Spectre?" Mask said. After a moment, he began to shake, and soft laughter filled Percy with indescribable hatred. "I am no spectre. I am only a man. Like you. Well, no, I suppose you are only a boy. Regardless, my message is this: Do not trust Marc. He will lead you to your destruction."

Percy wanted to scream at Mask, to denounce his lies and defend the man who spent the majority of their time together insulting and belittling him. He couldn't do it. For one, he knew Mask could very well be telling the truth, Marc certainly didn't seem to be any kind of saint, and he had already lied to Percy on numerous occasions. Secondly, the courage had vanished, and his knees were shaking, only the futility of the action kept him from fleeing again.

"Anyway," Mask said, repeating his annoying little hand wave. "I think I have been clear. You can go back to being arrested now."

The thuds of boots hitting cobbles caused Percy to turn his head just in time to see Grey round the corner, tackling Percy to the ground.

As Percy wheezed under Grey's weight, he was forced to watch as Mask dissolved into shadows.

Marcus

Marc was furious. It hadn't taken long to find out who had spirited Percy and Caitlin off the streets, and it took even less time to discern exactly where they were being kept, mostly because Marc had first-hand experience of the cell that they would currently be languishing in.

The Nordan Palace was not the largest palace in the central kingdoms, but it was certainly one of the most defensible. The bastion had been built before the Triman occupation of Aellis, a time when a warlord named Graakis Graklar held the majority of Aellis in his fist. Norda began as a keep, tall, with thick walls and thicker guards. Over time, people flocked to the keep, seeing it as a rock in a country continually at war with itself. As the city of Norda arose, the keep's defences became more robust. Eventually, Aellis was conquered by the Trimans, and the Graklar line was extinguished, Norda became a centre of Triman security in the Central Kingdoms. The defences were again bolstered with Triman techniques.

By the time King George graced the throne with his royal backside, the palace had become a fortress unlike any other, full of all the ingenious defences that two nations could devise.

That's perhaps why two guards were particularly astonished to find that a man had somehow bypassed every one of them and entered the throne room through a passage hidden behind an unusually large portrait of Graakis.

Marc stepped down; the portrait-door swung shut behind him. All around him, swords were drawn, and the royal guard rushed forward to greet Marc, a particularly nasty one with a swollen cheek and grey (though slightly bloodshot) eyes was pulling back his sword to cut down Marc before an order was roared from the throne.

"Stand down!" The strong voice commanded.

As one, the guard backed away from Marc, returning blade to scabbard and beast to cage. Grey took a long moment to comply, and Marc noticed the frustration. From the bruises, Marc could tell that he had already been bested today and yearned for a chance to reaffirm his place amongst the guard. Failure was not taken lightly in the palace.

"Back to your kennel, dog," Marc said with a smirk.

Disregarding Grey, Marc approached the throne, the guard stopped him twenty feet short of the dais.

"You have two of my travelling companions. I assume they did not commit any heinous acts while sightseeing, therefore I can only assume that you kidnapped them in the hopes of talking to me." Marc said. A huge stained-glass window framed the throne and the light pouring in from the setting sun wreathed the figure.

"You certainly have an ego. Perhaps I simply wanted to speak to your quite fascinating apprentice. Did you know he can recite the names of every one of Krowkis Hundred-sword's hundred swords?" The king replied. As the sun dipped, Marc could see that the king was resting his elbow on the arm of the throne, his head on his fist.

"No," Marc replied. "Once he gave me an accurate description of each one –including the number of notches in each, the names would have been somewhat underwhelming."

King George laughed. Well, it was more of a huff as he exhaled through his nose. He regarded Marc with a critical eye.

"It's been far too long, brother."

"If you say so."

Twenty years before

Marc's rooms were located in the northern tower. The windows were small and shuttered, lacking any glass. The rooms were large and cold, separated by narrow passageways and spiral staircases. The hour was late, and the shutters were closed, but the wind still whistled through the cracks, chilling Marc to the bone. The fire had long since died, Marc hadn't noticed.

Maps covered the desk before him, protected from the mischievous wind by various makeshift paperweights. Multiple charts of both the central and outer kingdoms, as well as large swathes of blank parchment that seemingly represented the Wastes Beyond. There was once a map created by Triivar the Wanderer that detailed the wastes, though it was quickly deemed a farce by the majority of experts for several reasons. The first of these reasons was that he would never reveal how he had passed the mountains. The second was that the map was utterly insane. It showed impossible geography, floating islands in the sky, ravines so deep that Triivar said he could hear the Underworld.

That particular map was buried somewhere amongst the desks papers, Marc had largely ignored it. He had little interest in the Wastes, he was hunting something different. He was pursuing greatness.

Raising his pencil, he marked another spot on his 'Master Map'. The Master Map was a thing of beauty, intricately drawn and expertly annotated, Marc had spent a great deal of coin having it made. As soon as he had it, he had set about making his corrections and markings. Symbols and words littered the face of the map, different symbols for different beasts. Stick-men for people, bubble-men for trolls as well as a hundred other symbols. His eyes always came back to the single spiral.

The spiral was a dragon.

A wedge of light crept across the chamber. Mark had delayed too long. He stood and began rolling up the maps, packing them along with several other essentials. He had to travel light.

With a pack on his back and a sword on his hip, he was ready to leave. Forever. So he did.

Walking through the palace, he didn't notice the guards and servants, he so rarely did these days. Conditioned guards and uneducated lackeys would not distract him, not today.

He passed through corridor after corridor, the walls lined with luxurious fabrics and somewhat rushed portraits to hide the ugly rough walls. He was avoiding all the main areas, including any routes that passed near the chambers of his brother and other assorted family members. The voice spoke from a grand arch-way, the passage beyond was unlit.

"Scurrying away as the baker's wake and the maids set about our breakfast, are we?" George said, stepping from under the arch. He was impeccable, as always. His golden hair was styled in the current fashion, his attire was perfect. He was a model prince, even his features were more regal giving a strong yet humble vibe, while Marc only looked vicious and blunt.

"I guess I just hate goodbyes" Marc replied with a little venom. He had been careful to avoid this situation, how had his brother known what route he would take, and how had he known he would be leaving at all?

"You're walking out on your kingdom."

"My kingdom is boring."

George shook his head in disbelief, crossing the corridor and taking position beside a portrait of King Phillip, their father. 'Well, that's why he chose this spot. The calculating fool.' Marc thought bitterly.

"Would you have shamed him so? Abandon everything we are sworn to protect?" George asked, his voice was calm, excruciatingly calm. Ever the politician.

"Protect? What do we protect? We protect nothing from here, inside our stone coffin. There are no wars, no rampaging orc clans and no dragons that ravage our countryside. The beasts hide in their holes, and so do we. I cannot build my legend here!"

"Legend? You are the king of Aellis!" George said, exasperated at his brother's stupidity.

"A king? I don't want to be a king! Every day since that spiteful old man named me instead of you has been a torture, a whirlwind of decrees, trade agreements and hour after hour of stupid, gawping farmers begging and pleading for just another field, just another concession!" Marc roared. George had a way of delving to the depths of people, he was always probing, always digging until he hit something raw. He was the polar opposite of Marc, who quite frankly didn't give a damn what people were hiding. It made him a terrible king, and he knew it. His coronation had not yet come to pass and he was already sick of the job.

"If you are so fond of the fools that populate this stupidly peaceful country, then you can take my place. I'll leave this morning and you'll never see me again. It's simple, you take the throne, and I become a new man. A free man."

"Father named you. You're the eldest. Perhaps not the smartest, but still the eldest."

"It doesn't matter. They'll all assume you killed me. I haven't been crowned yet, so if I go missing, there's no issue. King George Aurellis, not King Marcus Aurellis."

A flash of ambition flitted across George's eyes before he could catch himself, he instantly chastised himself. Marc sighed, and his bitterness faded away. George tried to be angry at his little brother, but it was impossible. He loved Aellis and its people, but he would always be an Aurellis, the family that had dismantled the Triman control of Aellis out of pure ambition rather than a civic duty.

"George," Marc said, trying a gentler approach. "You are the king of Aellis, you were handling 'civil disputes' when you were a child. Where was I when you were dealing with peasant arguments about who owned a specific square foot of mud? You know where I was, I was fighting in the yard or brawling in the taverns of our fair city. I'm no King, George. But I could still be something great."

"You reach and reach, Marc. Everything you need is here, you leave to hunt creatures long dead or chase after fables and myths. I can't stop you leaving. But I need to extract a promise from you, brother, a promise you will make if you have a shred of loyalty left in you. A promise you will keep if you are truly my brother."

It felt like the entire palace was listening, holding its breath. Marc couldn't bear the seriousness of the situation. It seemed such an unnatural state between him and his brother. But he knew what the promise would be.

"I will return. I swear it. In ten years, if I have not found my quarry, I will return and do my duties. But George, you will keep the throne." He said in a grave tone.

George thought for a long moment before nodding solemnly.

"Ten years." George agreed. No more words were exchanged, Marc walked away.

He walked down the palace steps. He glanced back. He hesitated a long moment. He had ignored so many, would be abandoning so many. He would be abandoning her.

And he was ok with that.

Present day

"It's been significantly longer than ten years, my long-lost sibling," George said in a level tone. He sounded tired. As the sun continued to dip below the horizon, Marc set eyes on his brother for the first time in twenty years. He had gotten old, streaks of grey marred the blonde of his hair, heavy bags hung below his eyes and his face looked gaunt. He was still handsome, but he had indeed felt the years. Though, hadn't they both? Unlike Marc, he was still free of scars and overall, the life of comfort had agreed with him.

"You look like heated manure," Marc said with a mischievous smile.

The corners of the king's mouth twitched upwards before he cleared his throat and sat forward in the throne, resting his elbows on his knees and clasping his hands.

"Might I remind you that you are speaking to a king? I'm somewhat of a big deal around these parts."

"No kidding? I thought you were the cleaner. And really, being a king of this country isn't all that hard. They'll give the title to anyone."

"Mhm. You're not wrong. Though I did solve the infamous 'square foot of mud' dispute."

"Oh? How did you manage that?"

"I took it. I'm thinking of building a summer house. Well, more of a shed."

Marc actually laughed, deep rolling laughter that his brother found infectious. They laughed long and hard, long enough that two of the guards shared nervous glances.

The laughter faded away, and the two men looked at each other in silence before George finally said the words that Marc had been dreading.

"You lied to me."

It hit Marc like a blow to the gut. He had steeled himself before coming, yet George had his ways of dismantling Marc. It was one of the reasons he had not returned.

"Twenty years you have stayed away, meandering as this ridiculous character. The Wandering Prince. How ridiculous."

"The wandering prince was your creation."

"Because the kingdom thought I had killed you, my own brother! My reign was marred by a fictitious murder and I was the hungry tyrant before I even planted my backside on this horrendously uncomfortable chair!" Marc did notice that the throne was considerably more cushioned than when he left. It's said King Phillip had an arse of steel.

"They call me King George the Hungry. It would be witty if I were fat, but in my emaciated state it is only embarrassing!" George had a habit of waving his arms when he was frustrated, as though he couldn't understand the world.

"You knew that would happen when we made the deal, George." Marc said, annoyed at his sibling's lack of foresight "Why didn't you tell them that I was as mad as a squirrel, why didn't you tell them that I'd been shipped off. Anything but the Wandering Prince. It's lazy."

George laughed bitterly. "Don't be a fool." He said "There was no story that they would have believed. Though I must say, it did our foreign relations a world of good. The inner kingdoms are ruled by a pantheon of cowards, and the 'Outies' are bloody shopkeepers. The Triman senate is composed of old men who just want to sit in comfortable chairs and indulge in their poisons once a week. And don't you dare mention the cushions."

Marc shrugged slowly "I didn't come to discuss your problems, George. I came for my companions."

George barked incredulous laughter "Why would I hand them over to you? By all rights, I should have you restrained. You are a prince of Aellis and it is time you did your duties, Marc!"

"I would be as useless now as I was then."

"Don't be so sure." Marc sighed as he lifted himself from his throne and began descending the dais. "We enjoy peace now. But it won't last much longer. General Brokk of Perda will soon attempt a coup. Once he succeeds, as he surely will, he will start to stretch Perda's reach. While no immediate threat to us, Trima is a prime target. Civvo certainly won't like the idea of Perda extending their border with them. Decades have passed, but the hate still lingers. Before long, Sar and Schorom will be involved, and we will find ourselves sandwiched."

Marc frowned; he knew of Brokk but had chiefly ignored politics for the last twenty years. The inner and outer kingdoms had been at peace for so long that he hadn't considered that a war could be brewing.

King George sighed deeply, despairing at his brother's lack of understanding regarding the political delicacies of Urn. "The issue is the same now as it was when Trima forged an empire, or when the first clans formed the kingdoms. We live in a world of limited space. The Mountain Wall ensures that we are confined. The only way to secure land for our growing population is through bloodshed."

"There is nothing to be done about the Wall, for all we know, there is nothing beyond it. I have been to the Wall, and I could not pass it." Marc said.

"Unimportant, even if we could surpass the Wall, we would still have to invade Trima just to reach it. I'm a decent king if I do say so myself. But I'm no warrior. The Wandering Prince, however, is, and he has a legend behind him. Be my champion, lead the warriors of Aellis. Just come back, Marc. Twenty years is more than long enough. Your quarry doesn't exist. It died long ago. How many have you killed in the pursuit? You've bested great beasts and fighters, you have created a legend, now it's time to use it to our advantage!"

George stood before him. When Marc didn't reply he sighed deeply.

"She's married now, you know. Five children. She's happy, I think."

Marc felt dread in his stomach. He knew who George was talking about. In truth, Marc couldn't bring himself to care about his once betrothed. He cared about the judgement in George's eyes.

The story of George's wife Mary was a tragic one. Death in childbirth always was, especially when the child was stillborn.

The message was clear, abundantly so.

You had a choice. You gave her up, you gave Aellis up. I never had any choice, you thrust the crown onto my head, and you threw away the loving wife and adoring children that fate tore from my grasp.

But he couldn't give it up. He simply couldn't.

"I will return, I will be your champion, brother." He lied. A genuine smile appeared on George's face.

"But..." Marc continued, the smile slowly vanishing. "I need to finish something. I need to accompany Percy home. I brought him all this way for nothing, I must be the one to return him. I will return in a month and begin my new life. Please. Trust me, brother."

And like the good brother he was, George did believe him.

Chapter 6

Percy had found his imprisonment most agreeable. Annoyingly so. Grey and the guard (still sore and frantically checking their surroundings for masked men) escorted them to the palace which loomed over the city.

Over the course of the journey, Percy envisioned every imaginable horror that would await them. He could see himself curled on the floor of a cold, draughty cell, or hanged from the ceiling by his ankles, or worse, he would be put in the stocks for the angry village-people (or in this case, city-people) to throw rocks and rotten produce.

The richly decorated room he found himself in had been somewhat of a disappointment. The drawing room was lavish with comfortable couches, luxurious chairs and ridiculous cushions the size of a boulder that you were apparently supposed to sit on. Caitlin tried one, and it slowly consumed her. It took about five minutes just to get her out of it.

This was a far cry from the hellish cell he had expected, which irritated Percy, at least the cell would have made for an exciting story, this was just boring. Percy had had enough boredom over the journey, while 'Big Smelly Bandit' wasn't trying to throw him off because he ate a crust too many and was now half a gram too heavy.

Caitlin, on the other hand, was having the time of her life as the room was filled with trinkets, portraits and beautifully-painted vases that she enjoyed flicking before grinning moronically at the resonating ting. Percy couldn't help but think of Landry Manor, he had not been able to see the manor in its full splendour, though he doubted it could match the wonders of Norda's palace, one of the greatest among the inner kingdoms. Still, it was the closest thing to home that Caitlin had seen since she joined Percy and Marc on their journey. Percy tried not to think of Caitlin's blood-soaked past, it always left him slightly sickly and overly wary of her.

For the sixteen-hundredth time, Percy made a circuit around the room, tentatively touching the treasures to alleviate his boredom and trying in vain to not to gawk

137

at some of the more valuable pieces. It dawned on him after a moment that this could not possibly be just a drawing room. The portraits were not only of Aellis' royalty but also champions, including several famous warriors and Marleen the Magnificent, a sorceress who repelled the great mountain wyrms some centuries before. This was an ambassadorial meeting room, where the royalty of Aellis would meet with foreign ambassadors and dignitaries. Every inch of this room was designed to impress and intimidate.

This realisation both annoyed and humbled Percy, while he had been imprisoned, he had been imprisoned in a room generally reserved for only the most revered individuals. This even further removed him from the tortures he had expected.

He stopped at one particular portrait. It was small, little bigger than his hand and the oval frame was plain and undecorated. It was not hung on the wall like the others, but it instead sat on the mantle above the fireplace, resting against the wall. It stood out quite spectacularly. The painting depicted two young boys, both couldn't be any older than ten. Percy assumed they were brothers as they shared the same steely eyes and hair colour. Despite the similarities, they were far from identical. One was taller with a familiarly severe expression while the other possessed gentler, more attractive features.

The taller brother was irritatingly familiar, and Percy couldn't shake the feeling that he had met this child. He knew it was quite impossible, the portrait had been well-kept, but the frame was showing its age and displayed all the tell-tale signs of a cheap frame that had been handled one too many times. For all he knew, this person could be an old man now, or even dead. He leant in to inspect the painting further when the door was thrown open. He spun and steeled himself for what was to come. A trial for his plentiful nefarious deeds no doubt, whatever they may be.

His breath caught in his throat as he found himself glaring at Marc's somewhat amused face.

"Expecting the executioner, boy?" Marc asked with a smirk.

"I'd rather that than being greeted by your ugly mug." Percy snapped without a thought. Marc's amusement faded. "I'll have it arranged then, shall I?" He turned to leave.

"No! Wait!" Percy yelped, betraying himself. "What I meant was… How are you here? For that matter, how are any of us here?"

"Philosophical."

"In the palace!"

Marc turned and shrugged lightly. "An unfortunate misunderstanding, that's all. You know how it is, you have a couple of meetings with underworld bosses, buy a few explosives and all of a sudden you're a Perdan spy or an arsonist." He said flippantly, waving a hand as though to dismiss the entire situation.

"Underworld bosses… Explosives… You've certainly had a busy day. How exactly did you clear up this misunderstanding?"

"You ask a lot of questions of your saviour. Just shut up and follow me, before I change my mind. Trust me, spies are not often afforded the same hospitality you have received and should I inform the guards that I was wrong, you will see the darkness that dwells beneath this palace. A darkness that few escape."

Marc turned and left, leaving a shaking Percy and a bewildered Caitlin. After a moment of indulging in righteous fury, Percy lost his nerve and jogged after Marc as they made their way back through the palace. No guards accompanied them, though all those they passed eyed them suspiciously.

"What now?" Percy asked tentatively as they exited through the grand palace gates. The streets seemed unusually quiet, and was that a figure lurking just out of view? It was most likely a stack of boxes, but once again, his imagination ran wild until Marc's voice brought him back to reality.

"We leave."

"We leave? Did you get what you came for then?"

"Mostly. We just need to pick something up first. Then we'll be on our way."

"What are we picking up?"

"I didn't bring you for your curiosity, you know."

"Shame."

The soft voice just behind him took Percy by surprise, entirely forgetting Caitlin was with them. That seemed to happen a lot, despite how dangerous she was.

"Shame?" Marc asked, glancing over his shoulder. Apparently, he had forgotten about her as well.

"Well…" Caitlin began, her face creasing in concentration, focusing on some memory that was buried a decade ago beneath bloodshed. Once she had successfully excavated it, she continued. "My da- my father used to say that curiosity could both make a man great an-
"

"And make him dead." Marc interrupted.

"Quite." Caitlin nodded. "But, the point is, that it makes things happen. Now, I might be wrong when I say this. But this journey is all about making things happen, no?"

Marc was silent. Percy guiltily took a small amount of pleasure from Marc's silence, Caitlin had put him in his place without even knowing.

"We're picking up two things. A package, which you two are not permitted to touch, ask about or even look at for too long."

"And the second thing?" Percy asked.

"Mercenaries."

Percy was getting a little tired of being shocked at Marc's announcements, so he could only really manage mild surprise this time.

"What do we need mercenaries for?" Caitlin asked.

"You know what mercenaries are? I wouldn't have thought the daughter of a Lord would need to know about them." Percy asked, raising an eyebrow.

"On the contrary," Marc interjected. "Nobles are the key employers. They have lots of coin and many enemies. They're also responsible for the people living on their land, so every time there's a bandit raid on one of their villages, or something unwholesome comes slinking out of the deep dark woods, they have to deal with it. That means mercenaries and lots of them."

"My father used to hire a man from one of the deep villages… Deep in the forest I mean. He was big and kind of smelly. Father called him Red, but I don't think that was his real name."

Marc laughed. "Well, no one knew any other. He was quite famous in his day, before he retreated to a cabin deep within a forest and took occasional jobs from a local lord. Which happened to be your father."

"I've never heard of him," Percy said with a deepening frown.

"You wouldn't have. He was never written about because he never did anything *great*. He did countless impressive things, and from what I've heard, he fought like a rabid warg." He glanced over his shoulder at Caitlin. "No offence. He did nothing *great.*"

"What happened to him?"

"The same thing that happens to everyone who fails to do something great. He faded into obscurity. Probably killed by some no-name bandit, or he was ravaged by a creature after he bit off more than he could chew." Another backwards glance. "It really doesn't matter. His name will be forgotten, assuming that was his actual name."

"Shame," Caitlin said. This one went unchallenged.

Percy smiled as they approached the Kings Purse Inn. It was without a doubt the shoddiest, roughest, most dangerous inn he had set eyes upon. Individuals with impossibly intricate patterns of scars lurked outside, sniggering and hungrily eying passers-by. Yells and curses cut through the air and every now and then someone would exit the establishment with more than a little encouragement from the thugs hired to protect what was left of the crumbling inn. Finally, he would have the rowdy tavern experience: fights, yelling and lots and lots of swearing. He pushed down the sick feeling of anxiety and forced a steely expression onto his face. His lip still trembled slightly, but overall it was passable.

Marc hadn't brought his longsword but stashed about his person were a range of daggers, throwing-axes and Percy's short-sword. Apparently, it was customary not to carry weapons openly in the Kings Purse, but hidden weapons were expected.

As they neared the front door, two bouncers disposed of another patron before locking their eyes on the small party. They were identical in height and once upon a time they were likely identical in features too. However, years of punishment had made significant variations: noses pointing in different directions and a bulbous cheek being the most notable.

"You lot are new." The brother with the left-facing nose said.

"Is this inn afraid of new patrons? How do you ever make any money?" said Marc.

"With great difficulty." The other brother said, smiling. "They're through the back, Marc."

Left-facing nose looked at his brother with a frown. Clearly, he was the less informed of the two.

The inside was everything Percy could have hoped for and more, everywhere he looked, shady characters lurked. They drank, they fought and then they drank again. The interior was surprisingly well-lit by lanterns recessed into the walls and protected by iron bars. The only possible weapons were the chairs (which appeared to be made from the cheapest possible wood) and the wooden tankards which the patrons threw from side to side as they sang a crude song about a woman of ill-repute and her long list of suitors. They jostled and swayed as they recited the list composed of pirates and bandits until they finally reached the big finale. The last name on the list was King George himself, at which they erupted into laughter.

Marc winced slightly at the mention of King George, Percy assumed he was insulted by the vulgarity. Percy smiled, the assumption amused him, and innocence in the travelling warrior was both worrying and reassuring.

They wove through the room, nearing a cluster of tables at the far wall. The occupants wore charcoal grey cloaks, and hoods hid their faces. On the shoulder of each was a small red insignia, as they drew closer Percy could see that the emblem was a single-headed axe, one more commonly used by a woodsman than a warrior. In a place of such movement and noise, their stillness was unnerving. By not standing out, they stood out. As they approached, two of the individuals stood and left their companion alone. Apparently, this was an invitation, and Mark took one of their seats. After a moment of apprehension Percy took the other. Caitlin hung back.

"Well." Mark began, studying the hooded mercenary who in turn studied their half-empty mug of a liquid so dark that Percy was fairly certain he could see stars in it. "You and your men certainly stick out like a sore thumb. I would have thought Merro would have more tact."

The mercenary chuckled. A soft, almost genuine sound.

"Do you have something to hide?" The voice was feminine. As the mercenary lifted their head, it became evident that that wasn't the only feminine part.

Marc smirked and leaned back.

"I'm looking for your captain."

"Can't say I have one."

"You are the captain? A woman?"

"A woman."

"...Merro insults me."

"Merro insults everyone, you're just the latest."

As Marc's face became increasingly red, Percy took the opportunity to study the mercenary captain. She wasn't huge, probably a foot shorter than Marc. The cloak was fastened at her throat and where it parted he could see that she wore an old tarnished chest-plate with thick leathers beneath it. This seemed to be the extent of the armour and her trousers were cotton. Percy was unimpressed, having expected a plate-clad beast with a necklace of teeth or something. Then he raised his eyes and met her eyes. They were dark green but held the coldness of steel. He was held by her gaze for what felt like an eternity before looking away, his face flushed red. He silently scolded himself for doubting the captain and showing his naiveté.

Percy's indiscretion had given Marc time to collect himself, and the business-like indifference was back.

"We're heading for a dangerous place. I need to know that you will be able to lead your men into the jaws of hell itself. You may actually have to."

"Could I lead them? Could I lead my *men*? Well, that's a good question. However, I think there's a better one. That being… Would my *men* follow me into the jaws of Hell? Better to ask them I think." With that, she looked over her shoulder at the tables further back, where the other cloaked individuals sat. One by one they stood and pulled back their hoods.

Percy laughed.

Marc scowled.

The captain smiled smugly. Around twenty women joined her.

"Y'know." The captain said, the smug look fixed upon her face. "I think they would."

Chapter 7

They say absence makes the heart grow fonder, but evidently, no one told Big Smelly Bandit. In fact, Percy was pretty confident that the horse's gait had become more violent and jaunty. Even on smooth roads the horse stumbled on imaginary rocks and looked back each time as Percy hung on stubbornly.

There's one aspect that the great odysseys of yore omitted. Adventures are one part action and nine parts travelling and tedium. That amounts to days and weeks sat in an uncomfortable saddle, largely in silence. Percy had thought having twenty extra people in the party would help with the quiet, but he was wrong. While none of the mercenaries were particularly cruel or cold, they just didn't see the point in having conversations with Percy, they talked plenty among themselves but tended to change subjects or disperse when Percy attempted to join in.

From listening to their conversations Percy had managed to glean some names, but nothing of their personal histories. Moira was the largest among them, towering over the others. She had a shock of red hair and a laugh that shook her entire body. Nica was much smaller, with dirty-blonde hair and a long face, she rarely spoke, but the way she butchered rabbits and deer left no doubt about her skills. The last name Percy had picked up on was Niv. Niv was likely the youngest of the mercenaries and to Percy's eyes, she was definitely the most interesting. She was far from beautiful, with a slightly crooked nose and a chin that ran the risk of being called sharp. The reason Percy was drawn to her was the simple fact that unlike the others, she didn't seem to mind his presence.

While being the youngest of the mercenaries, she was still significantly older than Percy, and her considerable life experience became apparent during their conversations. They had spoken about her adventures as a mercenary, which turned out to be far duller than Percy had expected, principally consisting of escort jobs for banks and merchants. While women can join Aellis' military this was still quite rare and other than the small

150

number of legendary female warriors, men still outnumbered them greatly.

"So…" Percy ventured nervously. "A female mercenary company… How did that come about?"

Niv looked at him with a half-smile, her hood covered her dark hair and eyes, but Percy could tell that this was the question that she had been waiting for, though he had assumed she would be sick of it by now.

"Well, like many great mercenary companies, it started with a woman." She said, her voice was soft, and she spoke quickly. Conversations with her tended to move fast. "A strong woman" she nodded further up the line of horses and their riders to where Marc and the captain rode.

"And a wolf!" Moira said in her booming voice.

"A warg," Nica said much quieter.

Percy tensed and thought immediately of Caitlin, who had been riding at the end of the line, staying as far from the captain as possible.

"A warg?" Percy said with a noticeable shake in his voice. If the mercenaries noticed it, they didn't show it.

"Well, it's only a legend, and possibly not a true one," Niv said.

"One better told by the captain," Nica said, a hint of warning in her voice. This was the most Percy had ever heard her speak.

"Probably. Anyway, the company itself was made some years later. I joined. That pretty much brings us up to today." Niv said with a mischievous grin.

"…You're not a born story-teller are you?" Percy replied with a sour expression, which made Niv's smile grow.

"Well, all I can tell you is that a mercenary company is rarely the safest place for a woman, especially when there's no one to fight." Niv's smile didn't disappear, but it didn't look as genuine anymore. Percy knew immediately that he didn't want to probe into that any further.

"Captain visited each company in turn, offering places among this bunch of malcontents. Some of us agreed, some of us didn't."

"The company's captains allowed this?"

"Well, after she killed the first two to refuse, the others got out of her way. It's not like any of them lost a great number, as you can see, we're a small band."

"And him riding up the back?" Percy said with a raised eyebrow.

Niv laughed, glancing back to the short rider at the end of the column, riding next to Caitlin. "You noticed him huh? You're observant. Well… Sometimes it isn't only women who have something to fear. It's not that we don't accept men, they just tend to not join. Jhon is… Special. He feels more comfortable with us than he does around men."

"So… I could join you?"

"Theoretically. Can you fight?"

Percy had to think about that one for a moment. Could he fight?

"I have fought."

"Were you successful in this fight?"

Percy's mind skipped through every vaguely violent situation in his life, from being beaten by the larger, less intelligent children to undoubtedly the most horrific experience to date, his encounter with the wargs. Had he actually fought in any of those situations? He didn't think so. He was beholden to stronger forces around him. The bullies went unopposed, it was Marc who stopped Caitlin from mauling him, and since then he had merely been swept along. When Mask made short work of the Royal Guard, he did nothing but run. To date, the most fighting he had done was contesting with Big Smelly Bandit for dominance.

"No offence pal, but you seem more suited to the quill than the sword."

Percy felt his ire grow. "You don't know that, you don't know me."

"No, but I know your kind. I bet your father was a scholar. Probably your mother too. Or possibly a coincount. The kind of person who would hire people like me to retrieve rare beast parts or to protect their boss's interests. You're the hirer, not the hired."

Percy shook his head before turning away from Niv. This was nothing new. Recent events had left him with little time to consider his situation here, or what he was doing here. He was Marc's apprentice, yet he had learned almost nothing of being a warrior, he hadn't fought, he had learned barely anything. Marc only insisted that he continued writing, 'Keep your pencil sharpened, then we'll worry about your sword' he had said. How long had he been following Marc now? Weeks. Weeks without a single real lesson.

"Never say never," Niv said with a shrug. "You'll never know until you use that sword though. As soon as you do. You'll know if this is truly the path for you. If it is. Well, a place in the Woodcutters might be possible."

"Woodcutters isn't a very intimidating name, you know," Percy said bitterly, though he appreciated Niv's words.

Niv laughed, shaking her head with a small smile. Moira joined her, even Nica joined in, though not nearly as forcefully.

"Is it not? You've never met a woodcutter then. Big burly folk with axes that could split a boulder. The captain named it so. I think it suits us just fine. We're all just thugs swinging steel at things immeasurably larger than ourselves."

"Poetic," Moira said with another punchy laugh.

"Are you sure it isn't you who would be better suited to the quill," Percy said with a wry smile.

Niv punched his shoulder. It really hurt.

They stopped just before dark to set up camp. The Woodcutters carried this out seamlessly, Marc chose the clearing, and within the hour there were tents, a fire-pit and a shallow latrine. The latrine seemed a little excessive, they would only be camped for one night, surely a few more... 'Piles' would be endured by the forest.

He didn't have time to focus on that though, too much had happened in the last few weeks that he had ignored. Some things he had pushed to the back of his mind out of necessity. Others he had nearly forgotten out of pure fear. He was unable to do anything about the font in the basement or Caitlin's terrifying affliction, but he was determined to do *something*.

Marc sat with the captain on a log by the fire-pit studying a map. As he watched the captain produced a strange cylindrical object wrapped carefully in leather. Marc took it carefully and was in the process of stashing it away among his many layers when Percy steeled himself and walked over to the pair. His fists were clenched, and he walked in overly long strides. This was how warriors walked, right?

Marc didn't look up at Percy, and neither did the captain. Percy stood in silence for nearly half a minute before clearing his throat. When that didn't work, he coughed. When that didn't work, he launched into a dramatic coughing fit, complete with spittle.

"What do you want Percy?" Marc asked. He didn't look up from the map. Captain did though, she set her eyes on him, and he immediately felt small and vulnerable. 'No! Be strong Percy! Percy the strong, right!' he thought.

"I entered into our contract under the belief that I would learn how to fight. The closest I've come to actually fighting is when we encountered the wa-" Percy cut himself off and glanced at Captain, who remained unchanged. "The wolves. Even then I learned nothing but how to run away. The same thing happened when that man attacked the royal guards!"

"What?" Marc said with confusing creeping into his expression. "I demand that you spar with me. I demand that you teach me." Percy continued.

Marc was silent. Percy had known Marc long enough to know that silence was dangerous.

"Fine," Marc said with an edge to his tone. Without another word he stood and drew his blade. "We have no training blades here, so if you don't block, you die. Agreed?"

Percy didn't have a chance to complain.

"Draw your blade."

Percy stood dumbstruck for a moment, not knowing what to make of this situation, now that Marc was doing what he wanted, he wasn't so sure that he wanted it anymore.

"Draw your blade!" Marc barked at Percy, and he fumbled to undo the scabbards catch and drew his shortsword, a blade that was untested and ancient. Percy began to worry.

"Block!" Mark commanded as he swept his blade at Percy's left side, the swing was wide, and Percy brought up the shortsword to intercept it. The contact almost shook the grip from his hand. The shock ran from the blade, up his arm and into his shoulder. There was a crack. The pain lanced across his chest but he had no time to think on it as Marc had already begun his next attack, an overhead arc.

"Block!"

Percy raised his sword above his head to block the blow. The strike forced him onto one knee, and the pain in his shoulder nearly blinded him. He felt faint, but resolute in his defence.

The next swing did not come with a warning and Percy nearly missed it. The connection threw the sword from his fingers, where it embedded itself in the log beside Captain. She didn't flinch, only scowled. Percy was relieved to see that the scowl wasn't for him.

"This is how you train your apprentice Marc? Through a public beating?"

The other mercenaries had gathered around the show, gathered to see Percy's shame. Though again, their ire wasn't for him.

"He asked to spar." Marc retorted. "We are sparring. I will not mother him. He's better than that."

Percy clung to the compliment.

"It's not mothering to ensure that the trainee comes out of training alive. He'll be of no use to you if he's dead." Niv said. Percy hadn't noticed her standing beside him.

Mark waved a hand dismissively before looking down at Percy. "Get up." He hissed through gritted teeth. Percy obliged painfully.

"Retrieve your sword. If you ever allow it to be retaken from you, I'll send you on your way home. I can assure you that you will not survive the trip home on your own."

Percy walked to the log, keeping his eyes averted from the captain in shame. He gripped the hilt and attempted to tug the blade from the wood. It didn't budge. He tried again, and it stubbornly refused him once more. He felt his cheeks flushing red and tears of frustration pricking at the corner of his eyes. Another few seconds of tugging and the blade finally came free. Percy stood triumphantly, the sense of victory overwhelming him. This victory, this incredible showing of strength and prowess would surely impress the others as much as he had impressed himself.

It hadn't impressed anyone else.

"Well done," Marc said in a deadpan tone. "Now, what exactly do you hold there?"

"Erm." Percy looked at the sword. He knew exactly what he held. "A Triman standard-issue shortsword of the first and second inner-kingdom conquests. Something every Triman Legionary carried." Percy looked up at Marc, expecting him to be impressed. He wasn't.

"No. What you hold there is life and death. Swords are the ultimate tools. A tool has no desires, no wants from this world, it is wholly dependent on its wielder for any kind of purpose. This purpose could be destruction or creation. In the end, they are one and the same, change can only begin when the old ways end. There is yet to be a time when the old ways end peacefully."

"Poetic." Said Niv from somewhere. Percy was awed. He had never considered his weapon to solely be the means through which the wielder exerts their will. To him, the weapon had always been its own character, like Gorelus and his mighty hammer, Giantsbane. The hammer had a name. Therefore it was a thing, not a sentient being of course, but a thing that had its own will, a non-sentient will of course. In the case of Giantsbane, its motivation was to become the bane of giants. What if Giantsbane had instead been in the hands of Necrus the Dead-Killer. Would the hammer have become Deadbane, blight upon the undead of Perda?

"However, after saying that. Look at your sword again. That was forged to be carried by a Triman legionary, you are not a Triman legionary. That sword was forged to aid in the conquest of the Inner Kingdoms. I don't see you attempting that anytime soon. You should be glad that weapons, therefore, do not have their own purposes, as you would not fit into that sword's particular fate. Forget its history, forget its original purpose. It is a sword, nothing more. It's not even your sword, it's one of many. One of many, mass-crafted in a forge in Trima. Do you know why I'm telling you this? Why this is your first lesson?"

"I believe so."

"Tell me. Tell us."

"When it comes to a battle… It is only my will that matters."

Marc actually looked surprised, and possibly a little impressed.

"Correct. Not your opponent's will, nor your kings. If you come face to face with a hellish dragon, even their will is nothing. Insignificant. Only your will matters, and you shall will death upon them. Stand up and attack me."

Percy raised the sword, it felt lighter in his hands, having shed the weight of memories, it was only, as it ever was, a length of steel with leather wrapped around the grip. It didn't matter who held the sword before him, he held it now, and his will guided it. Right now, his will was to beat Marc.

Percy resolutely raised the sword and charged, yelling a fearsome battle cry consisting of a long croak from a voice that occasionally cracked. He feigned to the left before attacking from the right. He masterfully swept the blade in a downward strike. This was promptly parried, and Percy was treated to a back-handed smack to the cheek in return for his efforts.

Percy spun on his heels before hitting the ground in a graceless heap. He looked at his sword, aghast and betrayed.

"Of course," Mark said with a rare chuckle and a half-smile. "It helps if you actually know how to use your tool of destruction and creation."

Most of the mercenaries laughed, even Caitlin's soft laugh from the outskirts of the group reached Percy's ears. Percy's cheeks blazed once again. A hand stretched down to him. Percy looked up and found himself fixed by green eyes once more. He didn't look away. Instead, he took the captains hand and was hauled to his feet.

"You kept hold of your sword this time." The captain said, nodding slowly. A tremendous sense of pride filled Percy, praise that should have come from Marc, but beggars cannot be choosers.

Karees

A century ago

'This is madness' Karees thought bitterly to herself. Her thoughts were echoed in the minds of the thousand legionaries that marched with her. They would never voice this thought.

The Triman Empire was built on discipline. Discipline did not begin with the general populace, but with the empire's soldiers. The warriors of the Triman legions were said to be the most effective and efficient fighting force in Urn, and possibly beyond the great mountain-ranges that encircled it. Above them were the centurions, and above them were the legates. It was a legate that led Karees and her thousand sworn-siblings now.

Since the march had begun three weeks prior, Karees had only seen the legate once. She was much more likely to see their resident mage. Friarn Fire-Finger was said to be the most gifted fire-mage to have ever walked. With one word he could transform a mountain into a volcano. Not a man you wanted to come up against in the arena. Perhaps this was why the legate followed him on this fool's errand.

Three weeks ago, Karees had been content and happy to lounge in Aellis, the empire's newest conquest. The small, pleasant nation suited Karees just fine, it was colder than her native Trima, and it was not built upon strict martial beliefs. She could relax. Then the order came. They abandoned their duty and headed south, back towards home. For a while, Karees had assumed this had been at the request of Emperor Augestius. This belief faded as several contingents of royal riders were turned away and the host went out of its way to avoid large settlements and cities.

Theories burned rampantly, and every night they would become more extravagant as soldiers embellished on things they may have possibly heard here and there.

Friarn's ambitions grew night by night around the campfires, and the prevailing theory was that this was ultimately a grab for the throne itself. It seemed ridiculous; A paltry thousand souls against the terrible might of Trima. Friarn was powerful, but the emperor's sworn mages would hold him off through sheer weight of number. This was a lost cause, and Karees could do nothing about it. The law was absolute, if she deserted, she died. Even if it was a legion of traitors she deserted. Discipline and obedience were everything.

At the end of this march was death. Though, perhaps if she ran she could blend in with the locals, live a quiet life as a farmer. She could marry, have children and slip away quietly as a wrinkled old woman. She thought about it for a while and eventually decided that she would rather perish in Friarn's flames than live such an excruciatingly boring life.

Karees glanced at the man beside her, he was short with grey stubble and a sour face.

"Oi, Terus," Karees said in little more than a whisper. "Terus."

"What? What do you want, let me march in peace!" Terus replied roughly, a tall figure in front of him half-turned his head. A growl from Terus and the man looked ahead once again.

"Are we going to die for this?"

"Probably."

"Do we really want to die for this?"

"What do you mean?"

"Well…"

"Disobedience means death."

"Even if you're disobeying a traitor to the empire?"

Terus shot Karees a dark warning glance. "Watch your tongue, girl. Just talking like that will get you a lashing."

"A lashing? Hah! We're going to die no matter what we do, and you're worried about a lashing, Terus?"

"If I'm going to die, I'd rather do it without my back in tatters, now shut up girl before I administer the lashing personally," Terus grunted. Karees made an obscene gesture but didn't bother the grumpy veteran again. Her eyes turned back towards the head of the column, they were cresting a hill, and as they marched down the decline, she could see the entirety of the army. A triman legion on the march was an extraordinary sight and had made more than one king cower.

She squinted against the sun, the legate and Friarn rode at the head. From her point high on the hill she could see the force moving to intercept them. They flew the standard of the empire. It was a small force, and therefore their intention was not to repel them through arms but to deliver an ultimatum. If the legion attacked, then they would officially be branded as traitors, and every Emperor-fearing man with a sword within a two-kingdom radius would descend on them in righteous fury. Every warrior was watching the confrontation with bated breath, sweating profusely. The smell could almost be tasted.

Three riders detached from the smaller force. Karees tried to make out the individual riders, but she was too far from the front, she could just see a broad chest and long shining blonde hair. The hair alone marked him as a man of some means. Men's hair in the legions was cut to the skull, this man was likely a local governor or lord under the thumb of the empire. The riders reached the column, stopping just short.

The exchange was relatively brief. The blonde man read from a scroll, even from this distance she could see the solid gold seal of the Emperor. Karees shared a nervous look with her neighbours. The emperor himself had heard of their treason and had taken steps to address it. Every one of the thousand souls willed the legate and Friarn to consider the Emperor's words.

Their hopes were dashed with such violence that Karees gasped. The eruption of fire from Friarn's hand was magnificent and terrible. It consumed the three riders entirely before he turned his attention to the small force which was already taking flight. Unfortunately, they were not quick enough, and two flaming projectiles saw to their demise. Karees could do nothing but watch in horror as any hope of survival quite literally went up in flames. From the edges of the column some soldiers decided that desertion would be a safer bet than treason and ran. Above their heads, Friarn summoned a roiling ball of flame which spurted precise streams at the fleeing men and women. Some escaped, but the majority ended their excessively controlled and regimented life in pain. Their agonised screams ceased any hope of further mutiny among the host.

Karees could only gawk at the scene in disbelief. Someone was laughing manically. Karees punched Terus' shoulder, but he ignored her and continued laughing. Before he stopped every man and woman around them had been thoroughly disturbed.

"Come on now, girl," Terus said, a wide terrifying smile on his face. The smile didn't reach his eyes. "You don't think this is funny?"

Karees waved a hand and decided it was best to ignore the insane. If only she could do the same to her incurably mad legate and the homicidal mage.

They all knew that they had no choice, if they ran, they would either be struck down by Friarn or hunted by the empire, if they mutinied they faced the same fate. They could only follow the two murderers in the hope that their terrible plan bore even more terrible fruit.

Chapter 8

There are several universal laws that must be obeyed. To deny these laws, these central truths, could tip the balance and cause the world, nay, the entirety of existence to come crashing down upon the heads of those unfortunate enough to call it home. Up is up, and down is down is one such law, this keeps the things that should be up, up, and the things that should be down, down. This prevents the sea from bleeding into the sky as you stare at the horizon and stops the sun from scorching the earth as it sets.

Percy was currently attempting to fight one such law, a fight that he could not win, and could prove to have dire consequences should he ignore its undeniability any longer.

The comfier you become, the more you have to pee.

Percy shook his head as he refused to abandon his comfortable sleeping place. Comfort was a rare thing on the road, and even scarcer when you stop to camp for the night. While he had collected possibly every remotely cushioned object within a square mile (this primarily consisted of leaves, hay from a nearby farm and what may have once been a badger), he still found it hard to find a position that resembled a viable sleeping position.

But he *had* found it. He wasn't going to give it up without a fight. He squirmed, careful not to lose the all-important position. For a while, he considered relieving himself in his cottons. The night air was relatively warm, and surely it would dry by morning. He scoffed at the idea and decided that if he could only fall asleep, he could hold it until Marc threw something at him in the morning.

Seconds passed. Then minutes. Maybe an hour passed and Percy squirmed, willing his bladder to share the load with some other organs.

It was not to be. Percy conceded and reluctantly lifted himself from his sanctuary and looked about the camp. Marc had opted not to pitch his tent and had instead hung the covering between three trees and slept beneath that using only a thin sleeping-matt. Therefore,

Percy had done the same, though his own matt was considerably bulkier and smelled faintly of badger. Like always, Caitlin slept close, even though she now had her own matt and cushioned bag to sleep in, gifted to her by the only male in the Woodcutters, Jhon. Before now she had always found her way under Percy's covers, claiming that while she was a warg, this gifted her no extra protection from the cold in human-form. Marc found Percy's terror hilarious and as a result had not sourced her own covers.

The Woodcutters well laid-out camp stretched around him. Eleven tents (two mercenaries to a tent with the captain claiming one for herself. Rank does have benefits), one dying fire and a latrine. Percy began moving towards the latrine when he noticed a figure sitting on the log beside the fire. The captain stared at him with impassive eyes. Percy felt the awkward seconds pass before he felt obliged to speak, though his bladder urged him to rudely ignore the captain and waddle at high speed towards the latrine.

"Ah, good evening, captain," Percy said, willing his bladder to be silent.

"Good evening Percy. It's late." Captain said softly. Her eyes didn't drift from him; instead, they locked him in place, giving no hope of escape.

"Oh, is that so? I hadn't noticed." Percy said, glancing longingly at a tree almost out of view.

"It is. I assume you need to relieve yourself. You had best stay close to camp." She said as her eyes travelled down to the fire, she used a stick to disturb the mix of twigs and ashes, sending lazy sparks high into the air before they blinked out of existence. Percy waited a moment, not sure if he should wait to be excused before he decided that his bladder would punish him worse than a little impropriety would. He waddled a quickly as possible towards a tree and began to frantically fumble with his belt, while doing so he allowed himself to glance backwards. He was still in sight of the camp, but the captain had disappeared from the log, likely retired for the night.

With the belt undone and the coast clear, he began to liberate himself from the tyranny of a full bladder. The satisfaction was incredible, and he wondered why he had ever tried to hold it back.

"Psst."

Percy halted mid-stream and glanced around, he tried to yelp as he saw the black-clad figure standing less than a foot away but a hand clamped over his mouth and the rest of the captain spun and forced him against the tree, where he finished his business involuntarily.

"Do you see them?" The captain whispered in a tense voice. It took Percy another few seconds before he even began to search for whatever the captain was referring to, once he did the captain gently removed her hand and released the pressure on his back, moving to crouch next to him. He followed her lead and adopted the same position.

A shadow shifted, flitting between two trees, Percy's breath caught in his throat as it was accompanied by several more, moving carefully from cover to cover. They were distinctly human-shaped, and a glint of steel showed that they weren't out for a midnight stroll.

Something was pressed into Percy's hand, something heavy and solid. He looked down and saw the grip of his shortsword and the blade.

"We need to wake the others!" Percy whispered in a panicked tone.

"No need. We're awake, aren't we?" The captain grinned. Percy wasn't sure it was an entirely human grin, something sheltering behind her cold, still eyes had come out to play. Whatever primal creature nestled within the captain was not the same one that gnawed at Caitlin. It was one entirely of her own making.

"That's mad," Percy said in a strangled whisper.

"Isn't it?" The captain looked around, looking for cover as she unslung her woodcutter's axe. Percy was forced to rethink previous conclusions on the weapon not being a thing of war as in the moonlight it looked as ferocious as any sword or hammer.

Percy looked back to his own weapon, reciting Marc's words, refusing to be intimidated by a lifeless length of steel. He was the master in this situation, the sword would enforce his will. Or he would die. There was no middle ground.

Though he had to admit, he wasn't certain his own will was going to be enough.

The figures drew closer, they still hadn't noticed the pair.

Percy took a deep breath, counting. Counting calmed people right?

One... Two... The captain began to lift her axe, Percy could virtually sense the explosive energy contained in her legs, ready to release and launch her at the prey.

Three… Four… The closest figure was distinguishable now, most of his face was covered by a grey cloth mask. He had surprisingly kind eyes, but he carried a cruel dagger almost as long as Percy's sword. It curved slightly.

Five… Six… Six. There were six of them. It seemed ludicrous, no matter how good they believed they were, they couldn't hope to win against a camp full of experienced mercenaries. This whole situation seemed to be full of tactical errors.

Seven… Eight… The peace shattered as the captain unleashed the energy and flew forwards. The axe took the lead bandit in the head before he could raise the odd dagger. The axes effectiveness was unquestionable. Have you ever seen an axe split a block of wood? Well, it has roughly the same effect on a human skull, but it's significantly messier. Before the first body had fallen the captain moved on to her next victim. This one put up a bit more of a fight, but the ending was inevitable, and the dark-clad man went down missing an arm and a good part of his face.

The remaining strangers exchanged quick glances and turned tail, sprinting back the way they had come. Watching them flee spurred Percy into action. Looking back on it he knew exactly why, it was that basic predatory instinct that he had assumed was never present in himself. He saw his prey (albeit very large and no-doubt dangerous prey) fleeing, and he had to give chase, he simply didn't have a choice in the matter. If he had thought for a moment, he would have recalled the ploy of Maximimius the sly who feigned retreat so that the shield-walls of his enemies would dissolve as they joyfully chased their beaten foes, only to be cut down in ambushes.

But he didn't stop to think, he was caught in the excitement of the chase. He barrelled through the darkness, following one of the figures as it weaved between trees and bushes. The strangers broke off from one another and headed in different directions, Percy chose one of the smaller ones and took after him, sword in hand. The captain called something after him, but within moments he was out of earshot. All that existed in that moment was the shadow he chased.

The stranger glanced back once or twice as he ran, after a longer look he came to a decision. He came to a stop and turned, looking at Percy with confused eyes. Percy realised too late that it was painfully evident that they were alone and had run a great distance.

The stranger looked to his own sword, slightly curved and thin, built for quick slices as opposed to his own short-sword which was better designed for thrusting and some chopping. Percy stopped and took up a defensive posture, or what he hoped was a defensive posture. His heart thundered in his chest and his breath became rapid, he clung to the adrenaline and excitement he had felt during the chase, it could very well be the only thing to keep alive. All thoughts of the impending doom were pushed out of his head by something that he didn't recognise, something akin to bravery. That couldn't possibly be so, he felt a cooling sensation wash over him. Moonlight trickled through the branches high above, illuminating the combatants in an eerie silvery glow.

The stranger attacked. He cleared the distance between them in moments and was upon Percy, reigning down an arcing blow that Percy parried with inches to spare. Any slower and Marc would be finding him in pieces, if he ever found him at all.

The next strike was powerful and thrust Percy backwards until he thudded into the tree behind him. The air blew out of him, and as he struggled to catch his breath, the stranger advanced. Percy saw death coming.

He decided that it wasn't coming for him.

As the blade whipped towards him, he slipped to the side, curving around the tree-trunk as the blade embedded itself into the thick bark of the tree. As he rounded the tree, he thrust the shortsword for the man's throat. Only a second too late as he let go of his own sword and fell backwards, narrowly avoiding the reaper.

The stranger hit the ground, and Percy followed him as the force of the lunge carried him forward. Percy gasped as a knee was driven into his stomach, he just couldn't seem to keep a hold of his breath during this fight. His foe rolled, just out of reach of Percy's sword and reached to the dagger in his belt. Percy saw his moment rapidly passing and with lungs still empty of air he threw himself across the distance between them, the point of his sword angled downwards. Time seemed to move at a crawl as the man saw the flying Percy. Percy could see the outline of his mouth open under the thin layer of cloth that acted as a mask and the realisation dawning in the man's eyes. Percy didn't reach the same conclusion until he hit the stranger and his sword slid between ribs, penetrating the heart and collapsing the lung. He wasn't sure how he knew both of those things had happened. The stranger didn't gasp. Instead, he spluttered, blood already filling his lungs and throat. He tried to cough, but the air wouldn't come, so he lay there with his mouth open. Similar to a fish, Percy thought.

Within seconds the person disappeared, and all that was left was an empty husk, with Percy's sword still planted to the hilt in the chest.

Roughly a minute passed, and the silence of the forest was not broken. Percy had not moved, still resting on the rapidly cooling body of his foe, his hand still gripping his sword so hard that his knuckles turned white. He couldn't bring himself to let go or look away from the still face of the stranger. This wasn't how it should be. His first victory should have been on a battlefield with fans and comrades screaming their adoration for him. It should not have taken place in a dark, damp forest with nothing meeting him but the silence he had created. It should not have happened in so lonely a place. He should have felt something, he should have felt pride at his accomplishment, why did he only feel sick? The stranger had died alone save for his murderer.

Slowly he lifted himself off the stranger's body, leaving the sword. He stumbled over to the nearest tree and bent over, spilling the contents of his stomach over the forest floor. Once his stomach was thoroughly empty he dry-heaved for a while, willing more vomit to come, wishing to purge his entire body. Only bile trickled from his lips.

He forced himself to look back at the body. Who had he been? This man who died in such a lonely place? Percy tried to push the questions from his mind, but the thoughts refused, and he began to invent a life for his victim. In Percy's mind he saw a family, a wife and children. He saw intense desperation. He did not see any choices in this man's past, but instead necessities driving him forward to commit acts like the failed antics of this night. Had Percy deprived a wife of a husband, had he stolen someone's father just because he got caught up in the chase? The body blurred as Percy fought back the tears that threatened to overwhelm him. After failing this, he slid down the tree and sat there, letting himself break the silence of the night with his sobbing.

He doesn't know how long he sat there crying, but by the time he gathered his thoughts he had a dry throat and his eyes stung. Guilt began to retreat out of necessity as he considered his current position. He was alone with a dead body, and he wasn't entirely sure which direction he had come from.

"They never really look human afterwards do they?" The voice caught him off-guard.

Caitlin stood a few paces away, her body was shrouded in the darkness as the moonlight only illuminated her face. He briefly wondered if the other strangers lay in pieces, scattered throughout the forest.

He considered her words before looking back to the stranger. He didn't look human, he looked like the pale imitation of a human, something an artist would fashion. It was a good imitation, but nothing compared to the living, breathing soul that had previously inhabited the flesh.

"No…" Percy said, barely above a whisper. "I don't suppose they do."

Feet pounded the forest floor, Percy looked back to Caitlin, but she was gone. A few moments later Marc, the captain and Niv stepped into the pool of moonlight. All three of them looked between Percy and the stranger with a mixture of confusion and disbelief. All the evidence was there in front of their eyes, but comprehension came slowly. Niv was the first to speak.

"Well. Now you know."

The rest of the night passed slowly. Percy sat near the edge of the camp, leaning back against the tree. His sword was wrapped in its scabbard in his lap. He could not bring himself to pull it from the stranger's cold body, so

Marc had done it instead. Marc cleaned it carefully, slipped it into its scabbard and handed it to Percy before they started back to camp together

Marc and Captain sat on the log once again, discussing quietly. No doubt they debated the stranger's intentions. It wasn't a bandit raid; they were too few. It wasn't a scouting party; they were too many. Had they hoped to steal something? One thief would have been just as good as six and less noticeable.

Mercenaries circled the camp, hidden in bushes and shadows, waiting for another attack as the two leaders settled on the theory that it had been more of a test than anything else. A way to check the camp's defences. No attack came, so either they had exceeded the stranger's expectations, or there were no more attackers at all.

Percy would have produced his own theories, but he was currently preoccupied with fleshing out his victim's fictional life. By now the man had become a saint who fed the hungry and clothed the poor.

"Very few people seem to understand just how addictive it is," Marc said as he loomed over Percy. Percy didn't look up, he couldn't face those judgemental eyes. Not now.

"Killing?" He spat at the man. Well, of course Marc would find killing addictive, he was good at it and from everything Percy had seen so far, the man had the conscience of a battle-axe.

"Guilt."

Percy frowned and forced himself to look up at his mentor. The judgement was still there, ever-present in the otherwise cold and indifferent eyes. Maybe it was merely his imagination, but he thought he saw something else there, a nearly unnoticeable softening of the usually hard features, the slight change in the angle of his eyebrows. Was it something similar to sympathy, perhaps even *understanding*? Percy dismissed the idea as being ridiculous.

"Guilt?" he questioned. He didn't see how it could be possible, this consuming hatred he had for himself couldn't be addictive, he hated it, despised it. However, he couldn't let go of it.

"Can't you feel it? The dependency you're assigning to the guilt. You begin to feel like you need to hate yourself. You feel like everyone else needs to hate you to ensure all is right with the world. You get addicted. It doesn't make you feel good, but it still feels right. That's the addiction." Marc said with a slight shrug.

"You're saying I shouldn't feel guilty? I killed someone. I didn't even know their name." Percy said. He could feel the tears pricking at the corners of his eyes, threatening to overwhelm him once more.

Marc shrugged again. "I'm saying that it doesn't matter. You can't change the past. Whether that man was a sociopathic killer or a doting father makes little difference to your life as a whole, assuming no avenging children hunt you down. Your guilt does nothing for his family if he had one. All you're doing right now only makes you feel *right*. It's self-serving and useless as a whole. You may as well let it go and get on with your life."

"That's possibly the worst thing you've ever said, Marc. If I don't feel guilt, then I'm not human." Percy said with a sneer.

Marc responded with a laugh that sounded more like a bark. "And what's so great about being human anyway?" He said before turning and walking back towards camp. The twilight was slowly turning to morning and light, diffused by the morning mist began to seep through the thick canopy. It would soon be time to pack up and be on their way.

Chapter 9

When they set off again, Percy had gained a new appreciation for the long hours of riding, the pure monotonous boredom of bouncing up and down for miles and miles. He even began to appreciate the cruel pain that it brought to his nether-regions. While they were travelling, they weren't being attacked. While he was on this horse, he wasn't being forced to kill people.

Niv rode beside him, glancing at him every hour or so, attempting to gauge his mood. Eventually, she decided that it was safe to speak.

"You're still thinking about it huh? Don't you think you're being a little... Cliché? I mean, I bet right now you're contemplating what it is to be human, did you have the right to take that man's life? Did he have a family? And all that… Stuff. The thing is, it's really much simpler than that. When two wolves fight, the victor doesn't worry about the poor losers' pups."

"I'm not a wolf," Percy replied, he couldn't believe that he would have to explain this to her, was she as much of a monster as Marc?

"You're no better than one. Sure, we humans believe that we're *different* and *special*. But, in my humble opinion, this couldn't be further from the truth. We sleep, we eat, we kill. We have rigid social structures."

"The old 'we're all just animals' argument? Really? I had expected something more profound from someone who specialises in killing." Percy said bitterly. He was annoyed, why wouldn't they just leave him to drown in his guilt? They weren't even attempting to convince him that he was in the right for killing him, they only insisted that it didn't really matter. He thought that was worse.

Niv didn't reply, after a few moments, he dared to glance at her. Her expression made him immediately regret his words. He opened his mouth to apologise.

"Niv, I-"

"I don't *specialise in killing*. No one here does. We specialise in *fighting*, we specialise in *protecting*. If killing is involved in either of those things, then so be it. None of us are ashamed of what we do."

"No, I know. I'm sorry."

"And what about you?"

"What do you mean?"

"Did you think your adventures would be peaceful? Bloodless? Did you think you'd come out of all this with a clear conscience?"

"Well, I don't know. I just thought…"

"Thought there'd be fanfare, right? Trumpets and war drums and glorious victories, which would be talked about for generations to come? Killing is dirty, and more often than not it's lonely too."

"You're wrong."

"Am I?"

"Yes."

"Care to elaborate?" Niv asked, a slight smirk tugging at the right corner of the mouth. She was attempting to lighten the situation again. Despite himself, Percy felt the seriousness of the situation lessen. He doubted he would ever see Niv's point of view, but he could try.

"No. Not really. I doubt a vicious killing machine like yourself would understand." Percy said with a forced grin. The levity in his voice sounded fake, even to himself. Whether Niv noticed it or not, she didn't comment. Instead, she laughed.

"Ah, yes, bloodthirsty Niv is what they call me. I'm as vicious as they come, you know." She shook her head with a small smile before looking ahead.

"Soon we'll be crossing into Perda," Percy said, attempting to change the subject.

"Oh, we have a few more miles to go yet, but yeah, it's not far."

"I've never been. Is it different from Aellis?"

Niv screwed up her face into an undeterminable expression before shrugging.

"Well… Out of the Inner Kingdoms, it's likely the most similar to Aellis. It's part of the reason the two kingdoms fought like cat and dog not so long ago. Similar industries, similar populations. Different kings. Trima didn't even class Aellis and Perda as different kingdoms. They conquered both and classified them as one domain."

"Well, that's what the books say. I was hoping they were at least a little wrong. Otherwise, the journey through Perda will be just as tedious as the one through Aellis." Percy said, crestfallen. He was hoping to see foreign lands where the most significant difference wasn't that the grass was slightly more yellowish in colour.

"I wouldn't worry, you won't be seeing much of it. We're taking the Low Road." Niv said, her tone not quite matching the gravity of her words. Percy looked at her, utterly dumbstruck by this revelation.

"The Low Road?" Percy exclaimed in disbelief.

"You've heard of it then?" Niv said with a sly smile.

"Well, of course I've heard of it. It's marked on every map with a little skull. No one takes the Low Road, no one!" Percy said, shaking his head at Niv's apparent ignorance.

"Oh, I don't know about all that. I'm sure they just put those there to try and keep people away because if you take the Low Road, then you will undoubtedly end up as a horribly mangled corpse, abandoned at the bottom of a forgotten ravine." Niv nodded sagely.

Percy's face turned red with indignation. "Well, that was a poetic way to mess with me. I maintain that you'd make a wonderful writer. However, you might wish to cut back on the sarcasm."

Niv laughed. "That might be so, but we're still going. Don't worry, you'll be safe enough with us there, I promise."

"Safe with you? You mean we'll be safe with him." Moira said as she pulled her horse alongside Percy and Niv's.

"Nah, he's still but a rabbit," Niv said, nodding to Moira.

"A rabbit? No no no, we all saw that bandit, the rabbit gutted him like a fish! Lovely bit of work that was my boy! If this whole adventuring lark doesn't pan out, you'd have a wonderful career as a butcher!" Moira yelled. Moira didn't really understand the concept of volume.

Percy lowered his eyes to Bandit's saddle.

"It was really more of an accident, in truth. I think we fell."

"Liar," Moira said with a half-smile before trotting on ahead, settling alongside the captain and Marc, no doubt discussing the suicidal journey ahead, perhaps deciding on the most gruesome way to ensure the party's demise.

"Well, if killing the bandit did anything, it at least earned you something that almost resembles a reputation. Something we mercenaries live and die by."

"I'm not a mercenary."

"You think young adventurers like yourself don't need a reputation?"

"It's better to not have one than have the wrong one."

Niv laughed and nodded. "True, countless young adventurers live on in legend purely because they died ridiculously."

"Unlucky Chucky."

"Unlucky Chucky."

Unlucky Chucky was a tale that was so old and had altered so much as it was passed from person to person that Percy doubted Chucky ever existed, and the original cause of his legendary lack of luck was lost in time. In the place of truth, countless stories had emerged, sometimes he had been cursed by a witch because he had expressed romantic interests, in others, it was a dragon that bestowed the curse because he stepped on its tale. In even more stories the dragon simply torched Chucky. Percy found the torching to be more believable as he always found the 'Wise and noble dragons' thing to be a touch ridiculous. Giant reptiles are surely more likely to be primal and savage, he was certain.

The sun was just beginning to set as they reached the Perdan border. He had expected some kind of physical boundary, a huge, intimidating wall with a wrought-iron gate built into it. This gate would, of course, be flanked by guards clad in plate-steel. However, though it was unknown to Percy at the time, the group had not exactly followed the main roads, and therefore there was not so much as a guard-post on their current path and if not for Niv, he would never have known they had left the country where Percy had spent the entirety of his life so far.

As darkness encroached, swallowing the yellow-grassed fields that surrounded them, Percy could just see the yellow twinkling of torches in the distance, approaching the party. Marc barked a command to halt. Niv pushed herself up, standing in her stirrups to see ahead of Marc and the captain.

"What's going on?" Percy asked with a hint of anxiety. Niv slowly shook her head before glancing back at her sisters. Nica positioned her horse beside Niv and shrugged.

"Well, they were going to find us eventually," Nica said.

"We're barely past the border. This is too soon. Look at that line, that's a full war-party. This isn't very good." Niv replied, still shaking her head. "They've been waiting for us."

Percy felt his heart-beat increase. He yanked on the reins, steering Bandit to the left and began trotting towards the forefront of the column. Bandit didn't fight him this time, prompting Percy to wonder if the horse actually understood the gravity of the situation.

As Percy reached Marc and the captain, Marc turned his head and nodded. "Stay close."

Percy felt fear grip him. The soldiers were now coming into view with torches held high. The flames glinted off their armour and illuminated their surcoats (which happened to be the ugliest shade of yellow Percy had ever seen). The rider at the head of the party wore a helmet with a plume of white and yellow feathers and his surcoat had a golden border. As they neared the mercenaries, Marc urged his charger forward to meet the Perdan commander, and Percy followed reluctantly. The commander stopped about six foot in front of them and eyed the pair. Marc's face was stony as he nodded at the commander.

"Turn around and go back." The commander demanded. He had the tone of a man who was used to being obeyed.

"No," Marc replied without a moment's hesitation.

The silence was terrifying.

"It wasn't a request. You are on Perdan soil."

"And what lovely soil it is too!" Percy blurted out. Both warriors regarded Percy with a mixture of annoyance and confusion before turning their attention back to each other.

"We're only passing through. In two days, we will be out of Perda, and you can go about your very important business. Harassing peasants, polishing your armour and whatnot." Marc said with no small measure of venom.

Percy could not believe his ears, Marc was openly taunting the commander and was pretty sure that the 'wandering knight' was actually enjoying himself, if the self-satisfied smirk was to be trusted.

The commander looked back at his lieutenants who dutifully drew their longswords, which shined like they had never been used, which was very possible.

Marc reached to the pommel of his own sword before Percy's hand stopped him. Percy had moved quite involuntarily. Marc's glare was dangerous, and Percy realised that if he didn't attempt to diffuse the situation, their entrance into Perda would be far from a peaceful one.

"Well, my friends, uh, I'm afraid your refusal is quite illegal, both in Perda and in Aellis. You see, we are the Woodcutters." Percy said, fumbling his words but having a general idea of what he was talking about.

"Indeed." The captain said as she joined Percy and Marc. "We are a fully registered and certified mercenary company with full rights to practice our trade in all inner-kingdoms. Including Perda. I have the papers necessary."

"Return to Aellis, or we will kill you. All of you." The commander demanded.

"But… This is illegal!" Percy protested. "Legally we can travel through Perda, attacking us would be an attack on Aellis! It's… It's illegal!"

"I don't think this is a question of legality. They're under orders from someone. Someone powerful enough that 'illegal' doesn't really mean much. I wasn't aware that Perdan soldiers were now for hire. If I had, then I wouldn't have had dealings with this lot." Marc led his horse forward and lowered his voice. "How much is my brother paying you to send me back there with my tail between my legs?"

The commander drew his sword, three feet of sharpened and polished death. "This is your last warning. Turn around and go back. Now!" On his last word the rest of his soldiers armed themselves with gleaming Perdan longswords. From behind him, Percy could hear the mercenaries following suit with their own collection of axes, swords, bows and other assorted horrors. Percy took a moment to admire the band of mercenaries, outnumbered as they were, they were ready to fight rather than flee. All because of Marc's stubbornness.

"We'll go! We'll go! There's no need for bloodshed here." Percy exclaimed. His last experience with violence had not exactly left him wanting more, and he didn't expect that he would come out of it the victor this time.

"I mean, no offence to you… Gentlemen, but I'm not sure the right to wander through endless yellow fields is really worth this."

"I agree." The captain said, looking pointedly towards Marc who kept his cold eyes firmly on the commander for another few moments before nodding slowly, moving his hand back to the reigns to urge Titan to turn.

"We will escort you back to the border," The commander said through gritted teeth. He slowly and reluctantly returned his sword to his scabbard. The commander had been expecting a fight, or even hoping for one. Perda was not at war and other than dealing with the odd thief or bandit, or the rare roaming monster, so the soldiers had precious little to do other than swing their overly polished swords at wooden dummies. Percy briefly wondered when the last time was they fought something that could actually swing back.

The journey back to the border was short, with the mercenaries riding in silence, occasionally glancing back at the column of soldiers. The Woodcutters were nervous, it went against every instinct to keep their backs to the potential enemy, but they had been left with no choice. When they reached what Percy assumed to be the border the commander yelled up the line.

"Halt!"

Percy could see Marc considering urging Titan onwards before eventually stopping.

"You are hereby prohibited from re-entering Perda. If you do, then you will be killed on sight. Is that understood?"

There was no response.

The commander clearly took the silence as confirmation and Marc didn't wait for anything further, he led the mercenaries back into Aellis. The sun had long since set and the great forest had devoured them once again before Marc called for the line to stop once again, summoning the captain, Percy and strangely enough, Caitlin. Percy nodded at Caitlin as she joined them, she had been doing a grand job of avoiding practically everyone, especially the captain.

"Well, we have encountered a slight issue." The captain said.

"It's not an issue," Marc replied, glaring back along the path to Perda. "We march back, charge their line and break them. Then we make for the Low Road without stopping."

"I'm not sure that's the best course of action. We are not the Iron Riders. We are outnumbered and out armoured. We can find a route through Civvo or Schorom."

"That will add weeks, possibly months to our journey. I'm not certain your mercenaries will extend their loyalty for no extra pay. Additionally, I expect the same thing will happen as soon as we enter either of those countries. From here to the mountains, we will be barred wherever we go."

"Perhaps you're being a little dramatic. You have no evidence that this will happen again. Perhaps there is no mastermind at work here. Perhaps the Perdans don't appreciate independent warbands travelling through their lands right now. There is talk of… Conflict brewing between Aellis and Perda lately."

"I didn't take you for one who listened to gossip, Captain."

"I would recommend that everyone listen to gossip. It can be handy. Gossip about war especially so for a mercenary like me."

"We can't straddle borders all the way to Trima."

"I have a suggestion," Percy pitched in.

All eyes turned towards Percy, and he very quickly realised why he rarely made suggestions. The searching glares were not worth it. He made a rare exception as he believed this to be important.

"Well... It seems to me that we are not looking at the simplest option..."

"That is?" Caitlin said, her voice almost scared Percy, who had forgotten she was there.

"We sneak in."

"We would be sneaking the entire way to the Low Road, which the entrance to is located within the bowls of the Yellow Fort," Marc said, but he was clearly giving the idea serious consideration.

"That's only a few miles!" Percy

"We number over twenty. Keeping a band that large hidden is nearly impossible. Especially in a country whose citizens wail and cry at the sight of a shifty gnome." The captain said, gesturing loosely to her warriors.

"Well, we wouldn't do it together of course. Your warriors are used to travelling unseen, I expect?"

"You might be expecting too much of us."

"Perhaps, though I hope I am not. We separate into groups of four or five and exit the forest at different points, at least two miles apart. Under cover of darkness of course."

"The sun will rise in a few hours."

"Then we sleep through the day, plan our routes and enter into Perda just after sunset. Simple. I will produce a map for each group and regroup not far from the Yellow Fort and... Well, from there we'll... Improvise."

"Improvise," Marc said. He was doing his best to sound sceptical, but Percy could see a hint of pride in the hedge knight's eyes. Percy took it as encouragement.

"It's what we do best, I think."

Chapter 10

They slept in a hastily made camp beside the road for the rest of the night and most of the day. All except Percy who fervently and carefully copied maps and planned separate routes on each, ensuring ample distance between each group throughout the entire journey. This was surprisingly easy as Perda was rich in farmland with hundreds of small paths that tended to act as barriers between each farm in place of fences and walls which required building and maintenance. Perdan farmers seemed to have a great deal of trust in each other, and the pests would not be stopped by a wall of mere stone. Percy shivered as he imagined the fang-toothed mud-rats that plague such farms.

The reverse of each map was then covered in coded instructions, which could be decoded using a separate sheet of parchment, which was to be carried by a different member of the party. If the group was discovered and had no hope of reaching the meeting point, then they were instructed to destroy the map and the decoder sheet to protect the other groups.

Percy was proud of his work, and though he would never admit it, he had enjoyed scribing, planning the routes and producing the maps. He was accurate to an almost excessive degree, even adding alternative directions should any of the groups be blocked at any point. However, he prevented himself from taking too much pride in the creations as it reminded him far too strongly of home. In his head he could see his short, balding, pot-bellied father sat in his chair, meticulously copying pages and pages of elegant, flowing script. His mother would come into the room, look at her husband's work before smiling her encouragement and placing a kiss on the centre of his bald-spot. They would be proud of the maps and his planning. He shook his head to rid himself of the idyllic image. That was not the life he had chosen, that was not the life he was made for.

"Are you ready?" Marc's voice came suddenly from behind, making Percy jump.

"Um… I think so, yes. Do we take the horses or not?"

"Well, there's nowhere to stable them here, if we leave them, we lose them."

"I see… Is it worth the risk then?"

"For now, if we find it too difficult to pass unnoticed with them then the horses will fair just as well on that side of the border as this one. The captain has separated her mercenaries into groups. She will be travelling with one of them. She has, however, assigned your new friend to move with us."

"Friend? Niv will be coming with us? I'm not sure I'd call her a friend, though let us be fair, she's an awful lot more civil to me than you are."

"I am your master, I'm not required to be civil. It's in our contract."

"The contract had one line; 'The apprentice will do as The Master says'. Hardly comprehensive. I should really never have signed it, my father would laugh at me for doing so."

"No point dwelling on the past. Come on, this is your plan, so you can explain it to them."

The others had gathered on the road, separated into their groups of four. Moira and Nica were together with Jhon and a fourth Woodcutter that Percy didn't recognise. Percy was certain that the captain had split up the mercenaries into groups that made the best of their talents and skills, though he certainly couldn't prove this. The captain herself was flanked by three of the smaller Woodcutters, she nodded to Percy as he approached.

"You have what we need?"

"Ah… Yes, I believe so."

Percy walked along the line of groups, handing out the maps and code-sheets. Nodding his encouragement each time he did. He then raised his voice to address everyone.

"Well, the plan is pretty simple. We're going to be sneaky. Very sneaky. I'm sure you're all capable of this. Moira, I think you should maybe just not speak for the duration of… Being sneaky."

"Understood!" Moira yelled, giving Percy a thumbs-up.

"You all have your maps and code-sheets. It's mostly self-explanatory. Those who have a decent knowledge of Perda should carry the map or anyone who has knowledge of map-reading and whatnot. Um…" Percy frowned, wondering if there was anything he was forgetting. "Oh! Due to the routes, we will be arriving at the meeting point at different times, but it should be before dawn, if you arrive early, lay low and wait. If the meeting point is compromised, then get out of there as soon as possible, retrace your steps on the assigned route until you're safe and return when the coast is clear. Is everything understood?"

The mercenaries didn't reply, they were too busy inspecting their maps, and the code-sheet holder was preoccupied with frowning at their sheet. Percy could see their lips moving as they silently attempted to first understand how the code-system worked and then memorise it. The system was as simple as Percy could make it. Each letter had been substituted for another, and then the order of each word was altered using a number of simple rules. Percy had almost gotten carried away, inventing cyphers and mathematical equations that required solving to determine the number of miles to follow a particular road. This system was not impregnable, but it would keep the Perdan soldiers busy for long enough to allow the others to reach their destination, whether or not there would be enough time to make it through the Yellow Keep and into the Low Road was slightly more doubtful, but that was a problem for future Percy.

The captain looked about her mercenaries and nodded slowly. "This is hardly the most trying task we've undertaken, but that's no excuse for getting complacent, keep an eye out for the soldiers and keep your heads down." She said, giving meaningful looks.

"Don't speak to any of the locals either. Nods and smiles, people. Nods and smiles." Marc added before everyone turned to look at Percy in unison.

Percy flinched at having so many eyes on him at once. "Wh-what?" He fumbled.

"It's your plan, you… Initiate." Marc said, crossing his arms and frowning at Percy.

"Oh… Right, yes. Well. Good luck and hopefully we will all be reunited in a few hours."

It had all been going so well. Percy had about two seconds to think this as he soared serenely from Bandit's back and hit the dirt-path with a dull thud. The arrow had appeared from nowhere, hitting Percy square in the shoulder, catapulting his small frame and causing Bandit to rear up in fright. Marc yelled and drew his blade with Niv following suit, swinging a bow from her back and notching an arrow with practised ease, within moments of Percy landing an arrow had been leased into the darkness, a cry to show that it had been received.

The soldiers appeared out of the darkness. They didn't make any war-cry. Marc didn't pay any attention to their example and roared like a mad man as he and Titan charged towards the emerging line of armour.

Caitlin's face filled Percy's view. She looked concerned. It's strange to see the concern on the face of a monster. Percy refused to look at his shoulder, refusing to acknowledge what he knew would be jutting from his flesh.

"Just tear it out! Do it quickly!" He said as he turned his head away and screwing up his face in preparation for the pain.

"Tear what out?" Caitlin asked.

"What do you mean? The arrow!" Percy cried in disbelief as he imagined the cruel barbed arrowhead embedded in his shoulder. He bet it was one of those arrows that needed to be pushed through and broken to avoid doing any more damage. This would be a nasty procedure and the first of many scars to come in his glorious career. Thinking about this distracted him from the battle going on nearby. He heard another bow-string twang and hoped it was Niv ending one of the Perdan's miserable existences. It's funny how pain will push someone to cruelty and violence.

"There is no arrow. It just glanced you. Your jerkin is stupidly thick you know. How do you even wear it without falling over?" Caitlin asked with apparent amusement.

Percy's eyes snapped open, and his head turned at roughly double the speed at which the arrow hit him. She was right, there was no arrow, what there was, was a deep tear in the shoulder of the jerkin and a fine, long cut in the flesh where the arrow had cut a ridge before vanishing into the night. She was not wrong though, there was no ugly wooden shaft jutting from his shoulder, and he doubted the wound would leave an overly impressive scar. He was a little disappointed.

"Are you ok?" Niv asked from beside them, she had slipped from her horse and crouched beside them, an arrow trained on where a still mounted Marc fended off four soldiers. Trained sweeps of the impressive blade combined with the devastating kicks of Titan had already doomed three soldiers. However, the situation was becoming dire as the soldiers began coordinating. A well-placed arrow from Niv was the only thing that saved Marc from a well-executed pincer-movement.

Caitlin helped Percy to his feet, and he painfully drew his shortsword, more out of a sense of duty than anything else. While there may not have been an arrow sticking out of it, the pain was very real and just holding the sword itself was a strain. Actually swinging the sword could prove to be problematic.

From what Percy could see there were only four soldiers left, circling Marc while keeping a safe distance. As he watched, one more figure emerged from the night and began a slow advance. He wore the same armour as the other soldiers and wielded the same longsword, but in an instant, Percy knew that he was different. It was difficult to explain, it was in each footfall. Each movement was liquid-smooth and refined. He didn't give Marc and the other soldiers so much as a glace.

Niv noticed him, and Percy could see that she had seen the same unnatural tendencies. Within moments she had sent him two welcoming gifts. Percy would never be able to say with any kind of confidence what happened to those arrows. One moment their course was true and the next it wasn't. Instead, the arrows careened out of view.

Niv dropped the bow and drew her sword.

211

"Percy, it's time to put that sword to good use again. Hopefully, you'll get lucky twice, eh?" Niv said with a forced smile.

Percy was terrified, but he was certainly not going to let Niv fight alone. He was a coward, not a *coward*. Percy stepped forward, dropping into the same stance he had adopted during the battle with the bandit. It had worked for him once, and he prayed it would work a second time.

Niv launched the first attack. A definite believer that the best defence is a good offence. She attacked low, hoping the soldier's height would prove a disadvantage. It didn't. Instead, he parried the jab with an apparent lack of effort. Niv was quick though and launched a series of practised thrusts, feigns and sweeping attacks. She moved more quickly than Percy had expected, and the sound of steel grating on steel filled the air.

Percy waited, Niv's attacks did not have much effect, and he doubted his own would add much to the situation, alas he was bound by a duty to his future, considerably more heroic self to at least attempt to help his friend.

He circled around the soldier until he was directly behind him. He waited for his moment. Niv entered into a complex sequence of powerful thrusts, Percy waited until he was convinced she had the soldier's full attention before showing his hand and thrusting his shortsword forward.

Percy was almost certain that the soldier hadn't turned. All he remembered seeing as he hurtled through the air backwards were two silver eyes that seemed to burn into his very soul. The more he thought about the eyes, the more they seared into his memory. He would never forget them. The eyes were cold, colder than those he had seen set into the faces of the Wargs, or the eyes of the Aellisian royal guard. They seemed to suck the warmth out of him and at the same time they made memories flood his mind.

He didn't know how long he was airborne for, but in that time he saw his home town, his parents sitting by a roaring fire, just as they had been the night before he left. Then he saw them sitting on the floor of his hallway, his father held his wife as she sobbed softly. Was this how they were now? Did they believe he was dead? Was he dead?

Pain quickly shook that idea from his mind. He was reasonably sure that the dead did not feel pain, otherwise, why would so many rush towards its welcoming, if slightly chilly arms. He let out a low groan as he lay there. He moved slowly, testing each joint and waiting for the pain

213

that would come with a broken bone or any permanent damage. When he was happy that he was intact, he propped himself up on his elbows, turning his attention back to the fight. The other Perdan soldiers had gone, fled from Marc's wild roar and biting blade.

As his eyes moved back to the strange soldier, he came to the conclusion that it was neither Marc, nor Titan that had scared away the other soldiers.

The attacker had changed considerably in the time that Percy had been sprawled in the dirt. Percy's very heart seemed to freeze as his eyes moved up the figure. He was still human in shape, he still wore the Perdan armour and still wielded the sword, but everything else had changed. From every crack and chink in the armour a silvery liquid leaked, streaming down the plate and chain-mail, degrading and staining the armour before dropping off the figure and evaporating. The two brilliant eyes had not been Percy's imagination, they shone all over the thing's body, and dozens of eyes plastered the armour. Percy couldn't quite believe his own eyes, and while his body refused to follow his orders, his mind worked at a speed he had never experienced before.

He saw pages from the Monster Manual flick by him. The creature certainly wasn't human and therefore had to be a monster of some sort. His mind lingered on many possibilities. Could this be a changeling taking the form of a Perdan soldier? No, the behaviour was all wrong. It could be some form of undead monster, but Perda had eradicated all necromancers some time ago. As Percy pondered on the beast's origins Niv was removed from the fight by a silvery fist, she spun on the spot before crumbling to the ground. Percy felt a jolt of concern as she lay there motionless but didn't have time to panic as a dark shadow passed over him and a black mass of fur, claws and fangs collided with the monster, knocking it off its feet and putting it on its back. The warg didn't halt its attack for a moment, and its murderous jaw snapped at the things face and throat. Unfortunately, it kept Caitlin at bay with armoured fore-arms.

A well-placed right hook gave the monster enough time to find its feet once more and put Caitlin on the defensive, which, as it turns out, is not what wargs are used to. As Percy began to push himself back up to his feet, Marcs war-cry echoed once again, and his blade bit deeply into the thing's shoulder. A high-pitched shriek made Percy cover his ears and grit his teeth.

They won't be able to defeat it.

Percy had heard this voice before, he had once foolishly mistaken it for his own thoughts.

'Caitlin?' He thought.

Guess again.

Caitlin lunged at the monster as it was distracted by Marc's attack, she latched herself to it by sinking her teeth into the steel of its pauldron, using the purchase to rake its chest with her claws.

'I haven't the time for this.' Percy thought angrily as he slowly and carefully stood. His sword was still in his grip. He took two steps towards the fight before the voice stopped him.

Oh, really now, you think that puny little sword is going to do anything?

"It's all I've got," Percy said aloud, pain and frustration getting to him.

Are you sure? Have you forgotten my gift so easily?

Percy felt it again. The coldness at his core. It twisted and strained inside him.

Use it.

The creature grabbed hold of Caitlin by the scruff of her neck and ripped her from its body. A horrible squeal came from Caitlin's nightmarish mouth as she left a tooth buried in its shoulder. It slammed the furry body against the ground with enough force that he felt the shock travel up his legs. He gripped his blade tightly and felt the prickling of tears in the corners of his eyes.

Use it.

It turned on Mark who ripped his sword from its shoulder before using the hefty blade to batter the things breast-plate. His assault was met with a plated fist, knocking the sword from his grip and Marc from his feet.

Use it. Now!.

Caitlin and Marc were down, vulnerable. The monster took a step toward Caitlin, its many eyes flared, brighter than Percy had seen. Something that almost resembled a roar burst from Percy's lips. He rose his sword high in a challenge. The thing turned to face him.

USE IT!

The voice roared in his ear and in his soul as Percy clumsily lurched forward. The world exploded into white, incandescent light.

About time. The voice whispered.

Chapter 11

Percy was getting a little sick of waking up on the ground, but it was something he was at least very good at. He sighed as he saw that the sky was taking on the pale blue colour of early morning, he had been out cold for most of the night.

His frustrated moan brought a familiar face into view. Caitlin was much less hairy than when Percy had last seen her. She treated him to a full, toothy grin. Her right canine was gone. Percy sighed, he couldn't just put the night's events down to some bad cheese and a nightmare then.

"You're alive!" she exclaimed happily.

"Remains to be seen," Percy said with some difficulty. He pushed himself up and looked around. They were in a dilapidated barn that was missing most of its roof and half of one wall.

"Where are we?" Percy asked. They could not have travelled far, everyone was unconscious the last time Percy saw them. They must have woken, bundled Percy onto Bandit and found the nearest barn.

"This is your meeting spot. Well, a few hundred feet from it. Turns out the spot you chose has no cover." Marc's voice came from nearby. Percy could see the fight had lefts its mark on him too. The right side of his face was covered in a livid bruise, and his eye had begun to swell.

"Don't worry, we can see all around from here. If anyone appears, we'll see them," Niv said, perched on what was left of the hay platform. She offered him a small smile, slightly crooked now as the beast's fists had delivered the same damage to her face as it had Marc's. As she spoke, Percy could see that one of her teeth had been cracked, but other than that they all seemed to be intact. Not bad after an encounter with a hellish, otherworldly killing machine. As he moved the pain in his shoulder flared, he inspected the cut he had received, seeing that it had been bandaged expertly.

"That's my handiwork," Niv said with a proud if slightly smug smile. Percy bowed his head in silent thanks.

"The monster… What happened to it?" Percy asked, afraid that he already knew the answer.

"That is the question, isn't it?" Marc said, his eyes fixed on Percy.

"I woke first," Niv said while scanning the horizon for any familiar figure arriving at the rendezvous point. "There was nothing left of it. Just a pile of armour and… Dust. Silver dust. Might have been worth something, actually."

"There was also this," Marc said as he tossed Percy his short-sword, safely encased in its scabbard. Percy caught it clumsily. "Buried up to the guard in the monster's helmet. You killed it."

"Two for two, Percy," Niv said before chuckling. It sounded painful.

"I… I don't remember that…" Percy said. He remembered the voice, he remembered charging the… - thing-, and he remembered being incredibly frustrated at how useless he had been during the fight. Other than that, he only remembered the burning light that engulfed both him and the beast. He was not keen to dwell on any of those points.

"What was it?" Percy asked, his eyes not moving from the sword. He slowly pulled it from its scabbard and inspected the blade. The edge had still not dulled, this was an extraordinary blade.

"A golem, I think," Caitlin said as she circled him and took a seat, the grin was still there and Percy suspected it was for him. He didn't know how he felt about that, Caitlin had clearly turned into her warg form to protect him. Did she see herself as some kind of protector?

I'm supposed to protect you! The fountain has blessed you!

Of course, she did. It seemed so long ago that she had said that, at a time when Marc was prepared to kill her.

"A golem?" Percy's mind flicked through the pages of the Manual until he found information on golems.

"Shells pumped full of a specific kind of magic," Marc said, finally moving his eyes from Percy to his sword. He ran a stone slowly along its edge.

"Indeed…" Percy said slowly, deliberately. "But they're usually made out of stone or clay, right?"

"Usually, yes. Those made by regular mages and sorcerers. The more advanced a magic-wielder is, the more… Options they have. This option was a suit of armour… and the body within it." Marc said, his stone made a grinding noise as it did its work. Percy's blood ran cold.

"A human body can be a golem? That's… That's necromancy!" Percy exclaimed, suddenly feeling like he was covered in cobwebs. He brushed himself down just to make sure.

"Not quite," Caitlin said, looking thoughtful. "There's no soul or anything, just an incredible amount of magic, it wasn't moving on its own, and someone was controlling it. All those crazy moves just show how much magic was in it. I mean, the thing was literally leaking the stuff!"

"In the dust was an arrowhead with a broken shaft," Niv said, distractedly watching the road.

"The first soldier you killed," Percy said, understanding a little about the situation now. "Then there's a powerful mage following us?" he asked, glancing towards the door of the barn, expecting a horde of shambling bodies to burst through it at any moment and tear them apart, eating their most valuable parts. He could not get this image out of his mind even though the golem had looked nothing like the clumsy horrors that plagued his imagination.

"Incredibly powerful!" Caitlin said with the same stupid grin "So powerful that their power literally ate the body away and left nothing but dust! Quite fascinating really."

Percy was a little taken aback by Caitlin's glee at the situation, had her father's ill-conceived exploits in practising pale magic given her an unnatural interest in magic and the monsters it spawned? Marc was only interested in killing them, and Percy agreed with his point of view, the only good horrifically powerful magic creature was a dead horrifically powerful magical creature.

"There's no point worrying about it now, we have to remain focused on our goal. We still have to get through the Yellow Fort and survive the Low Road before we get to our destination… Which is… Marc?" Niv said, glancing down at them.

"A surprise," Marc said, inspecting the swords edge. He placed the stone down and began using a cloth instead.

Niv stood up suddenly, her gaze fixed on the rendezvous area. "Someone's there. I can't tell who it is, but I think it's the captain."

"Go and collect them. Take Percy, he needs the walk."

An hour later and the small barn was crammed full of mercenaries. The captain's group had been the first to reach the point, and as Niv and Percy met them, they had both received an overly enthusiastic hug from Moira and a nod from Nica.

One group never made it to the meeting place.

"We cannot wait for them forever. We must assume they met similar resistance." Marc said, speaking to the captain in the centre of the barn.

"Yes. A golem is quite distressing. But I won't abandon my warriors."

"You're not abandoning them. They're dead."

"They might just be lost?" Percy offered meekly.

"If they can't follow simple instructions then I have no use for them!" Marc barked, anxious to continue.

"Why the rush? We have yet to deal with the Yellow Fort. We can at least wait for them while we form a plan. From the sounds of it, you killed several of their soldiers and others fled, while you believe those soldiers were hired, that doesn't mean that the deserters didn't find their way back here." The captain said. Though her face was still expressionless, Percy could tell that she feared for the missing mercenaries, the tale of the body-possessing golem had put everyone on edge.

"They didn't," Marc said with certainty. "Niv."

Niv nodded and walked to a pile stashed in one of the barns shadowy corners, she returned with a chainmail coat and a yellow tabard, there was a thin gash with a hint of red along its edges.

"We made certain of it."

"You cannot be serious." The captain said, for the first time he saw genuine surprise on her face. "You are going to play dress up?"

"I have spent some time in the fort, I know its layout and interior. I plead for sanctuary, spin a tale about the big bad Aelissean mercenaries and find a way to let everyone else through the other entrance."

"There's more than one entrance?" Percy said with a frown etched on his features. "Seems like a design oversight."

"It's a remnant, constructed by the Trimans in case of an uprising, they needed a way to flee the fort so they could return with a legion. It can only be opened from the inside."

"And the entrance to the Low Road? It must be guarded." Moira said before adding in her characteristically cheerful tone "Not that I ain't lookin' for a fight, you understand. Just that startin' one in a fort ain't usually the best idea."

"It was guarded, once."

"No longer?" Percy asked.

"No one has tried to access the road for nearly a hundred years, and nothing has slithered out of it in two hundred. The road is dead and cursed, so it's locked, but not guarded. Luckily enough, I have a key."

"Should I even bother asking how you came about a key?" The captain asked.

"Probably not, no."

"Grand. Well, if it's the only plan we have, then I guess it will have to suffice."

"For now, your… *men* can get some sleep I suppose, I'll approach the gate just before nightfall and open the door an hour before dawn. If your lost little girls haven't appeared by then, well, that's too bad." Marc said, taking the tabard from Niv's hands and studying the tear.

"As you wish, until then I will search for them. Percy, do you have a copy of their map?" The captain said, jolting Percy slightly.

"Ah, no, the maps were unique. However, I'm sure I could produce another. Its group C we're missing who followed a path just to the west of here, find the path and follow it back. If you get to the crossroads and still have not found them, then I think it might be folly." Percy said with a small shrug of his shoulders. "There were alternative routes plotted for them, but it would take all day to search all of them."

"You do not have time to make more maps! If the captain wishes to waste her time looking for corpses, then let her." Marc said bitterly. "Percy, you will need to know precisely where the door is, open your notebook and write down my instructions *exactly* as I give them."

The captain's eyes lingered on Marc for a few tense moments, and Percy began to slowly back away from the two, any fight between these two was not one that he wished to be a part of.

Niv broke the stalemate. "I will join you, captain."

The captain nodded and finally stopped boring holes in Marc's back. The two left in silence, Nica slinked off after them a moment later.

Marc motioned for Percy to follow him to a corner of the barn.

"I am not sure that was wise," Percy said.

"I'm not sure I care, Percy. These people have been hired. Do not be fooled by the 'honourable mercenary' act.

They trade lives for coin. They're nothing more than our guards, you understand?"

"I'm with Percy on this one," Caitlin said, making Percy jump and Marc scowl.

"I don't remember inviting you to this conversation, little monster," Marc said.

"No, but aren't you glad I'm in it now?" Caitlin said with a mischievous smile. She honestly had no sense of fear whatsoever as long as the captain was not present.

"It's important to read a person, I think. If these… Ladies are to have our lives in their hands, then I would prefer they thought our lives were a little valuable." Said Percy.

"That, Percy, is why you pay half before the job, and half after. Now, are you quite done berating me on how I treat the hired help? Good, then we can get on with some actual work."

Percy could not decide if the location of the hidden door was intelligent, or moronic. He imagined their route in his bedroll. He had picked a spot where the grass was fullest and mostly alive. However, it was now early afternoon, and he was struggling to sleep. This was not helped by Caitlin's frequent sleep-mumbles and the fact that she had a tendency to kick every few hours. He could

228

have tolerated this had she not insisted that she could not sleep more than a few inches away from him.

The door was actually a trapdoor. A narrow but deep river actually runs through the centre of the keep, with an arrangement of grills and bars protecting where it enters and exits the keep. Percy wondered if it was a tactical move, but apparently as the fort expanded the planners simply did not know what to do with the river, so they left it where it was. The first grill at the exit of the river is set into the fort-wall. The instructions were simple. Enter the river by the depression in the wall, pull yourself along the grill until you reach the wall on the right and force yourself under water and continue for ten feet, then come up for air.

Percy should find himself in a small alcove, with a trapdoor. The more he thought about it, the cleverer he thought it was, those fleeing the fort could use the door and then allow the river to carry them until they reached one of the many small watch-posts that watched the traffic on the river.

Footsteps drew his attention, and he watched the captain, Niv and Nica enter the barn. No one followed them, and Percy felt a tinge of guilt. If he had recreated the map, perhaps they would have found their missing brethren. The three spoke in hushed tones for a few moments before Nica climbed to the higher platform. Niv made to follow her, stopping halfway up and returning to the ground. She scanned the barn and the many bodies that littered its floor before locating Percy. They locked eyes for a moment, and she treated him to a sad smile before crossing the room and lying down next to him, she didn't bother with a bed-roll and closed her eyes immediately.

"No... No sign of them then?" Percy asked nervously, acutely aware of the fact that he was now sleeping between two women, the fact that one was a battle-hardened mercenary and the other frequently transformed into a beast that may have been spawned in hell didn't even factor into the equation.

"No. Nothing," Niv said softly, opening her eyes and gazing up at the mid-day sky. "No golems in sight though, so that's something, eh?" she said with the same sad smile. Did these mercenaries really feel the loss of their comrades so profoundly? Was there really something to this 'bond between rogues' thing that he read about so often in his legends? He suddenly wanted to tell her everything, he wanted to tell her about the font, about Caitlin's... *condition*. He even wanted to tell her about the voice and whatever strange gift he had received that night. He wanted to tell her that the golem was his fault and that it was there for him. He wanted to tell her that her missing comrades might even be dead because of him.

"Niv…" Percy began delicately, running a dry tongue across dry lips as he considered his options.

"Yes?" Niv replied, turning her head to look into his guilty eyes.

"…You'll need some sleep; it's going to be a long night."

Niv frowned slightly before nodding and rolling onto her side, away from Percy. Percy cursed his cowardice.

Good decision.

Chapter 12

It did not surprise Percy to see just how well the Perdan suit of armour and surcoat suited Marc, he had the face and frame suited to a high-ranking officer and the way he carried himself like royalty. His commanding voice and gaze showed that in another life, Marc could have risen to the heights of a commander or even a general in any military he wished.

"You look like an idiot." The captain said.

"Maybe so, but I look like a *Perdan* idiot," Marc replied as Percy fussed over the armour, tightening straps and securing buckles. While Percy didn't dare say it, he did have some doubts in Marc's acting abilities. Luckily, the captain was much less timid.

"I'm not sure you can do this. You'll have to act helpless and weak." The Captain said.

"I appreciate the compliment. However there are few other options, and in all honesty, I'm not certain I trust any of you to be able to carry out this job."

"Charming," Niv mumbled to Percy as he stepped back to appreciate his own work. He didn't respond or look at her, he wasn't sure he could. Marc was right, guilt was addictive.

"We don't have time to form another plan. This is it, this is what we are going to do. Percy will lead you to the door when darkness falls, and there you will wait. Nice and simple."

"And if they see through you or have men there who recognise you?" The captain said, folding her arms.

"Then I die, and you are all free to return to the King's Purse where you may wait for the next poor soul that Merro wishes to make a mockery of!" Marc snapped. "And you may attempt to collect the rest of your coin from my corpse, though up to this point I have seen little reason for you to deserve it."

"Your corpse? Don't be silly, I wouldn't charge a fort for that. Your debt will pass to next of kin. Or in your case, it will pass to your apprentice." The captain said as she glanced at Percy, her eyes were cold and hard. He didn't doubt that she would pursue this debt like a hound after a fox. He didn't look forward to such an eventuality.

Marc laughed and waved a dismissive hand. "Two birds with one stone, I rid myself of debt and have the opportunity to aggravate young Percy one more time. I will go laughing into the underworld! Do not fret, Captain, I will open the door, you will get to experience the horrors of the Low Road first-hand and then you will be paid."

Marc walked through the barn to the door, stopping just short of the threshold and looking back at Percy.

"You're in charge. Be at the door, I'm counting on you. If you're not there… Well, then I suppose we will see if someone can survive the Low Road alone." Marc said before slipping the Perdan helmet onto his head, patting the domed helmet until it fit snuggly on his over-sized head. With a final nod, he left the barn, and Percy felt his chest swell with pride. He had been placed in charge and as happens so often when a horrendously unqualified individual receives any position of power, he certainly was about to let it go to his head.

"Well then!" Percy exclaimed, pushing out his chest. He addressed his waiting audience. "Well, I think we should form into two groups, a small group that will scout ahead and ensure our route to the door is unobstructed and the co-"

"With all due respect lad, the captain is… Well, the captain." Moira said with a sympathetic smile that Percy actually thought might be genuine. Percy's mouth hung open as he slowly looked around the barn. The Woodcutters regarded him with a mixture of sympathy and mild annoyance. The captain's eyes had not changed, and while Percy did not believe she was a spiteful person, he could see the restrained frustration, he decided a swift apology was appropriate.

"Ah, captain, I-" He fumbled before being cut off once again.

"There is no need to apologise, boy. Your master is our benefactor, his word is therefore law." The captain said through gritted teeth. "Does everyone understand? Marc is our employer, Percy is his… second in command, as it were. Therefore, Percy is in control, and you will follow his orders. If you do not, then you will not only be disobeying him, but you will be disobeying me, and you certainly do not wish to disobey me."

Percy didn't quite know what to say, and he hadn't expected the captain to defend him, and certainly not as passionately as she had. Then a small smile crept onto her face, it was not kind or sympathetic, it looked like victory, and it scared Percy.

"Right, well, yes, I'm glad that's all sorted then. Now, if you would kindly form into the afore-mentioned two groups, that would be grand."

Despite how much he despised the acting profession, Marc liked to believe he had generally understood the main concepts involved. Namely, do not be yourself, be someone else. Therefore he was not currently Marc the wanderer, he was not even Marcus Aurellis the wayfaring prince. He was... Luc. Luc Bordo. The name had been inscribed into a small square of iron that hung around the dead man's neck on a strip of leather. The Perdans called them dog-tags due to the Perdan slang for a soldier being 'mutt'.

The Yellow Fort was imposing. It was no Norda, and many of the Triman forts put it to shame, but within the Inner Kingdoms, it was a piece of art, assuming the artist had been a strategically minded veteran with severe paranoia. The walls were high and turreted to provide vantage points for archers. The wide portal was protected by a portcullis constructed from thick timber that lifted through the use of a complex network of chains and pulleys. The fort gained its name from the stone used to build it. The fort was unlike many of the buildings in the area which largely made use of whatever stone they could find, normally resulting in some very drab, grey buildings. The fort, however, was constructed from stone from a quarry several miles to the south, it was much more robust and had a yellow tinge.

The overall yellow-ness of the fort was increased by the variety of Perdan flags that dotted the walls and the yellow-coated guards that patrolled the ramparts and stood as sentinels behind the portcullis. Marc stumbled up to the portcullis, frequently glancing behind himself to give the impression that he was fleeing from something.

"Halt!" The more observant guard called from behind the bars. "Who are you? What regiment? Name and rank lad!"

This guard was significantly taller than the other and had the forts insignia stamped into his breastplate, the sign of a guard-sergeant.

"Luc Bordo, sir," Marc said, exercising a well-polished Perdan accent and adding a hint of desperation to his words. "Private Bordo that is, Just a path-plodder sir!" Marc was proud of his masterly use of Perdan phrases, path-plodder referred to a regular patrolman, one of the lowest in the Perdan military.

"Private Bordo? There is no Bordo assigned to this fort!" the sergeant replied, scrutinising Marc's uniform. Marc silently cursed the sergeant; he was one of the more involved sergeants who made it his business to know every soldier in the fort. A busy body, if you will, the kind of sergeant that Marc had detested in Norda.

"Not from this fort sir, I'm stationed in Riverrun, but, well, that's gone now, sir!" Marc lamented while mentally congratulating himself on his quick thinking. Riverrun was a day's travel with no forts or outposts between it and the Yellow Fort. The sergeant would be unable to uncover his lies until riders were sent to verify his story.

"Gone? How?" The sergeant asked as he came nearer the bars so that Marc could see his face. His suspicions were confirmed, he had the look of a busy body. Quite a shame really, with a face like this he had been destined from birth to be a nuisance.

"Reckon that's a story that I should be telling the lord-commander, sarge," Marc said, anxious to get inside the fort. The sun had just dipped below the horizon, plunging the fort and the surrounding fields into darkness.

He still had a few hours until he was scheduled to be opening the door. If he were late, then Percy and that unbearable Captain would never let him forget it.

The sergeant regarded Marc with evident suspicion. But, alas, Marc was correct, protocol demanded that Marc be escorted to the lord-commander immediately before the story can be retold in case the tale requires immediate 'hushing' to avoid panic.

The sergeant barked a command, and a few seconds later the great gears of the portcullis began to screech painfully. The iron lattice rose slowly. When the gate had raised far enough for Marc to duck under it, he did so. The sergeant promptly seized his arm.

"You will accompany me to the Lord-commander then, let's see what he makes of your vanishing town, Bordo." The sergeant spat. His breath smelled like cheese, the horrible blue stuff that the Perdan's ate by the barrel and somehow managed to keep down. The king of Perda had once made a gift of twenty wheels of the finest sapphire cheese to the Civvon royal family. This resulted in the first time in history that a royal family engaged in synchronised vomiting. It became somewhat of a diplomatic nightmare with Perda's king being accused of attempted murder and the Civvon patriarch being accused of insulting Perda's highest delicacy. Marc agreed with the Civvons wholly, it was vile stuff.

"Quite right sarge, quite right," Luc replied with force civility. The inside of the fort was much the same as Marc remembered it, behind the fore wall there was a courtyard that was mostly deserted at this time of day. Though Marc could see a few of the residents of the fort coming and going, as well as soldiers following some arbitrary circuit around the fort's interior, designed to keep them busy and distract them from how useless they had become in past years. Each of the inner kingdoms had begun scaling back their defensive standing forces and most forts now only contained a skeleton crew of soldiers with the extra room being used as stores with very thick walls. However, the Yellow Fort was Perda's showpiece and therefore never had fewer than two hundred of the most impressive-looking soldiers. Pir, the capital city of Perda, was the commercial hub of Perda, but The Yellow Fort was the centre of Perda's military. If Perda were to be invaded, the fort would become the centre of the kingdom's defences.

They crossed the courtyard at a measured pace and passed through an arch that led into the heart of the fort. Marc mapped out the fort in his mind as he walked, comparing it to his memories of the place. Nothing had changed, the tapestries were a little more frayed but still depicted the same battles and feats of much-exaggerated heroics. The corridors led to the same places, and as he expected, he was brought to a small waiting area where a diminutive clerk sat behind a cluttered, comically large desk.

The clerk did not lift his head from his diligent if slightly mind-numbing work, so the sergeant demanded his attention.

"Sergeant Picard to see the General, sir!" the sergeant said with exaggerated syllables, the kind that buffoons use to feign intelligence. Marc really could not fathom his dislike for this man, it was unreasonable and petty, but it was not something he was willing to let go.

"You were not summoned, Sergeant Picard. Who is your friend?" The clerk said without raising his eyes from the papers that threatened to overwhelm and consume him.

"No sir, I was not, this here is Private Bordo, a patrolman from Riverrun."

"Quite a long way from home, Bordo."

"Ah, yes sir," Marc said, attempting to sound as humble and meek as possible, a difficult task for a man with such an ego.

"Private Bordo claims that there has been a happening in Riverrun of catastrophic proportions sir!" Picard said, forcefully pushing Marc forward into the spotlight. The clerk finally raised his head and rested his tired eyes on Marc.

"And what exactly has happened in Riverrun, Private?" The clerk asked, his gaze wasn't suspicious, merely the look of a man who detested distractions.

"General's ears, sir. Regulation nine-two-two-Bee and all that sir!" Marc said confidently. In truth, he hadn't the foggiest clue if regulation nine-two-two-Bee existed, and he hoped that the Clerk had not been brushing up on his obscure regulations. His hopes were soon dashed.

"Nine-two-two-bee. When on manoeuvres, no soldiers are to relieve themselves in the Commanders helmet. Is that the one you are referring to, Private?" the clerk said without a hint of mirth.

Behind every regulation, there is a story.

"Eh, apologies sir. Must be nine-two-two-dee."

"Quite."

The clerk regarded the two of them before giving a tired shrug and rising from his seat.

"I shall ascertain whether or not the general is available for entertaining, private. Though if this turns out to be nothing, I would not like to be in your shoes." The clerk disappeared through the tall wooden doors.

"Was once stationed in Riverrun y'know," Picard said, by the tone of his voice, Marc could tell that the sergeant was about to suspiciously test his knowledge of the dreadfully dull little town.

"Is Marie still flaunting her goods on the corner of main street?"

"Marie Luz?"

"Nah nah."

"Marie Florenz?"

"Who?"

"Ah, you must mean Marie Senclir the flower-girl, amazin' that a flower-girl could ever make a livin' in such a small town. 'Course, doesn't matter now." Marc said as a deep depression came over his face, selling the terrible tragedy story with everything he had. The sergeant said no more as Marc was a far better liar than he was a detective.

The clerk reappeared a few moments later and gestured for the two to follow him. They passed through two further corridors that led off to the lord-commanders private rooms. The last passage led to a large study, lavishly furnished and well-decorated with the portraits of Generals past, including an intimidating portrait of the man who had been in charge when Marc had last visited. The portrait did not do the ferocious man justice. The general that now sat behind the polished oak desk was much less imposing. He was small and wiry with a bald spot on the centre of his head. Marc could see from the man's hard stare that he was no weakling, however.

"My man says you have some terrible news. Out with it." General Brokk commanded, with an uncharacteristically high-pitched, whiny voice.

"Well, general, I believe it's something best told with less company," Marc said, glancing at Picard and the clerk. The few people hear the lie, the fewer there are to contest it.

"Just speak," Brokk said. There would be no flexibility on this point.

"Very well sir. Riverrun has been attacked by a creature most foul. Some undead monstrosity!"

Instantly everyone in the room was very still, including the lord-commander, the mere mention of undead was enough to send Perda into a panic.

"Private, it is imperative that you think very hard on your words. Describe exactly what you saw."

"Well…" Marc began, spinning his lies into a tapestry that the old masters could have been proud of. "It began about a week ago. People started to go missing, sir. Then, two days ago… That's when it happened, sir. That's when *it* attacked."

The entire room had become silent, and Marc was confident that his small audience had been holding their breath since he began his fictitious story.

"When… What attacked, Private?" Brokk asked, breaking the silence when he could take the suspense no longer.

"I would not rightly know what to call it, sir. But I can describe it. It will haunt my dreams until my dying day. It was huge, sir, twice the size of any man and three times as wide. I wouldn't say it walked, sir. It shuffled. It was a mound of flesh, in it, I could see the faces of our missing townsmen. I suppose you could only call it an *abomination*."

The general stood up slowly but made no indication for Marc to stop talking.

"It had these… Tentacle-like things made from entrails and limbs. They whipped around the town, grabbing everyone! Sergeant Turn charged the thing, but it wrapped him up in a tentacle and used him as a club! That is how I was… Removed from the situation you see, Sergeant Turn's lifeless body saved me, if you will. He landed on me sir."

"I see, I see." The general waved a dismissive hand. "What happened to the abomination?"

"Don't rightly know, general. I came to after the sun had risen, somehow found the strength to move the sarge and began walking here."

"I see. You have done the right thing private. However, it is imperative that you do not mention this to anyone else."

"Regulation nine-two-two-dee, sir."

Confusion flashed across the man's face before continuing. "Quite right, private. Birno, arrange for a host of riders to confirm Bordo's claims, have them led by Murn. You will forgive me, private, but this is a matter of some importance, and I cannot begin a necromancer-hunt on the word of a private alone."

Birno nodded to his superior before leaving the room silently to go about his orders.

"I quite understand, m'lord. I barely believe it myself."

"Until Murn returns you will remain here. You will not reside in the barracks but one of the private quarters. Sergeant Picard, you are responsible for ensuring Bordo does not interact with anyone else or leave the fort. Picard, the same restrictions apply to yourself, of course."

Marc glanced at Sergeant Picard, the colour had drained from his face, and Marc could almost see the images of undead horrors dancing behind his eyes.

"Sergeant Picard, do you understand?"

"Oh." The sergeant said as he snapped back to the conversation. "Of course, my lord."

"Good. Escort our guest to one of the lower private rooms, when Birno returns he will see that food is provided. Dismissed." The Lord-Commander waved them away and returned to his seat behind the desk.

Picard wasted little time, and again Marc felt the tugging at his arm. He followed the man out and through the familiar corridors, planning his next move.

Chapter 13

On Marc's previous visit to the Yellow Fort, Prince Marcus Aurellis had stayed in one of the most lavish rooms in the fort, a place reserved for royalty, both Perdan and otherwise. It was a room designed to intimidate or impress. This time he had been provided significantly less lavish surroundings.

The small room could have been described as being Spartan. It had a bed, a wardrobe, and a table with a simple wooden chair. The small square window looked out onto the courtyard and the wall beyond it. He would not be able to see the mercenary's journey from this viewpoint. He had to stick his head out of the window to see the soldiers below. Soon the others would reach the secret door, and he would not be there. As he watched, a captain barked commands at his riders, each wearing a bright yellow cloak and straddling sleek, powerful horses. Another command and the portcullis rose, the riders trotting out before picking up the speed when they were clear of the portal.

Sergeant Picard had been frustratingly diligent in carrying out his orders. He had escorted Marc to the room, brought the food in himself and then remained outside the door ever since. The only useful thing that Marc had gained from his encounters with Picard was the knife that the sergeant had provided him to eat with, currently stashed in the waist of his trousers. This would require some extraordinary inventiveness.

"Need to use the privy, sarge," Marc said through the thin wooden door. His own genius sometimes amazed him.

"There's a piss-pot under the bed, Private."

"What? No piss-pot here, sarge."

"No piss-pot?"

"No piss-pot sarge."

"Right, 'ang on."

Marc considered himself to be a wise man, and a wise man ought to be thankful for a few things. Beautiful women, for example, or good food. The thing that he was most grateful for at this particular moment in time was stupid sergeants.

Sergeant Picard had a fatal flaw, one that Marc was surprised had not become apparent before now in a military career. Sergeant Picard had a weak jaw. Picard hit the desk hard, and Marc was momentarily worried that he would go through it. Luckily the desk held and Marc had been hidden away in such a remote part of the fort that the noise went unnoticed.

Punching Picard had possibly been the most satisfying thing Marc had done in weeks and took a moment to appreciate his work. The right-hook was always a speciality of his, but he had really outdone himself this time.

Marc padded slowly to the door, listening for the sound of footsteps before quickly poking his head through the opening and checking in both directions. The passage-ways were empty, but that did not mean they would be for long.

He was not in a part of the fort that he was familiar with due to it being too unimportant for a royal to take any mind of. He crept out of the room, quietly shutting the door behind him. He had made no effort to hide Picard, his absence would be considered as serious as the unconscious body, and a man-hunt would be initiated regardless.

Marc moved quickly, he knew well that the real trick to sneaking through a highly-populated fort was not to hug walls, peek around every corner and duck into shadows at the sight of every servant. Confidence was key, and he was nothing if not confident. Private Luc Bordo strode through the corridors, passing soldiers who offered him no more than a bored glance or occasionally a preoccupied nod. Marc had been relinquished of his armour and weapons and now only wore the cotton trousers, long shirt and leather sandals that the soldiers wore when they were not officially on duty. While some of the more observant soldiers may have briefly wondered why the private was not within the barracks or visiting the civilian buildings that lined the courtyard, none of them challenged him.

Marc scoffed at the lack of care displayed by the soldiers. 'This is what happens when a country goes too long without a good war.' He thought to himself as he descended a spiral staircase leading to the lower levels of the fort. 'Soon, rumours of undead will sweep through this fort, and each man will analyse every little thing they have let slide, I hope I feature in their worries.'

"Oi!" A voice called from down the corridor that Marc had just passed through. He didn't stop. Instead, he picked up the pace, taking the first right available and turning into a narrow passageway missing the paintings, tapestries and rugs that cluttered the more popular areas of the fort. This was a sign that he had reached the lower levels where he was less likely to meet any others, but it would also be more difficult to pass without incident if he did.

Heavy boots beating against the stone floors echoed through the bare corridors, and Marc broke into a run. His last visit to the secret door had been under similar circumstances, and luckily his only experience of locating the door was through doing it at full-sprint. He rounded two corners without slowing, at the next one he was forced to push himself off the opposite wall. At the next, he collided with a six-foot-tall slab of muscle and plate-steel.

When two large men collide, there's always a second or two of complete silence as the immediate area reviews what just happened. In this particular instance, Marc, being the more lightly armoured of the two came off worse, bouncing off the soldier and hitting the floor with a painful thud.

"Ooof." Said the living wall. Though as 'Ooof' is not really a word, perhaps it would not be correct to say that he said anything. The next things out of his mouth may have been words, but certainly not ones intended for polite company.

"What're you doing down here? Take a wrong turn?" The unnamed sergeant demanded of him. Once Marc had stopped seeing random spots of light, he could see the man more clearly. He had the same pointed features as Picard but did not share the man's blank stare or fair hair.

"Eh, guess I must have, sarge. The latrine isn't this way by any chance?"

"Latrine? Where exactly do you think you are?" The sergeant asked, extending a hand to Marc, which he took.

As the sergeant hoisted Marc to his feet, he saw his chance and took it, he launched his other fist into the man's vulnerable face. The impact was nowhere near as satisfying or as powerful as Marc had hoped and succeeded only in aggravating the man who responded in kind, snapping Marc's head to the side with such speed and ferocity that he was a little surprised that it had not twisted clean off.

It took Marc a few seconds to clear the grogginess that generally comes with a body-shaking punch. In that time the sergeant had spun him and twisted his arm up his back painfully. Marc gasped as the pain fired up his arm and through his upper body. The stranger continued to force the arm upwards, and Marc could feel the bones creaking.

Marc jabbed his elbow back, but it only hit the steel that protected much of the man. As pain racked his body, he desperately strove for ideas. His fingers curled around the grip of the stolen knife. It would not make it through the plate or the chainmail so he would have to aim carefully, something that was exceptionally difficult when all you can see is pain, and you're currently facing away from your assailant. He swung his arm back and hoped for the best. Lady Luck reared her beautiful head, and the sergeant screamed in agony as the knife sank into unprotected flesh. The grip on his arm became weak, and Marc was able to free himself, turning to face his opponent.

The knife had found a point of penetration in the man's leg. Marc used the momentary distraction and executed perhaps the finest tackle of his life. He wrapped his arms around the sergeant's thighs and lifted while simultaneously throwing his shoulder forward. Both of the men hit the ground. A sickening crack resounded through the corridor, and the sergeant stopped resisting immediately.

Marc slowly lifted himself off the still body. He was silent as he regarded the sergeant and the small puddle of blood that was growing around his head.

He glanced around himself once more before retrieving the knife, cleaning it on the sergeant's tabard and continuing on his path. It was not far now.

Percy flattened himself against the massive stone wall that encircled the Yellow Fort. They had crept from the barn, cutting loose their horses. Bandit did not even glance over his shoulder as he parted ways with Percy. Percy didn't care. They silently made their way through the darkened fields and found their way around the fort. The silence with which the mercenaries walked amazed Percy, and he was quickly put to shame as he stumbled through the darkness, almost revealing them all on more than one occasion. Luckily Niv had been close enough to catch him and pull him to his feet before he rolled into the light.

There were more guards on the walls than Percy had imagined, and torches burned every few meters, with soldiers patrolling relentlessly along them, occasionally stopping to scan the horizon, then moving on.

The water outlet was only a few meters away now, he could hear the gentle rushing of the current, and the occasional splashes as rocks and pieces of detritus hit the metal bars of the grill.

As they came to the edge of the river, Percy clung to the rock and slowly and carefully swung himself out to see the other side. The river was narrow here, spanning possibly three metres. In the darkness it was difficult, but he could just see the rock-face of the short tunnel in the wall. He swallowed hard; the current looked much more violent than Marc had described.

"No, no, that's quite alright. I'll just knock on the front gate and ask if they're absolutely certain they won't let us in." He whispered as he attempted to get around Niv and back along the wall. Niv's arm barred his way.

"Percy!" She hissed impatiently. "If you do not do this right now you will forever be known as Percy the coward. How does that sound?"

"Preferable to Percy the drowned, I must say." He replied, his eyes not meeting hers.

"Percy." She said calmly, waiting for his eyes to finally find hers. "You have fought bandits, faced off against Perda's finest and stood up to a golem. This is water, only water."

"I think that in sufficient amounts, simple water could have overcome all of those threats," Percy said, forcing a smile. She did not return the smile.

"Oh alright," Percy said, resigning himself to his fate and turning back to the water. With one last look at Niv's reassuring if somewhat threatening smile, he made his decision and swung his entire body around the edge, clinging to the wall and balancing precariously on the thin ledge. He reached out to touch the grill, it was just out of reach. He cursed under his breath and awkwardly shuffled as close as he could. His breath caught in his chest as his right foot slipped on the wet stone. He flailed desperately, attempting to grab whatever he could, but there was nothing in reach apart from the wet, slippery rock.

He hit the freezing water in an undignified half-bomb, half-flop. As his face was submerged, he opened his mouth to scream, allowing the vile water to fill his mouth He thrashed desperately and could feel the current begin to drag him away from the grill. Something else entered the river, he was not sure how he knew, but they certainly had. An arm gripped him roughly by the shoulder and forced him towards the metal bars until he was close enough to grasp the cold iron himself, pulling himself forwards and hugging the grill like a dear lover.

Once he had regained his breath and steadied himself, he had the presence of mind to thank his saviour. He had expected Niv, or possibly Caitlin. Instead, the calm eyes of the captain regarded him with little sympathy.

"Tha-thank you c-captain. You may have saved my life." He said through chattering teeth.

"I believe your survival is somewhat of a requirement for our payment. I always protect my payment." The captain said before gesturing for Percy to continue.

Percy didn't waste any more time. He began feeling for the next bars, pulling himself along to the opposite wall. The iron bars were rusted and covered in slimy green algae. Percy tried to ignore this and focused on the task in hand. As he reached the wall, he readied himself for the next part of the journey. This was possibly the most dangerous part of this ordeal. He looked back along the grill, the captain, Niv and Caitlin looked back at him, each soaking wet and clearly impatient to be out of the river. He got the message.

He filled his lungs with the almost fresh air and forced his head under the surface. He attempted to see the short underwater passage-way but all he could see was oily blackness, he would have to trust that Marc had not been lying or mistaken. If the recess were not there, then Percy would drown. Percy did not even hesitate. He pulled himself along the grill as quickly as he could as the air in his lungs strained to be free of him. He felt his muscles begin to burn.

Had he travelled the required ten feet? It occurred to him that he had no way of measuring this. If he overshot the small opening, then he may never find it. He could hold his breath no longer and in desperation, pushed his head up. It touched the stone ceiling of the passageway and Percy felt panic grip him. Had he passed it or had he yet to reach it?

He had to make a decision.

If this is how you die, I will be most displeased.

Percy cursed the voice, but as he did something began to grow in front of his eyes. He watched in astonishment as the thread of silver light grew and led away from him, it shone in the darkness like a thread of pure light. He didn't know what else to do but follow it.

It didn't lead him far. As soon as Percy reached the end of the thread his head broke the surface, and he pushed himself up, spluttering as he simultaneously tried to empty his lungs of toxic air while also trying to suck in the fresh air.

Wherever he was, it was pitch black. He felt a ledge that continued to a solid floor. Without hesitation, he hauled himself onto it and lay flat-out on the chilling rock.

As he lay there gasping and staring at nothing, he heard the splashing and gasping as enough found the entrance. He waited until he heard them find the edge before speaking.

"Captain?"

"Yes, Percy."

They said nothing more. Instead, the captain found him with a prying hand, and in the blackness, she led him to a back wall to allow room for the others who broke the surface of the water every few seconds.

"Do we have any light?" Percy asked.

"I do," Niv's voice answered. "I wrapped my matches in leather. They should still be dry."

There were a few more seconds of blind fumbling before the match flared into life and illuminated Niv's tired face. She reached out, providing the alcove with what little light she could. The space was as small as Percy imagined it and it was a tight fit with all the mercenaries cramming as close to the walls as possible. In the centre of the space was a metal door set into the floor. There was no handle or keyhole, and the edges were recessed into the ground, making it almost impossible to open from this side.

As Niv let the match die they huddled as close together as possible to warm themselves after the biting coldness of the water.

"Stay quiet, we don't know who would be able to hear us," Percy whispered to the captive audience.

"These stones are thicker than Moira's head. I think we should be ok." Somebody replied. Niv thought it might be Nica.

"Oi." Said an unmistakable voice.

"Nevertheless, this door might not be that thick." The captain warned.

Silence reigned supreme as the mercenaries followed their captain's instructions.

In the darkness, time was impossible to judge. He felt someone sit down beside him, their arm just brushing his. He opened his mouth to speak but thought better of it, sitting quietly with his secret companion.

You think they are your friends.

'I have yet to see any evidence that they are not. The mercenaries are hired, that is all they need to be.' Percy thought, wondering if this omnipresent voice could actually hear him or if it just anticipated his answers.

You think she is your friend.

Percy did not know who the voice was referring to, but the image of Niv filled his mind regardless.

She would sell you if she knew. You cannot trust her. She will try to take you away from your purpose. She will try to draw you from your goal. She will make sure you never become the hero you need to be.

'I'm not sure if I should really be trusting a disembodied voice either, no offence.'

The voice didn't laugh, but Percy was hit with a wave of feeling. It felt like delight.

There is only one you need to trust.

'Who?'

A screeching noise filled the alcove and light spilt from a crack in the centre of the floor. With a tortured squeal the trap door began to open. The light grew until it lit them all. Percy glanced to his side to see who had shuffled beside him. Caitlin stared at the trap-door, his ever-vigilant and entirely unfathomable protector.

From the opening the trap-door left, Marc's grizzled face appeared, looking a little worse for wear. The bruise left by the golem was now accompanied by a less severe mark on the other side of his face.

"You're late." The captain said.

"I just successfully infiltrated one of the most well-protected forts between the Great Lake and the Mountain Wall, I think I can be forgiven a minute of two," Marc said, gesturing for them to follow him through the door.

Percy was the first to descend into the room below. This room was not actually that different from the one above, plain and cold. A dark passage led away. Percy walked to the door and peered down the corridor. He thought he could see something moving, something just beyond the light.

"Percy, I will lead the way if you don't mind." Marc said as he gently pushed Percy aside and strode down the dark corridor. Percy quickly followed him, passing no demon in the darkness. He could hear the others following, their stealthy footsteps sounding monstrously heavy in the utter silence.

"Is that the reason you were late?" Percy asked nervously as they passed an unmoving body. The bloody puddle around his head had begun to run along crevasses between the stones.

"A momentary distraction," Marc said, not slowing.

Upon seeing the entrance to the Low Road, Percy felt a tremendous feeling of satisfaction as for the second time on this journey, something actually lived up to his standards.

The great door was nearly twice the height of Marc, constructed from solid iron with laborious carvings covering it. Percy approached the door warily and inspected the images that stretched from corner to corner. He felt his heart grow cold and his stomach queasy. The carvings were grotesque and depicted horrors of all shapes and sizes, there were hunched human-shaped beasts with extended talons and no eyes, and there were small monsters that looked like insects with dozens of legs that ended in a spear-like foot. The thing that dominated the majority of the door was what really terrified Percy.

Whatever the thing was, it was clear that the artist had never actually seen it as it had no discernible shape. Instead its body coiled into impossible shapes, with human-like arms and legs sprouting from its body as well as segmented chitinous spikes and fur-covered paws with claws like scimitars. In addition to this, the length of the central spiralling coil that made up its central body was covered in mouths and eyes that came from every creature imaginable.

"It doesn't really look like that of course," Marc said as he appeared beside Percy. After a few seconds, he smiled slyly. "It's much, *much* worse."

"You're just trying to scare me."

"Am I?"

"Of course, the Low Road is documented in Legate Chassius' 8th journal. It was used for over a hundred years, primarily by the Trimans."

"And then?"

"Eh, it's a little vague on how, but the road flooded with… 'Hellish beasts and unknowable evils'. That's how Chassius put it, anyway. One of life's mysteries. The road was sealed, whatever the monsters were, they're all dead by now."

"Assuming they were ever alive. They say Perda's necromancers came out of the road."

"No, the necromancer's were always here. They're just people, no more mysterious than you or I."

Marc raised an eyebrow quizzically at Percy. Percy quickly rethought his statement.

"Well, no more mysterious than I am, at least."

Marc smirked before turning to regard the mercenaries.

"Well, it's time for you lot to earn your coin. Young master Percival may believe that the Low Road is devoid of all the horrors it once held, but I'm not so sure. Personally, I would rather have twenty swords to prove his assumption. You are the swords I need."

Percy was stunned, this was possibly the closest thing to a motivational speech that he had heard from Marc so far. He thoroughly doubted it would undo the damage caused by his usual insults and quips, but it was a start. For their part, this was the readiest that Percy had ever seen the Woodcutters, they had their weapons drawn, their armour strapped tight and across each face was an expression of pure determination with only flickers of doubt or fear here and there. Percy could see that the one harbouring the most fear was Niv. As with the rest of them, the encounter with the golem had left her shaken and possibly a little more open to believing the impossible. To her, it was entirely plausible that the monsters that stopped a Triman legion could still be lurking in the murky depths of the road.

In light of this, Percy's own lack of fear was surprising.

266

"Let's just get on with this." The captain said, her axe grasped firmly in both hands.

"As you wish," Marc said with a small tight smile.

Percy didn't see where Marc produced the key from, one moment his hand was empty, the next it grasped a simple key that was as black as a witch's heart. It was small and delicate. It was not made from dragons' bone, and there was no skull in sight, it could be mistaken for the key to any Aelissean lavatory – something no Aelissean would misplace.

Mark slid the key into the hole located in the centre of the door and attempted to turn it. The key would not twist. Marc grumbled in frustration as he placed his other hand on the key and applied more force.

"Need a hand?" The captain asked, satisfaction behind the words.

A low grinding noise marked his victory over the door and without warning it slid into the wall. Gaping darkness stood in its stead.

Percy felt an immediate draw to the darkness beyond the opening. He felt the same way he did when he first approached the Landry estate, and the open door beckoned him inside. He opened his mouth to protest, to warn the party that nothing good could come from this.

He couldn't speak, the words didn't form, and he found his tongue numb. He wanted to back away from the opening, but his legs wouldn't carry him in that direction. Instead, they propelled him forward.

He was stopped when a heavy hand landed on his shoulder.

"How about we let the captain lead the way. It is what she's paid for." Marc said, warning in his voice.

The captain strode past them and into the darkness without hesitation, followed quickly by Niv, Moira, Nica and several more Woodcutters. The rest of the mercenaries waited for Marc, Percy and Caitlin to enter before following them. Percy stepped into the darkness.

Karees 2

A hundred years ago

Karees tore her blade from yet another ancillary. His gasp became a gurgle as blood welled in his lungs and slowly drowned him. Karees drew upon every ounce of her training and faced the next foe. He was more boy than man, but he held his sword in a sure fist. He tried to hide his fear behind feigned confidence, but Karees saw through him, and he knew it. The boy charged, his face contorting into something almost frightening. His final assault was halted prematurely as Terus rammed his shield into the boy's face. As he fell back, instinctively raising a hand to his broken nose, Terus used the opportunity to plunge his shortsword into the boy's throat. He couldn't even scream to mark his departure from the world.

The ancillaries acted as supporting cohorts to the legions and were supposed to be filled with the veterans of each conquered kingdom. The truth of the matter was that very few veterans remained after said conquering, so anyone without a damn good excuse or a significant coin purse was drafted instead. The cohort currently attacking them came from Eastern Aellis. Karees recognised the tactic. Friarn was simply too dangerous, and at this delicate point in the empire's expansion they could not afford to lose a legion or two to the mages fury, so instead, they sent the faceless masses of the ancillaries. They swarmed up the hill toward the defending legion's shield-wall. The charge would be suicide for hundreds, but they could not be repelled forever. Soon another cohort from Aellis and finally the 7th legion would descend on them to mop up.

Terus gripped Karees' shoulder and tugged her back, the shield-wall opening to readmit them into the fold.

"What are you doing girl? Trying to die?" Terus asked. In front of them three rows of their siblings battled wave after wave of the ancillaries. Each push forced them back just a little bit further, and each charge whittled down their number by just a few more. Little by little, the once great legion was being chipped away.

"Would it really matter?" Karees replied sarcastically.

"Don't be so melodramatic. This is a battle, this is what you were bred and trained for. This is our business, Legionary."

"This is insanity, I don't remember training to kill our own ancillaries."

"Don't be naive, half of the strategies we learned were for use against our own people."

"Under orders from the emperor."

"The legate is your new emperor, isn't that clear?" Terus said, straightening suddenly and turning back to the shield-wall.

"Legionary!" A voice barked. It was coarse and rough. She turned to salute the centurion.

"Centurion!" She replied. He was tall and dark-haired with a stern face and a hooked nose. He didn't look afraid of the carnage around them. He looked her up and down. "I need more bodies around the legate, Aelissean infiltrators are aiming for Friarn. You too Terus."

Despite Karees' traitorous talk she almost jumped at the chance to fulfil her orders. Her training was still deeply ingrained within her. Together, she and Terus took a moment to compose themselves and travel further up the hill to where Chassius and Friarn looked out over the battle below, looking as imperious and sure as ever, even in the face of insurmountable odds. Friarn's flames burned gently around them, creating a perimeter but they extended no further. Karees wondered for a moment if his strength was failing him. It had to happen sometime she supposed.

They had no sooner come to join their meagre contingent of brethren upon the crest of the hill that a yell of triumph erupted from below. The legionaries ran to identify the source and saw their worst fears becoming a reality. The ancillaries, led by an Aelissean brute nearly twice the size of his comrades wielding a ridiculous axe had broken through the shield-wall and were streaming up the hill towards them.

"Shields! Form up! Defend your legate you maggots!" Terus commanded. His voice sounded hoarse. Karees joined them and stood shoulder to shoulder with Terus and another. She glanced around. There were only ten of them. She prayed and didn't really care who she prayed to.

The goliath hit them with enough force to push the entire shield wall back. He had impacted with Terus and

Karees could hear the bones crack in his shield-arm. She wanted to assist him, but the ancillaries were now throwing themselves against them, and she had three Aelisseans beating at her shield with swords and axes. She thrust her sword at them every chance they gave her, expertly demonstrating the benefits of a shortsword in confined spaces.

It was hopeless. They could hold off one wave only to be devastated by the next. With a crash the huge Aellissean had knocked Terus to the ground and was through them, stepping over the downed veteran and charging at the ultimate prize. She expected flames to engulf the man. She expected flaming rocks to rain down from the sky and obliterate the entire hillside to avoid the loss of the legate. She had expected everything except what she actually saw.

The man just stopped and stared at Chassius in utter horror. Chassius' eyes were no longer vibrant but had turned a pale silver that seemed to flow and warp like a river of mercury. The battle around them seemed to stop, and Karees' hair prickled, as though there was static in the air.

"Him," Chassius said quietly, and the Goliath fell to his knees and let out a wail of torment that sounded almost inhuman. She watched his transformation with a mixture of abject terror and morbid curiosity as the body distorted into something that resembled a man, but its skin was cracking and leaking a liquid silver which overflowed from its eyes and mouth. He had doubled in size, and the armour had welded itself to his body. It took perhaps a minute before he stood again. Silent.

Chassius waved a dismissive hand at him, and the Aelissean turned to face the shield-wall. He charged. If not for Terus tackling her out of the way, she would have been swept away by the abomination into the stricken ancillaries. The horror tore its way through its former allies, tearing men apart as though they were straw-dolls.

Karees felt sick, but the monster was immediately effective, driving the ancillaries back with as much terror as it did with its terrible strength and soon the Aelisseans were fleeing. Karees looked back at Chassius who watched the carnage with grim satisfaction.

If the man could create such warriors with ease, then perhaps his quest to become emperor was not so ridiculous. Though, who would become these warriors? Karees shuddered and helped Terus to his feet.

Chapter 14

Percy wasn't happy in the Low Road, but being there still felt right. The mercenaries had lit glass lanterns pilfered from the walls of the Yellow Fort, as well as several torches that were found just inside the tunnel. Percy could only assume that the torches had been stored there when the road was used regularly, forgotten when the only ways in or out were sealed. In truth, they were not yet in the Low Road itself, they were instead walking through another tunnel cut by the Trimans to link the Low Road with the Perdan surface. This tunnel sharply descended and took them ever deeper into the earth, down the throat of the beast and onwards towards the stomach. Though in this analogy, Percy believed he would enjoy the last part of the journey the least.

This tunnel was crudely cut into the earth with the walls and ceiling being clad with wooden beams which were silently rotting away. The ceiling was supported by thick timber. For all intents and purposes, this tunnel looked no different than the iron or salt mines that dotted the north of Urn.

The first door had closed behind them, powered by some unseen time-operated mechanism.

"Marc!" The captain called from the head of the column. "There's another door."

"Open it then!"

"Eh… I think you should see it first!" Niv said, walking back up the line and gesturing for Marc to follow her.

Marc followed Niv silently, Percy did the same after a moment's hesitation.

The walls were solid rock here instead of the wooden beams, Percy could see no evidence of this rock being carved. There were no tell-tale chisel-marks; instead, it was as though the stone had been poured and moulded. There were cracks, and the line that separated the Triman-built tunnels and the older Low Road was evident by the deep gouges into the older rock and missing segments.

The old tunnel had been destroyed and dug again by the Trimans.

The captain and Marc stood in front of something less like a door and more like a steel wall. In the centre of this wall was a metallic panel with rows of small circular domes that extruded from it. A tiny symbol was carved into each dome.

"What is it?" The captain asked, looking at Marc expectantly.

Marc didn't answer. Instead, he stared at the panel as though he expected it to answer the question for him. He slowly reached out a finger and pushed one of the domes. The dome sank into the panel, and there was a quiet click. As he retracted his hand, the dome pushed itself out of the panel again.

"Is it Triman?" The captain asked.

"No, it was here before the Trimans," Percy said confidently.

Both the captain and Marc looked at Percy with confused expressions. Percy enjoyed their surprise and savoured knowing something that they did not.

"Well, it's all documented in Legate Chassius' journal of course."

"Of course. Refresh my memory." Marc said, his expression unchanging.

"You know that the Low Road was not built by the Trimans, it is far older than Trima, or Aellis or even Jorlund. For all we know, it is as old as Urn itself. This mechanism could be just as old. According to Chassius, you must enter a sequence of pushes. There is only one sequence. You know, that door in the Yellow Fort is just for show, this thing is the real gate. Nigh impregnable you see. Chassius tried everything, rams, black powder, even managed to coerce a Bull Orlo into the Road and painted another Orlo onto the door. The Orlo killed itself and didn't even dent the door."

"How did they get through then?"

"Figured out the code."

Marc barked a laugh and pointed at the panel.

"Figured it out? There could be thousands of possible combinations."

"Millions."

'Million' was not a number most people in Urn had any business with, it was inconceivable, but it still existed.

"Then how exactly did he figure it out?"

"We don't even know how many symbols are required," Captain said, still inspecting the panel.

278

"It just came to him. Let's just call it 'divine inspiration'."

"And then he wrote it in his journal?" Marc said.

"Well, yes, but he encrypted it before it was published. It has driven my father mad for years. I, of course, figured it out in less than a day."

"And you have now been savouring this while Perdans could come flooding down this tunnel any minute?"

"…I understand now why that may have been wrong."

"Open the door, Percy."

Percy nodded and quickly stepped up to the panel, squinting to examine the dome and their corresponding symbols. The symbols were a little different from how Chassius had described them. They were more angular, but Percy could see the resemblance.

He carefully and slowly input the sequence of symbols that he had taken from Chassius' use of them in his journal. The symbols had been scattered throughout the journal, with small puzzles and games determining which of the symbols were correct, and in what order.

He put in the final symbol and made a flourish with his hands, expecting the door to slide open. It was very dramatic in his head.

"It's not opening, Percy," Marc said.

"Oh…"

"What?"

"My copy of the journal may have been… Missing a few pages."

"Percy, this does not please me."

Percy stared at the panel. Praying for some kind of sign. Perhaps a little of that divine inspiration that Chassius had enjoyed. Nothing came. Percy closed his eyes and pushed a dome.

The squeal of old gears filled the tunnel, and with a metallic grinding noise, the door began to slide into the wall of the tunnel. It stopped when the opening was large enough for two wagons to pass through side by side.

Percy couldn't move. He stared into the darkness just beyond the light of the lanterns and torches.

"Well," Marc said as he passed Percy, keen to be getting on. "Fate favours you, Percy. Let us hope some gods do too."

"That was lucky," Caitlin said as she walked beside him once again.

"Was it lucky?"

"What else would it be?"

"Well, it could be… You know. The thing."

"Well, I suppose it could be. Might not be though. What does it matter? It worked didn't it?" She said with an optimistic grin. How was she not afraid? They were descending into a place that once contained horrors that most people in Urn could not even imagine. Was it the same reason he did not feel the fear that he should?

"Well, then there's something that wants us to be here. It wants us on this path."

"Us?" Caitlin said, her grin growing to split her face. Percy felt a chill shoot up his spine. It didn't want them, it wanted him.

This section of the Low Road was similar to just before the sequence-door, smooth, grey walls with a streak of what looked like red paint that travelled and turned sharply, making geometric shapes across the walls and ceiling. Every few metres there was a long glass bulb like a lantern, though Percy could see no way of lighting them. Percy was fascinated with the tunnel. About half a mile along the road two metallic rectangular poles extended along the floor about the width of a carriage apart. These continued into the blackness.

"This is amazing," Percy said to Caitlin as quietly as possible. "Think of the people that made this road, while we can barely get our wagon-wheels circular, they could build permanent tunnels, complex sequence-based locks and impregnable steel doors."

"Impressive," Caitlin said passively, clearly not finding the Low Road as fascinating. Her eyes stared into the blackness just beyond their light. Percy briefly wondered if her warg eyes could see dangers that he could not. At this moment, he would rather not know.

"What happened to them?" Nica said from behind him in a small voice that made Percy jump nonetheless.

"Oh, uh, I don't know. There's little information on Urn's history before the Jor Clans took up residence in the north and created Jorlund. Before that there may as well have been no Urn. There may have been dragons or ogres or something, but one has disappeared entirely, and the other isn't the best at recording their history." Percy whispered.

Nica nodded slowly. Moira opened her mouth to speak but thought better of it.

"Any theories?" Nica said.

"From me?"

"Who else?"

"Well… There really is very little to go on. Though, look at those."

Percy pointed to their right where a door was set into the wall, just as impregnable as the code-gate but with no panel on it. These doors would only ever open from the other side.

"They're taller than we would need but no wider. This tunnel is much larger, but I expect these… Things on the floor are like wagon-tracks, they're for something much heavier. I don't know of any species that could build something like this… Other than humans. Therefore, I believe they are not unlike us. Additionally, this is not the only underground structure made by these… Beings."

"There's another?"

"Well, there was. Or at least, the Jor's have a legend of an entire underground city. Personally, I believe this is probably an exaggeration, but tunnels are not out of the question."

"So, human-like beings crawl from those tunnels. Beings that could do all the things you just said… And became the Jor clans?"

"Of course not. They were killed by the Jor clans." Caitlin said, cutting into the conversation.

Percy was shocked by the brutality that Caitlin suggested.

"Still doesn't answer where the Jor clans came from."

"Well, you're not going to learn that answer right now so shut up!" Hissed one of the woodcutters. Nica turned her gaze on them, and they quickly slunk to the back of the column.

"She's right," Percy whispered, nodding. "We have to be quiet while we're on the road."

You could almost say that the Low Road had been boring so far. It was uniform and unchanging, the size, wall-patterns and the distance between the doors were constant. Here and there the stone walls showed more decay, and in one part, half of the tunnel was filled with dirt and stone.

The column stopped, immediately the mercenaries dropped into offensive poses, brandishing their most threatening weaponry. At the front of the line, someone was waving a torch, as they lowered it, Percy realised that it was Marc and he was looking right at him. Percy swallowed hard and made his way to the front of the line.

"Is that a problem?" Marc said as he pointed to one of the doors that led off from the main tunnel. This one was slightly more interesting because it was hanging open.

"How should I know?"

"You seem to know the most about this road."

"Which still means that I know very little."

Marc's glare made Percy consider the question more carefully.

"I don't know. It could be. Though, we could investigate."

"Why would we investigate?"

"Well, it would certainly teach us more about who built the road."

"I don't really care who built the road, I only care about getting to the end."

"It could be where the beasts that decimated the Triman legion came from." Captain said.

"We continue then," Marc said while Percy wondered what he was actually supposed to add to that discussion. He stood and stared, lamenting at having lost the opportunity to explore further, to see if this door led to the answers about the maybe-humans. The mercenaries seemed happy enough to leave him there gazing into the void until Caitlin gently pushed him onwards.

Percy didn't know how long they had been walking, but he had found his way to the front of the line once again as Marc bombarded him with questions, seemingly believing that Percy was an expert on the Road, or if he wasn't, then he ought to be. He insisted that Percy take constant notes about the road and everything they saw.

"No one has travelled along this road in a long time, this could make for an interesting story. You wish to make your own legend, don't you? This is a good place to start." Marc said with a sagely nod.

"It'll also be a good place to end if you don't keep quiet." Captain hissed.

"We've been walking for hours now. I think if we were going to encounter anything we would have by no-"

Marc was cut off by noise.

The noise itself was tough to describe, and instantly Percy attempted to assign it to a creature. It was not the proud roar of a wall lion, it was too guttural and wet, but at the same time, the dry skittering noise put Percy in mind of spiders or insects. The foreboding door in the Yellow Fort very quickly came to mind and the monsters that it depicted.

Marc gripped his sword in both hands, staring ahead. Something moved just beyond their view, too far to gain a full silhouette or outline, just a glint here and a sharp line there.

"There's something there," Percy whispered, suddenly feeling the fear that had been mysteriously missing from this leg of their journey.

"We should go back," Niv said, she had already notched an arrow and was aiming blindly into the darkness.

"We have to make it to the end," Marc said. "There is nowhere else to go, the only thing on the other side of the steel wall is Perdans."

"We could use that door."

"What makes you think there's anything better on the other side?"

"It's a chance, isn't it?"

"No."

"Fine then." The captain said, she stepped forward, taking a torch from one of the Woodcutters and tossing it forward. It spun through the air before hitting the ground at the feet of a monster.

What it illuminated had stepped out from Percy's latest nightmare. This thing almost looked human. It had two arms and two legs, but it was hunched, and its limbs were long and spindly with lean muscle. Its skin was a pale, almost translucent white and each long skinny finger ended in a curved black talon. Its face was the least human part. It lacked a nose and eyes; instead a mouth dominated its face, and just beyond its black lips, Percy could see a row of pointed teeth.

The thing let out another wet roar and leapt back from the torch, the heat shocking it. Its eyeless face turned in their direction, and the lips curled into a snarl, showing off those impressive pearlies that Percy had seen hints of.

The captain nodded to Niv who let loose her arrow. It flew true and struck the thing in the throat. Its intimidating roar became a pathetic gurgle, and then silence took over once again. There was a collective sigh of relief from the mercenaries, but they did not relax, listening carefully for any signs of reinforcements. When they came, there was no sound. The next thing was taller and broader, less stooped, it stepped into the light with obvious purpose, unlike its sibling. It had the same eyeless face and oversize mouth as the first but was immeasurably different.

"Doesn't take much to draw out the strong, eh?" Niv said in little more than a whisper.

The things head twitched at the words and in jittery, unnatural movements. It lowered itself into a crouch, spreading its nightmarish hands and bellowing a low-pitched challenge. As the noise echoed through the claustrophobic tunnel more took their place at the nightmare's side. They came in all shapes and sizes, some smaller than children while others towered over Moira, each looked like they could tear an orlo apart with vicious, blood-stained claws.

"How on Urn does a desolate underground tunnel sustain so many?" Percy whispered, fear having sent his senses packing.

Both Niv and the captain looked at him, Niv in mild shock and the captain in light amusement.

"Asking the important questions are we? Here's a better one… How do we survive!?" Niv hissed.

"There is only one way, Niv." The captain said, the same excitement creeping across her face that Percy had seen on the night where he lost whatever innocence he had managed to cultivate in his short life. At that moment he wasn't sure which he feared more, the eldritch horrors that stood in their way, or the woodcutter that would face them.

"Woodcutters! You have a job to do! Anyone who dares to die... Well, the death itself will be nothing compared to what I'll do to you in the Underworld! Am I understood?" She yelled, raising her axe.

"Understood Captain!" The Woodcutters replied as one, their collective roar making the monsters flinch. Seamlessly the mercenaries moved together, those with shields took to the fore with Moira anchoring the line.

Marc looked at the captain, and Percy thought he could see something that almost resembled respect, or at least it was not as insulting as most of the looks his face was used to pulling. Behind the shield-bearers, the long-range combatants took up position, Niv with her bow and Nica with an assortment of throwing-knives. It would seem that any weapon was a ranged weapon to the Woodcutters assuming that they could chuck it with sufficient force as one proved by launching a battle-axe at the largest of the nightmares. The axe embedded itself in the beast's chest, raising a cheer from the mercenaries. This cheer quickly died as the thing tore the axe from its chest and promptly returned it to sender. Moira raised her shield and braced, the wayward weapon bouncing off the shield but transferring enough energy to throw Moira back into the axe-thrower.

Volleys of arrows, knives, axes and what Percy was sure was a boot tore into the front line of the monsters. At another roar from what they assumed to be the leading nightmare, the tide of pale aberrations hit the shield-wall, sending a shock-wave through the mercenaries. The ranged combatants moved back, allowing room for Woodcutters with spears, swords and axes to jab, slash and hack between the shields. Marc and the captain fought side by side, at the captain's call the bulwark before her would split and she would deliver a crushing blow with her axe while Marc would thrust his long-sword into the nearest enemy.

The Woodcutters had the width of the tunnel on their side, it was too narrow for the nightmares to use their superior numbers to full effect. This advantage quickly melted away as one of the taller horrors launched themselves clear over the shield wall, crashing into Niv.

Percy was frozen on the spot as Niv struggled with the monster, she threw punches while it slashed at her, tearing with its claws. Percy drew all his courage and advanced on them, raising his short-sword and bringing it down on its shoulder. The monster screeched and turned to Percy, allowing Niv to scavenge a dagger from her belt and drive it into its neck. Percy looked on in horror as the screeching noise stopped and it turned its attention back to Niv, raising its hand, ready to sink its long claws into her face.

A flying dagger saved her just as the claw began to face, hitting the beast with enough force to throw it off Niv and wrench Percy's blade from its shoulder. It shuddered before going still. Percy reached a hand down to Niv which she took as Nica retrieved her dagger. Percy turned to thank her for her intervention, but she had already moved onto the next monster that had jumped the shield wall.

A scream came from the front-line, the shield-bearer beside Moira had lost most of their face, and they were dragged forward into the writhing throng of pale, gaunt bodies. Woodcutters rushed forward to fill the gap, Marc picked up the fallen shield and forced his way to the front just in time to deflect a large piece of ceiling turned projectile.

"There is no end to them!" Niv called from the rear, relieving a nightmare of its malformed, eyeless head.

"How can there possibly be so many?" Percy replied, having to yell over the screams of pain, monstrous screeches and the sickening wet sound of claws ripping through leather and armour. The battle was beginning to turn, and more and more nightmares made it through or over the shield-wall despite Marc's resilient defence and the captain's frenzied, well-trained attacks. Percy felt helpless as one of the Woodcutters met their gruesome end and was tossed aside like a broken toy.

"Percy." A small voice beside him said.

Caitlin looked so out of place there. She carried no weapon and gave him the same whimsical smile as always. Amongst all this bloodshed and horror that most people would have trouble even contemplating, she seemed to not notice it. As a warg, this had been her life, blood and killing were all that Caitlin had known.

"You know that I am here for a reason." She said, gesturing idly to the sea of pale bodies that stretched back into the darkness as though they were a throng of rowdy children.

"You can't. Not here. The Woodcutters will kill you!" Percy said.

Caitlin chuckled and looked around doubtfully. "I think they're a little busy."

She turned and walked back along the tunnel, away from the front. "Don't worry so much!" she said as she vanished into the swirling blackness. Percy watched, ignoring the battle that still raged around him. Everything seemed to become very. Percy shook his head as the warg prowled into the light. Its growl cut through the sound of battle and made the Woodcutters turn. It even made the nightmares stop and inspect the curious new creature.

Caitlin gave them no time to study her as she pounced onto the nearest nightmare, nearly tearing it in two. The next fiend did not fare any better, and any Woodcutters were knocked out of the way as Caitlin sprinted for the front line. The captain turned, and upon seeing the warg a number of emotions washed over her usually passive features, first there was confusion, then there was hate, then there was only anger as she raised her axe to end Caitlin. She did not get the chance as Caitlin soared over her, crashing into the horde. The warg vanished for a moment beneath the lanky bodies, and when she reappeared, she thrashed and tore at them, throwing some and tearing others apart.

The nightmares that slashed at the shield-wall turned and squealed in delight as they pounced on her, biting and clawing her thick hide.

"Kill it!" The captain said as she attempted to force her way past Marc and closer to the warg. He refused to allow her.

"Kill it? She is giving us a chance! We have to leave now!" Percy yelled over the snarling and screeching that echoed down the tunnel.

"She?" Niv said from beside him. She glanced around, her face turning from shock to anger as realisation struck her.

"That *thing* was travelling with us?"

"This is not a good use of our time," Nica said. She was depleted of throwing-knives and held only two longer fighting knives. They were covered in blood.

"Marc! Please! We can leave now." Percy said, pushing his way to the shield-bearers.

"They would run us down before we reached the entrance. The little monster cannot hold back the tide forever." Marc said.

"We don't have to make it there."

"There is no guarantee that there is anything better on the other side of that door, Percy! Forward is the only way!"

"You're smarter than that Marc, no matter what's at the end of this tunnel, it's nothing if you're dead. You'll just be another man, consumed by the Low Road!"

It seemed that the only thing Marc feared more than not reaching the end of the Low Road, was being another one of the forgotten men who has fallen to it.

"Lead on then!"

Percy wasted no time and sprinted ahead with Niv joining him. She was running with a slight limp, but she held a torch high to light their way. Behind them the shield-wall began to recede carefully, arrows and knives continued to pepper the monsters as they gleefully tried to subdue the mound of claws and teeth that continued to tear through their ranks. Once they had left sufficient distance between the beasts and them, they unceremoniously turned tail and ran.

Percy and Niv reached the open door and briefly stopped to stare into the darkness just beyond it.

"There is no other option!" Percy argued as he saw Niv's hesitation. After a moment of indecision, she nodded unhappily and stepped through the entry-way. Percy looked back along the tunnel, he saw the torches of the mercenary's approaching. Marc and the captain were at the rear, a small detachment of the monsters was following them down the tunnel, delighting in the chase, their huge mouths pulled into terrible grins.

"Here! It's here!" Percy said, waving a hand which was ultimately useless in the gloom of the tunnel.

A hand grabbed the back of Percy's jerkin, and he was yanked back through the doorway. The light died as the door slammed shut.

Chapter 15

Percy stood in the all-consuming blackness, shivering uncontrollably.

"Niv? Niv? Why did you do that Niv? Open the door." Percy said uncertainly, partly wanting answers and partly just wanting to break the silence.

"Not Niv I'm afraid." The voice said. A voice that instantly transported Percy back in time, to a time before he had killed, before he had met the Woodcutters and before he had dared to enter this place where even the moonlight did not find a home. Even though there was no light, he could see the mask clearly, silver and eyeless with the split crescent on the cheek.

"Mask. I knew you were a spectre."

"Mask? Do you make up names for everyone?" He said as he stalked around the room.

"You have to let them through."

"I cannot."

"You can. You already opened it once."

"That is an assumption."

"An incorrect one?"

"I didn't say that."

"Please."

"I just said that I cannot."

"Where's Niv?"

"She is safe."

"Why are you here?"

"You ask a lot of questions."

"The more you talk, the less time you have to kill me."

Mask burst into surprisingly pleasant laughter.

"You think here, in this darkness, time is relevant?"

Percy still had trouble placing Masks odd accent, it sounded almost Triman but some words were too elongated, and others clipped off harshly.

"I think that you're getting philosophical in order to avoid my question. Time always matters, especially when my friends are about to be eaten by horrible monsters!"

"Your friends? Which ones are your friends? The hired help or the man who would sacrifice you to ensure that his story remained alive and well? Perhaps you mean the beast that has been bound to you. You have only one friend, and that is me."

Percy's mouth gaped at the disembodied mask. "Friend? You're a friend? In what way? As of yet, you have done absolutely nothing friend-like!"

"I did warn you that all of this would happen, you did not listen."

"You did no such thing!"

"I told you not to trust Marc, you did not listen, and he brought you here."

"Perhaps, but you didn't really say 'If you trust him, you will almost inevitably end up as a snack for a hellish monster with no eyes and a mouth like a knife-drawer!'" Percy snapped, trembling with a mixture of fear and anger.

Mask laughed again; Percy heard no venom in it.

"Perhaps you have a point, I will ensure that I keep it in the mind for next time."

"Next time?"

"I am certain that you will not be the only one chosen by The Stranger."

"The Stranger? Another masked stalker I take it?" Percy said, stepping back from where he thought Mask was, holding his sword at the ready, he had had quite enough of mystery on this journey and was confident that it was about time that someone gave him a straight answer.

"Sorry, bad translation I suppose," Mask said, a little further from the right than Percy had imagined. "I did send some ruffians to discourage you, I assumed that a little blood on your hands would deter you."

"You evil son of a bi-."

"Many times over, yes," Mask interrupted.

"Are you Triman?"

"Yes."

"The Stranger... That's what Trimans call the moon, yes?"

Mask didn't reply.

"So, I assume this is all about that font in Aellis? You know, it really hasn't benefited me much, I think you can take back this pale magic thing as so far it hasn't really done anything. Really, I cannot believe that I'm having troubles with the moon of all things. Wargs? Certainly, I understand how they could be an issue. I don't even find the idea of mouthy monsters in the depths of the Low Road inconceivable; I mean, ogres are pretty weird.

However, I refuse, I draw the line at the belief that the moon is the thing that has caused any of this misfortune to befall me. The moon didn't choose me. How could it? Something else lived in that font, some magical parasite that calls to golems and wargs and maybe even those monsters out there." Percy gasped, tears pricking at the corners of his eyes as he finished his rant, he had raised his sword, so the point faced where he hoped Mask was. The triman was silent for what may as well have been an hour in the darkness. Screams, clashing and happy shrieks could just be heard through the door, muffled but still pulling Percy towards it, encouraging him to open it and let the others inside. He took a step towards where the noise came from. A hand gripped his shoulder.

"You are intelligent. More so than I ever was." Mask said, quiet and close to Percy's ear. "The monsters that prowl out there are endless. Out there, they are already dead."

From the other side of the door, a commanding voice cut through the cacophony of noise, slowly the sounds of battle moved away, but the screeching and odd roars continued for several minutes before silence won over again.

"You killed them," Percy whispered. "They would have been safe in here, by stopping them from entering here you are as guilty as those monsters. You are just as much the monster as they."

The hand lifted from his shoulder, and Percy gritted his teeth and span, slashing the sword at the darkness while yelling his frustration at the masked stranger. The sword passed through nothing but air and his assault was ended as the back of a hand shook his world and snapped his head to the side.

"I never claimed to not be a monster. This is a world of monsters."

"Who are you!?" Percy yelled; his cheek burned with pain.

"Someone who has walked the exact same path as you! Someone who has seen where you will go! Someone who has seen what horror lies at your destination!"

"I don't even know my destination. Marc leads!"

"And you follow like an obedient dog."

"I am his apprentice! That's all, I'm just an apprentice. What else am I supposed to do?"

"You were just an apprentice, but after the font, you have become something that could change everything. You

303

will have the same choice that I did. It speaks to you, does it not?"

"*Something* speaks to me."

"It spoke to me too. Told me to place my trust in a man. I did. I lost everything because of it."

"I don't care."

"You do not now, but you will, I am certain of that."

"I'm not the caring type!"

"Liar. You and your master are not the same person. I'm afraid that you appear to have the heart, which is why the stranger chose you, and not him."

Percy slashed wildly at the air, anger and confusion taking over his most basic faculties and reasoning.

"This was supposed to be simple!" Percy yelled as his arm became tired, his muscles burning. "Kill a monster, become a hero! Now everyone is dead, and I'm nothing because you shut a damn door!"

"You're right, it all starts so simple. It certainly did for me. I was to make my name, I was to become a hero of my people, and my name would be carved into the Triman Stone, where all the great heroes live on for eternity. It was all promised, and I believed it."

304

"The Triman Stone was destroyed nearly a century ago! Who are you!?"

"My name is Chassius."

"Chassius? *The* Chassius? You're going to start making jokes? You murder all those people and then you make jokes?"

"I am Chassius Mornis, legate of the Triman Empire. Leader of the third legion, spearhead of the campaign in Aellis. I was the first to traverse the Low Road, and until you and your companions made the ill-fated decision, I was the last."

"Chassius Mornis is dead."

"He is, and I live."

"You might think that you're being mysterious, spouting curious riddles, but you're really just being a pain in the ass. I'll make sure you pay for what you just did."

The light almost blinded Percy. It burned an unnatural and garish yellow, he raised a hand to guard his eyes, but after a moment he spread his fingers to inspect the source. Several of the glass tubes he had seen in the broader tunnel were also here. They did not flicker like fire but were constant and uniform, protected by metal bars. The hallway in which they stood was similar to the rest of the Low road but much narrower and with a lower ceiling. In front of him stood the door they had entered through.

He turned slowly. At the end of the corridor stood the focus of his anger. Mask hadn't changed since he had last seen him. He stood unarmed but confident.

"Where is Niv?" Percy asked again, his short-sword raised threateningly, confident that now he could actually see his opponent he would stand a better chance.

"Like I said, she is safe."

"Why don't I believe you?"

"I thought you were going to make me pay? Do you not want your revenge?"

"I do."

"Then attack me."

Percy gripped his sword so tight his knuckles turned white, he gritted his teeth but did not advance on Mask.

"I can't beat you," Percy said, there was no shame in his words, it was simply a statement of fact. Mask responded with a laugh that almost spurred him forward into action.

"That may be true, but it is a very defeatist attitude. I thought you wanted to be a hero? Does a hero not fight despite overwhelming odds? Could it be that you are no hero at all?"

"You're right, I'm no hero."

Percy lowered the tip of his shortsword, looking to the floor. Images of his journey so far flitted through his mind. He had to agree, he had not exactly been the definition of a hero so far, at best he had been a failure with good intentions. Nevertheless, he raised his arm and prepared.

"I'm a hero in training!" He declared as he threw the sword with all the strength he could muster, it was not a refined throw like Nica's, and it was not as strong as Moira's. Alas, it was still a good throw and the sword span through the air. Mask turned and stepped out of the way just a moment too late. The sword glanced off his mask, taking a triangular splinter with it and cutting the face beneath. The sword bounced away and clattered against the wall.

There was silence in the corridor, Mask did not move, and Percy did not dare.

"We will meet again young Percival."

With that, the lights went out. When they came back to life, Percy was alone in the corridor.

The tunnels that branched off from the Low Road were much less straightforward than the road itself, these twisted and turned, branching off and converging again. Some ended in a ceiling-collapse, but many led to larger rooms. Some of these rooms were boring, grey stone cubes with little in them, others contained snake-like metal pipes that stopped carrying their intended fluid long ago. Some chambers were filled with desks, chairs, shelves and metal cabinets. On each desk was a beige cube with a shiny grey face. Percy left them alone.

This place was fascinating. The language was different from any that he had seen before. He could see elements of it in each modern Urn language, they had metal plaques on the walls covered in words and diagrams, as well as many in a material that he had never seen before, it was like metal but brightly covered and it held more of a sheen. He wanted to stop and inspect everything, collections of papers and ancient books were piled on every shelf. He flicked through a number of them.

One of these books he found especially interesting. The album contained maps of places that he had never seen before, maps that made no mention of Urn or any of the kingdoms that it was comprised of. He couldn't even find the mountain-wall that encircled Urn. They could just as easily have been maps of an alien world.

Those who built the Low Road inhabited a world magnitudes larger than Urn. It contained a coloured painting of green and blue. It took Percy far longer than he would admit to realise that it showed the entire world. The green must be land. Therefore the blue was water? This made no sense, how there be so much water? In Urn, the only large body of water was the great central lake, though some rivers and streams came from the mountains and either left the same way or drained into the lake. There were only two semi-logical answers that he could imagine. The first was that these maps were a fabrication, a fantasy invented by the ancient people that once inhabited these halls. The second was that this was indeed another world entirely. Adventurers had long theorised that an entire world existed beyond the great mountain-wall, but precisely what that world consisted of was purely up to speculation. The mountains were considered impassable by most and those who found a way to traverse them were never heard from again.

Limited space had been the main driver of the centuries of war that had engulfed Urn before the Triman Empire asserted dominance. With the fall of the empire, there was a period of relative peace in which the majority of monsters were hunted to extinction in search of glory due to the absence of war. The confirmation that there is indeed land beyond the mountains would lead to great exhibitions and attempts to pass the mountains. Would any of these succeed? Percy doubted it. There was more than just mountains standing in their way.

He continued on his way. He didn't know how long he had been wandering these corridors, in some places they led to wide open spaces with racking along the walls covered in strange, sleep contraptions about the length of his forearm. He reached out and touched one of the objects and instantly his mind filled with pain. He looked down, and his body was riddled with holes that oozed thick red blood, he gasped in horror. He blinked, and the holes disappeared, he was whole again. He knew what they were. They were weapons. They were weapons, unlike anything Urn knew.

He walked along the rows of stands. The weapons came in so many shapes and sizes, but each was painted black. The world above had barely just grasped the concept of siege-weapons. Controlling this room would mean controlling Urn.

Adjacent to this was a room of equal size that had long tables with attached benches that ran down the centre like the great feasting halls of the Jors in the north.

310

Everything was covered in a thin film of dust. He moved through the room carefully, touching the tables. They were cold, and he left a trail through the dust of neglect. He wondered how many had seen this place before him, had anyone been here since the days when these halls were flooded with almost-humans? Two more corridors brought him to a room that was long, against the walls were beds. They were stacked on top of one another.

On the walls were small paintings. Or, at least, Percy thought they were paintings, as he inspected some he wondered how there had ever existed a painter so skilled, the detail was exquisite. It was as though the artist had captured a moment in time and put it on paper. He dared not touch them for fear of what power they might hold. This was the first time Percy saw them. He stood in shock. They were not almost-humans. They were humans. Two eyes, one nose, a mouth and a mop of hair. Some were beautiful, some were ugly. He blushed as several of the paintings depicted unclothed women in lewd positions.

He stopped at one of the images. It was a painting of a boy with unruly red hair, if not for the broken nose and pointy chin Percy would have believed he was staring at a picture of himself made before he was born. He found it difficult to tear his eyes from the beaming boy who even shared his eyes. After too long he turned away and left the barracks.

He couldn't tell if he had been wandering for minutes or for hours. Niv had to be in here somewhere, he must have travelled miles from the first door, and he found it difficult to believe that Mask could have taken her this far.

'Is this maze endless?' He thought to himself. 'Is this it for Percy? To ceaselessly wander ancient corridors, to eventually collapse from exhaustion and be buried in the memory of this awful place?'

That is very pretty, you should write it down.

Percy flinched at hearing the voice, he had become so used to his thoughts going unchallenged that the sudden answer thoroughly unnerved him

"Somehow I didn't think you'd be able to reach me down here." He said aloud if only to hear something other than his footsteps.

Unfortunately, I can reach you anywhere.

"I was right, wasn't I? You're some kind of parasite."

That's mean.

"Is it wrong though?"

I wouldn't put it that way, but no, it's not wrong.

312

"I need to find my friend."

The mercenary? I told you she's not your friend. So why would you want to find her?

"Like I said, a disembodied voice that may or may not be a side-effect of my poor, shocked mind is no competition for that of a living, breathing person in terms of trustworthiness."

You really are very smart. Stupid. But smart. I can help you find her, if only to move this whole thing along.

"Move what along? Marc and the others are dead. This is the end whether or not I find her."

You should have more faith in your teacher.

'Marc is still alive?' Percy thought. It couldn't be possible, he had nowhere to go and too many to fight. Marc must be dead.

He lives, yes. Now, moving on.

Before his eyes, a glowing silver thread materialised and hung in the air, leading down the corridor and off to the right. He took a deep breath and began following it.

'Who were these people?'

I don't know.

'You don't know? Aren't you the Stranger?'

A rather grand name, I think. Too grand. No, I'm not. I only work for them.

'Does the Stranger know?"

I expect so. The Stranger arrived before they destroyed themselves.

'Arrived? So, the moon wasn't always there?'

The moon was there, the stranger was not. Listen, Percy, all of your questions will be answered, but not now. Everything will become apparent at the end of your journey. You're so close. So close.

"Percy?" Niv said, her voice barely more than a whisper and so weak that Percy wasn't sure if he had actually heard it, or if it was a creak or the murmur of dust.

"Niv?" He said tentatively.

A cough drew his attention to a corner of the corridor, the lantern had died long ago, and he could only see the faint outline of a person. He hurried over to her side.

"Where am I?" Niv asked. She looked around with bleary eyes as Percy fetched the water-canister from his bag and lifted it to her lips. She drank thirstily.

"It's some kind of underground city. The same people who built the Low Road built all this. It's been under Urn all this time."

"Is there a way out?" Niv said as she gently pushed Percy's hands aside and clumsily rose to her feet.

"Not that I've been able to find. If there is, it'll just open onto the Low Road again. Open onto those monsters."

Niv's face dropped as her mind caught up to the present. "Everyone else?" She asked.

Percy waited a moment before answering. "They didn't make it to the door in time."

Niv was silent, but in her eyes, Percy could see the loss, and for a moment she herself looked lost and confused. It occurred to Percy that while he had lost friends that he had only known for a matter of weeks, she had lost family who she had fought alongside with possibly for years.

"I'm sorry Niv."

"That doesn't make sense. They had plenty of time."

"…The door shut."

Niv looked at him with distrust in her eyes. "By itself?" She asked. The accusation was blatant, and Percy felt it like an icy dagger to the heart. Or a golem-fisted punch to the stomach.

"By itself," Percy said sheepishly. Whether Mask had closed it or not, Mask was only here because of Percy.

The realisation that he was still responsible felt worse than any punishment that Niv could deliver. He hoped.

Niv nodded slowly. She didn't believe him, but her self-preservationist ways rose to the surface as she forced down her grief. Priorities were set, and she spun slowly, assessing all the routes she could take. Each was identical save for different levels of degradation in the walls and ceiling.

"I've been making a map of sorts," Percy said as he showed the rough map of the underground city to her. It was far from the meticulous plans he had produced for their journey through Perda, but it showed the majority of the corridors he had passed through and little notes regarding what was in each chamber. She took the map, and her eyes fell on one particular area.

"Armoury?" She said, glancing over the top of the paper at Percy.

"I think so."

"Any black powder? We could blast our way out."

"Eh, I'm not sure I'd recommend that. We have no way of knowing how deep we are. Also, their weapons are… Strange. We could just as easily kill ourselves. More easily, I expect."

"The corridors lead to one place," Niv said.

"What?" Percy said as he took back to the map and inspected it once again. Sometimes his own stupidity amazed him. Niv was quite correct, while the corridors might meander and branched off into a myriad of oddly-shaped rooms, ultimately they would all converge on one point while in the other direction they led to the locked doors which shut off the Low Road.

"Whatever they're converging on must be of importance."

"A door?"

"Let's hope so."

Percy led the way, continuing to add to the map as he moved. When they came to a dead-end or cave-in, they found an alternative route and eventually they located where the corridors converged. This cavern was huge, greater than any that they had passed through so far.

The size of the room was not the most exciting feature of the room. Instead, it was the mass of black chitin attached to the floor. Percy and Niv froze as a shiver ran through the thing, and the tiny spear-like legs became visible. The hulk was not a pile of rubble, nor was it a single creature. It was instead some kind of hive.

317

A rumble ran through the room, and the hive broke apart like glass, the fleeing beasts exposed a hole that led down to a black abyss.

"I think we should probably leave," Niv whispered as she began backing up.

It was the noise that stopped them. It was alien but familiar, it was otherworldly while still sounding right and normal. It started small but quickly grew. From the lip of the hole, a face appeared.

"Caitlin?" Percy said. The lights had faded to a dull glow, and through the gloom, he could barely see her, though he was sure it was her. Her hands clawed at the edge of the hole.

"Percy! Help me!" She screamed.

Percy leapt forward, but Niv wrapped her arms around him, anchoring him to the spot.

"You see Caitlin?"

"What?" Percy asked in disbelief. "Of course I do! Let me go, or she'll fall!"

"I see the captain."

"It's Caitlin!"

"It's neither." She said quietly.

Percy struggled from her grasp but did not run to Caitlin's aid. As he squinted to see through the murk, he

318

saw something protruding from her back. A limb reminiscent of an arm but with far too many angular joints. The fleshy appendage led into the darkness of the hole.

"This… This is it. I think we should run, yes."

The sound grew until Percy could feel it in his legs. A black snake-like body rose from the gaping hole. It was difficult to describe, and Percy was not sure if his eyes were to be trusted or not. It didn't really have a head, the body just ended in a gaping circular mouth with rows upon rows of serrated teeth. It had no scales; instead, it was covered in pink veiny flesh, and a veil of transparent mucus cascaded from it, leaving a trail where it slithered. It disgusted Percy in a way that he couldn't fathom, he was terrified and repulsed. Niv saw something completely different. To her eyes, it was still vaguely snake-like, but it was covered in glossy black scales, each as large as a shield and it had one bulging eye atop its head. Whatever it looked like it reared out of the hole, looming over the two and making every noise Percy could imagine, it let out deep, rumbling roars as well as screeches that made Percy's teeth vibrate. Around the base of the creature, the black insects congregated, flowing over each other and making the ground a writhing black blanket that moved and swayed as the monster slithered.

Percy and Niv wanted to run as fast as they could, they both willed their legs to carry them back down the maze of narrow corridors as quickly as they could, but they didn't move. Instead, the beast slowly encircled them, its body filling the cavernous room and yet it still emerged from the hole. Percy took a moment of relief from the sheer terror that had gripped his mind to contemplate the beast and how it managed to survive in the Low Road. It was colossal, the heftiest creature that Percy had ever heard of and a monster like that required food, a gargantuan volume of food each day. Percy could not imagine where it was acquiring such a quantity. The insects and human-like creatures of the Low Road could not possibly sustain it. Therefore, unless there was some kind of underground feast at the bottom of that pit, this was not a mundane creature of flesh, but instead, it was a thing created from magic, like the golem. The Caitlin-shaped lure still dangling from its head only supported that theory. He winced as he looked at the doll-like representation of Caitlin, it was lifeless with a blank face and its limbs swinging limply as the worm moved. Percy was not sure if he would ever forgive himself for thinking it was the vibrant young girl. He would certainly never forgive the creature that used her likeness. He felt a coldness in his heart, but it burned like fire.

Well, look who is considering using what he has been given.

'I don't know how.' Percy thought in desperation.

Creatures born of dark magic can only be defeated two ways, as all dedicated disciples of the great heroes of the past know. The first requires a mountain-sized barbarian with blazing yellow hair, a battle-axe stained with the blood of his foes and of course, the traditional and highly practical loincloth. The second way to destroy a creature so heavily influenced by magic is through the use of magic.

It's really not that difficult. Can't you feel it?

The coldness spread but Percy fought it. It didn't feel natural, it didn't feel right.

Don't fight it.

'It isn't right!'

Well, of course it isn't. Do you think that thing looming over you is right? Do you think it's natural? Do you think Urn is natural? Use your unnatural power to slay this unnatural beast and go on to live in your unnatural world.

The coldness spread through his chest and down to his stomach, making him feel unimaginably hungry. The worm finished circling the room and reared up over its

321

trapped prey. Its uncountable rows of vicious teeth undulated in its cavernous maw.

'Does this power make me a monster?' He thought as the coldness continued to spread to his shoulders, he felt suffocated as it reached up his throat and down his legs.

More of a monster than this thing before you? I can't imagine that it should be a concern right now. You're overthinking this. It's you or it. Just like the Golem. Just like the bandit.

'The bandit I killed using my sword, not an unnatural power'.

I see, so it's not killing that you have a problem with, merely the method. Is the barbarian with the axe so much more honourable than the sorcerer with his magic?

The insects swarmed around the trapped pair, Percy wanted to recoil from them as they repulsed him to the very core, but whatever foul magic the worm had worked on them kept them fixed to the floor.

Don't think. Just act.

The coldness spread through his brain, for a moment it felt like he had eaten ice-cream too quickly, but it quickly subsided. He felt peaceful, in control, as the coldness stretched all the way to his toes and his finger-tips he was able to move once again. Everything he looked at seemed brighter, with silvery outlines. Each living creature had ethereal silver tendrils that reached from their bodies, gently stroking the ground and air. The insects had a weak outline, and the tendrils only stretched a few inches while the worm was so covered in the silky threads that they almost obscured it entirely. Its shape had changed. This version was much more boring. It was a dull grey without scales but instead thick leathery hide. It still had no eyes, but its mouth was much more reasonably shaped and sized. It was a good deal smaller as well, its body was skinnier, and the end had exited the hole long ago.

He looked at Niv. She had no outline and no tendrils. She was as she had ever been, a boring, plain human being. Percy reached out his hand and the insects scattered, but not quickly enough. He balled his fist, and the weak threads reached out to him, flowing into his closed hand. They writhed and shook, letting out a chittering noise. Niv did not see this as she was still focused on the worm. It now regarded Percy curiously.

The insects ceased their chattering and became still, littering the floor with their husks. Percy turned his attention on the worm which lunged at him, faster than he would have imagined for a creature of its size. He held out his hand and opened it. The light was blinding. It reached from his palm in a lance that struck the worm as it opened its jaws to clamp down around him. The stream of brilliance travelled down its throat. The worm's own unnatural tendrils turned inwards, wrapping it like a cage. It squealed like a kicked dog, shaking and whipping its body from side to side. Percy let it suffer, taking a perverse pleasure in it. He knew exactly what was going to happen, he was going to close his hand and tear the life-sustaining magic from its body so violently that its skin would rip and its blood would wash over them.

Before he could do this, he felt Niv's arms wrap around him and pull him away from the still corpses and the pain-wracked worm, back the way they came.

"Let's go while it's having a fit!" Niv yelled, almost drowned out by the worms tortured scream. Percy felt the coldness recede to whatever recess it resided in when it was not called upon. Percy released himself from her grip and took to running as well, he hurriedly found his self-drawn map and began yelling out which direction to take at each intersection. The squealing stopped, and it was quickly replaced by a roar. As this roar died, it was replaced by the dry skittering of thousands of spiky little legs that grew in volume very quickly.

"We can't outrun those things!" Percy panted before calling out the next direction.

"Just do what you did before!" Niv yelled, glancing behind her. Whatever she saw behind Percy made her run just that little bit faster.

"You… You saw that?" Percy asked. He had hoped Niv's mind had been so gripped by fear that she had either not seen Percy's magical moment, or had found it so fantastical that she had dismissed it as a figment of her fear-heightened imagination. No such luck.

"I saw something, I wouldn't like to guess what it was."

A noise caused Percy to look over his shoulder. The insects had caught up, they covered every surface, the floor, walls and ceiling, the corridors behind them turned black as their bodies drowned the antique lanterns. The sight sent a surge of shock through Percy, and he picked up the pace. He didn't know how fast he could run, but he was determined to outrun his highest estimation on this occasion.

"I can't! I don't know how to!" He yelled, he hadn't called out the last three turns in time and now did not dare look at the map in fear that they were doomed to run into a dead end and then be consumed by thousands of angry insects.

They emerged into a larger room, and it took Percy a moment to recognise it. It was the armoury. He saw Niv's moment of confusion before turning, grabbing the edges of the door and slamming it shut. Screeches erupted from the passage beyond as the insects rebounded against the metal. Niv thrust her shoulder against it and yelled out as the weight of the insects competed with her strength. Percy joined her, throwing his meagre weight against the door. On the door was another of the panels that he had first seen on the entrance to the Low Road. He quickly punched in the code he had used before, and an angry fuzzy bleep signalled that this was very wrong.

Percy stared at the panel, suddenly feeling very helpless. Niv saw the issue, took a moment to assess it and decided on the best course of action. She punched the panel. Her grunt of pain showed that ancient panels are actually quite durable. However, a blinking red light came on, and the bleeping started again. Thick metal bolts slid into place as the locks engaged. At the same time, at the other side of the armoury, the other door slammed shut, a similar lock ensuring that it remained that way.

Chapter 16

Niv slowly backed away from the door that she had locked.

"So… What happened there?" She asked, slightly nervous.

"Well, I can't claim to be an expert in ancient doors and their locking mechanisms…" Percy started before Niv interrupted.

"You realise that your actions in the past day or so might actually make you Urn's leading expert in ancient doors and their locking mechanisms, right?"

"Well… I think your violence might have caused it to believe that there is some kind of emergency. In which case it has sealed all the doors."

"It? What is it?"

"Whatever controls these doors?"

"Like a spirit or something?"

"Nothing so complex, it's just a mechanism. It's a machine. The Civvans make little toys that if you turn a handle so many times, then they jump or clap or do something equally ridiculous until the handle is back in its original position. This is kind of like a really advanced version I think."

"How do you know that?"

"I... I don't know. How do I know that?" Percy said, directing it at the whisper in his mind.

I am but a muse, an inspiration. A spark, if you will.

"How do we get out?"

"I don't know."

"You're not really living up to your 'Leading expert in ancient doors and their locking mechanisms' title you know."

"I'm newly qualified."

Niv was no longer listening, she was already browsing the racks of weapons slowly, stopping to inspect some while others didn't take her fancy.

"You said this is an armoury... Then these are the weapons? Maybe we can use them." She said as she tentatively touched a pear-shaped object with little bumps extruding from it.

"We don't know anything about these, we could kill ourselves or bring Perda down upon us," Percy said, still inspecting the panel. He willed for something to happen, he wished for the correct symbols to appear in his mind. He tried several combinations, merely trying the first one that came to mind. None of these worked of course, and it was only after the third attempt that he realised that had he stumbled upon the correct code he would have been overwhelmed by the insects and no doubt the worm was working its way through the myriad of passages.

"What do these even do? There are knives but no swords. There are shovels but no axes." Niv said as she lifted a long, glossy and incredibly dangerous looking object, it had a handle and the butt at the end of the weapon fit snugly against her shoulder. It was so well-designed that holding it felt instinctive and effortless. It was designed so even an idiot could use it. She extended her finger and found the trigger, she pulled it experimentally, but it only clicked harmlessly. "It feels like a crossbow."

"It… Fills you with holes." Percy said, crossing the armoury to the other door, believing this one to be safer to experiment on.

Niv looked at Percy quizzically but didn't stop her exploration of the weapon or the shelves. She came upon boxes and boxes of small metal cylinders with domed heads.

"What exactly are you trying to do? We can't take any of these with us." Percy said.

"Why not? Weapons made by whoever made these tunnels must be better than anything I have. They could make mercenary work a lot easier. I'm going to be doing it alone now after all." Niv said, a tinge of sadness to her words. Guilt did not lessen the force of Percy's reply, this was too important.

"We can't risk any of these making it up to the surface. Can you imagine the wars they would ignite? We still don't know what happened to the people who built all this, for all we know, they could have destroyed themselves!"

"I guess we'll just have to keep a hold of them then."

"I don't think we can be trusted any more than anyone else."

"Then what's your plan for when we get back to the Low Road? Ask the monsters very nicely if we can pass?"

"I'll use my power. I'll use the magic."

"The magic that you just said you didn't know how to use? Percy, this is necessary. These weapons might have destroyed them, but they could save us." Niv argued, irritated at Percy's lack of foresight.

"Niv, if any of this reached the surface it would be the end for Urn. Look how efficiently we kill each other with swords, imagine what would happen if we could use these. Up there it's relatively peaceful, this discovery would change that."

"So, we just allow ourselves to die, Percy?"

"I didn't say that."

"I thought you wanted to be some kind of big hero, I thought you wanted books to be written about you? This would secure that. With what is in here you could write your own story."

"I know I could, but I don't want to be known for genocide."

Niv looked at Percy, her mouth hanging open, not quite believing what she was hearing.

"Percy, I understand you're still clinging onto the whole 'honour in heroism' thing, I'm sure Marc taught you well. The fact is, these will be found one day and on that day war will ignite, whether that's one day or one thousand days from now it doesn't really matter. People will still die."

"And death is profitable I suppose?" Percy spat at Niv, all present danger forgotten.

Niv frowned, waving an angry hand as she turned away, walking down the row of weapons. "My captain and my sisters are dead. Your master is dead… And whatever Caitlin was, she's dead too. It's just me, you, and them."

"So, you're going to kill me and do as you like then?" Percy said, his hand finding the grip of his shortsword. Niv rounded a rack and looked down at his hand with open confusion. This shifted to hurt and then to a coldness that Percy had not yet seen in her. Percy didn't know where this mistrust came from, perhaps the whisper was not lying.

"No. Because I don't think I can get out of here without you, Percy."

"So you'll use me and then kill me? I guess it was right."

"It?"

"Just give me five minutes to think. I'll find a way. If I don't, then you can blow everything up."

The five minutes were excruciatingly short even though they had no way to actually record the time. In that time Percy moved from weapon to weapon to inspect and calculate, attempting to find something, anything that could help them open the doors without causing too much damage to the armoury or themselves. Finally, he slumped to the floor beside the door.

"I don't know. I don't know." He said in a quiet voice. After a moment Niv joined him on the floor, leaning her weight against his shoulder. She had a small, sad smile on her face. He looked into her eyes, seeing a friend once again.

"Well, if it had to be a choice between dying of dehydration and being torn into pieces by a swarm of giant bugs or being eaten by a giant snake, then I think this is for the best," Niv said, nudging him slightly. He almost smiled.

'Why won't you help me?' He thought, aiming the accusation at whatever entity he had been speaking to.

I believe I have helped you enough already. What makes you think I have any power here? It asked, the non-voice reverberating through his mind and blocking out whatever Niv said.

'You showed me the last symbol before, and you gave Chassius the entire sequence. You can do it again!' Percy directed at the voice angrily.

I didn't help Chassius then. He had not yet visited a Pale Font and therefore I had no influence. The Stranger assisted him.

'You're the same thing!'

I'm a fragment, as you said, I am a parasite. I have no help to give you. Besides, I have helped you quite enough, you're not really proving yourself.

'I can't prove myself if I die here.'

Not dying here is how you will prove yourself. Good luck, young one.

Percy angrily scoffed, causing Niv to look at him curiously. Percy shook his head slowly.

"Niv isn't an Aellisian name," Percy said. It was so off-topic that Niv laughed.

"I guess it isn't." She said with a slight smile, letting the silence worry Percy for a moment before continuing. "It's short for Niveer. I chose it myself. The Woodcutters thought it was much too fancy."

"Where are you from?"

Niv thought for a moment "I'm not sure. Like so many others I'm an orphan of one of the many small fringe wars on some border. Just another tragic but tedious backstory. I travelled with many caravans, doing small, unpaid odd jobs."

"Where did you see?"

"Where did I travel? Oh, many places. Aellis of course, Perda, Trima, Civ, Bukkin. I even made it up to Llev and Jorlund with the Woodcutters. The captain…" A moment's hesitation. "The captain loved travelling, you see, and the Inner Kingdoms were becoming a little sparse in terms of jobs. We were in Jorlund before Merro's word reached us. We travelled all the way back from Jorlund for this job." Niv nodded. Her eyes looked empty. Percy attempted to change the subject.

"Any good stories from the snowy north?"

Niv laughed, a little shocked by the question, she rested her head back against the wall.

"Good stories? Well, perhaps you would like to know the story of Moira's stone forehead. Well, you see, Moira has an incredibly thick skull. About a week after we first reached Jorlund we heard of a bounty on one of the snow-trolls up there. Massive beasts with fists like boulders and jaws like a wall-lion. They're absolutely vicious as well, they'll take your head off for doing nothing more than looking at them wrong, or walking over their bridge. Oh yeah, they take ownership of bridges. The Jors say that most of the time a traditional dance will do for a toll, but every now and then you get one that prefers warm flesh to a quick jig. This was one such troll.

So, we took this hunt, racing at least ten Jor hunters. Though we had numbers on our side, so the Jors kept their distance for the most part. We reached the bridge just as the sun died and the moon offered little light that night. We surrounded the bridge, the captain, myself, Moira and Nica approached from the north side. It was pitch black under that bridge, but we could hear it. Oh, we could hear it. It breathed like an enraged bull, in the faint light I could just see the plumes of its breath. We had to be careful you see, a spooked troll is a dangerous troll.

However, I guess Moira was never one for subtlety, so she decided the best course of action was to throw an axe at it. It bounced off but succeeded in pissing it off royally. It charged out of the darkness and in its hand it was holding a bloody great log wider than a man." Niv grinned as she looked back on the memory. Percy found it difficult to imagine it as anything other than utterly terrifying. Though he couldn't help but be a little jealous that he had no such stories to tell that Niv did not already know.

"So, Moira calmly steps forward, stares down the troll and then waited for it to pull back the log to hit her harder than a charging Orlo, and then she head-butted it. That's it, she just head-butted it. There was a crack that sounded like the wall itself had broken apart. The troll swayed once or twice before it hit the ground like a wet sack of potatoes. Then these Jor hunters come up and try to claim that the trophies were theirs by right. So Moira head-butted them too."

Percy laughed like he had not in a long time.

"What about yourself?" Niv said, drawing Percy's mind from the guilt that threatened to consume him once more.

"What do you mean?"

"Well, a great adventurer such as yourself must have your own collection of heroic stories," Niv said, her eyes focused on Percy, clearly expecting something.

"Well, no, not really, before Marc found me I was just the son of a teacher preparing for a long, tedious life of academia or something equally as boring."

"Oh, so you mean you ran from a long comfortable life of books where you could have found a nice woman, had a few pretty little kids and died in a warm comfy bed? And you ran away so you could experience every horror that Urn could throw at you and eventually die in a forgotten underground world?"

"Shockingly, this wasn't the intended outcome of my choices."

"Well, I guess we rarely see the 'intended outcomes'. Nonetheless, you must have a story or two from your boring life before you made some questionable life-choices?"

"Well, I guess there's the time that Jim Joanus stole my mathematics book. This required punishment. I copied his handwriting and left him notes in various books, then made sure he found them. Convinced him that I was him from the future and warned him that a dragon would soon turn the school-house into an inferno. He did the right thing and came into the school-house ranting and raving like a madman. They took him away, bound in leather straps."

"They… Took him away?" Niv asked, looking shocked.

"No… I confessed. I was not welcome back in the school for months, but my father found it hilarious. Jim recovered, but he never stole my books again."

Niv grinned.

"Or there was the time that Fargi Nerdum decided it would be terribly funny to pour itchy-seeds down the back of my trousers."

"What ingenius punishment did you devise for him them?"

"Oh, I mainly just cried a lot and had to walk home trouser-less."

"Manly."

They both laughed for a long time. Niv stopped, but Percy continued. The sheer ridiculousness of the situation hit him. He was a boy born of a family that had never strayed far from the path, here he was, in a place that no human had seen since before Urn existed with giant insects and a hallucination-inducing monster on one side and nightmares on the other. He had seen wargs, a golem and had briefly been detained by the royal guard of Norda. At this moment, how could he think about his heartbroken parents never to see their child again, how could he reminisce about how bullies had treated him as a child?

"I've decided that we're not going to die here," Percy said resolutely.

"Well, that's comforting."

Percy stood defiantly.

"We're going to live."

"Well, for a few more hours I suppose until the air runs out."

"It's not going to. Because of farts."

"…Because of farts. Oh, I see, you've been trapped for less than an hour and already gone insane."

"Ventilation! A huge underground place like this must need a whole lot of air-flow. Otherwise, a single fart could empty the place!" Percy said excitedly as he pointed to a metal shutter in the wall, near the floor. He ran to the shutters and clawed at its slats. In a moment of desperation, he managed to remove two. His face fell immediately. Just behind the slats was a metal barrier, blocking the vent.

"It… It must have closed with the doors."

A beeping started, the infernal headache-inducing beeping that seemed to penetrate Percy's skull and bounce around the inside of his head until his brain was bruised.

"Percy!" Niv shouted as she leapt to her feet and rushed to his side, facing the door with her sword held threateningly. Percy turned from the vent in shock, he drew his shortsword. The bleeping was coming from the panel. The door would open, he knew it.

'Well, Percy ol' chap. At least you can go out with a sword in your hand, it's better than fading away, right?' He thought. He wasn't so sure anymore, but he clung tightly to the last scraps of his crumbling dream.

The door wailed on its hinges. The figure that stood in the doorway was terrifying, over six foot and built with enough muscle to put an ogre to shame. It wore armour that was coated in fluids of all different colours, the deep, dark red of blood, an oily black and green that looked like it could have seeped from a horribly infected wound. It carried a sword in its bloodied fist, gripping it so hard that Percy thought he could hear bones cracking. Its face was a visage of anger, pure, unfiltered rage. It was softened with surprise, but the fury was still very much present.

"You left us," Marc said, entering the armoury but not sparing the amazing array of ancient technology a glance, all of his focus was on Percy. "You shut the door. You left us to die."

"No, no Marc, I didn't. There was another, they closed the door… You're alive!"

"We retreated all the way to the entrance but it was shut, and without you, we didn't know the code. They hit us hard." Marc stood just before Percy, towering over him. A bloody tower of muscle and anger. "We had no option but to drive a wedge into them and try to make it through. Most of the mercenaries died in the process, but the captain and I came out alive. She wouldn't leave her girls. She started hacking away with that… damned axe of hers. By the time I got back the door was open again. Guilt get to you?" Marc said. Percy was afraid and could feel it rising in his throat, threatening to seize his tongue and hold it hostage.

"I told you, it wasn't me."

"He's telling the truth, neither of us closed the door. I was knocked out, and Percy had to search this entire place to find me. There is someone else here."

Marc regarded Niv like a bear would a mouse. She instinctively tried to make herself taller and kept a firm grip of her sword.

"How did you open the door?" Percy asked, able to rationally think now that Marc's eyes had moved away from him.

Marc held up what looked to be a piece of paper, it was perfectly square and bright, luminescent yellow. Scrawled on it was a series of symbols "It was stuck to one of those beige boxes, it opens most of the doors."

Percy shook his head in amazement, perhaps the people who built this place were not so intelligent after all.

A heavy thud sounded through the armoury, it took a moment to realise that it had come from the other door.

The worm had reached it and was becoming impatient. Marc looked at the door, not knowing what was beyond it.

"We need to move, now."

Marc didn't move, his bloodshot eyes had locked on to Percy once more, he slowly raised his blade until the tip touched Percy's chin.

"If you closed that door, then I'll send you back to your town in pieces, understood?" Marc said in a voice that convinced Percy that he wasn't lying. On that homicidal note, they turned and ran. They ran out of the armoury and down the next passage, they ran through a network of rooms that were filled with desks and cupboards. It only now occurred to Percy that while the tunnels showed some degradation and even a few cave-ins, the rest was immaculate save for the thick layer of dust that covered everything. A crash echoed through the halls, heralding the destruction of the armoury's door and their impending doom at the hands, or tail of a giant worm.

Percy felt his legs speed up though he didn't remember commanding them to do so. Marc ran leisurely, using his long stride to easily keep pace with Percy. Niv limped slightly, Percy wasn't sure where she had picked that up, but this hardly seemed like the best time to ask.

343

"Where are we going?" Niv asked through wheezing breaths.

"The main road," Percy said.

"Great, I get to die after all then. I was starting to get worried."

"I thought I made it clear just what was waiting for us on the road." Marc said.

"You did, but this time we have back up."

"You think they'll fight each other?" Niv wheezed.

"They have to. It's the only way this plan will work."

"You're insane."

"Maybe."

"There it is," Marc yelled. The door to the Road stood before them. The Road was deserted. That is, it was deserted save for the bodies. Percy had never seen so many corpses. They were strewn across the ground, and many were in pieces or had fatal gashes. Several torches lay on the ground, still burning defiantly, lighting this section of the road with flickering yellow. One of the nearest corpses looked familiar, Percy didn't want to know who it was, but Niv fell to her knees beside it.

"Nica…" She whispered, lowering her face and placing her forehead against that of the corpse. Percy turned away. It wasn't only Woodcutters that littered the ground, but also dozens of the eyeless creatures. The Woodcutters had not gone down easily, Percy thought they could take some pride in that. Though he wasn't sure if they would have traded that pride for their lives.

A howl vibrated through the road, drawing all eyes. Just beyond the light given by the torches stood a figure that Percy would forever see in his nightmares. The tall, confident fiend bared its teeth. Niv reluctantly left Nica's body, taking a dagger with her, without hesitation she threw it at the creature, following it with a scream of pure hatred. The knife slammed into its shoulder, causing it to screech and fall to a knee. As before, the other nightmares slowly crept out of the darkness, hissing and wailing at them. The leader yowled and began its charge, aiming for Niv. As the party turned to run a giant head burst from the doorway and clamped its jaws around the waist of the leader. It shrieked in confusion and pain as the worm, now restored to its former terrible glory closed its jaws, severing the leader in two and raining its blood over its companions. The throng stopped momentarily but quickly overcame their initial shock. They made their war cry and attacked as the insects swarmed through the doorway, meeting them.

The carnage was magnificent, limbs were shattered, heads were removed, carapaces were cracked, and the ferocity of each side made Percy stop and observe, terrified and fascinated in equal measures. Niv grabbed his arm and together they ran from the bloodbath. Marc had retrieved one of the fallen torches and was holding it aloft to light their way. Percy was exhausted, it felt like he had been running for hours in the deep darkness of this subterranean world and he had decided that he would give an arm or two just to be able to peacefully lie in a field under the unending blue sky for an hour or so. He wasn't sure he had ever done that before.

After an eternity of sprinting, they slowed to a rushed jog before it turned into a worried hobble. Their legs burned and they had no way of knowing how far they had run or how far they still had to go. There was nothing but silence from the tunnel and whatever battle was raging in the Low Road, they were a long way from it, no agony-filled echoes reached them here.

After what must have been a day or more of uninterrupted walking they reached it. The Road split into two, the entrance to one of these tunnels was barred by the most catastrophic collapse Percy had seen, it looked as though half of Urn had fallen into the Low Road, the other shaft was guarded by a door. The door was colossal, identical to its twin in Perda. It had the same panel, and Percy prayed that it also shared a symbol-sequence. He hobbled to the panel and entered the code, a code that he would remember until the day he died. The door opened slower than its counterpart, excruciatingly slow given the situation. He hated it when ancient technology didn't understand urgency.

Nothing came for them, and when the gap was wide enough, they slipped through. Beyond the door the ground sloped upwards towards the surface, they ascended the incline until they reached another gate, this one resembled the yellow keep door though it was not covered in depictions of monsters, but instead words in Old Triman. Percy could read some of them, but the majority were nonsensical. They broadly described horrible ways to die and what would become of trespassers in the afterlife. Marc slid the same key into the door and turned it. As the door opened, warm sunlight flooded them. Percy did not think he had ever welcomed the light with such fierce devotion before.

Karees 3

A century earlier

In the past few weeks, Karees had felt herself in somewhat of a haze. She hovered after her legate like a zombie. She killed what he ordered her to kill, and she took what he ordered her to take. Even the horrors of the Low Road had only briefly brought her back to herself through sheer terror. She looked around herself and despaired at what her once proud legion had become. They had shrunk in size and strength and what remained was the hard but ultimately rotten core. Each carried a haunted look in their eyes. It was a legion of murderers and the murdered.

The abominations strode alongside them now. She counted about ten of them. They broke down eventually, but Chassius had been busy experimenting, and they could now fight for days before the bodies broke apart and the foul magics seeped into the earth, silver flowers growing where they fell. One turned its many eyes upon her, and she hastily averted her gaze.

Their path through the Low Road had allowed them to avoid the Imperial City and the seat of the emperor himself and now they headed in the opposite direction, towards the edge of Urn, towards the barrier that penned them in. The legionaries had given up trying to guess Chassius' and Friarns true intentions. It was pointless. There would be no redemption for them. They had slaughtered Triman and Aelissean alike just so that Chassius could raise both into something so abhorrent that too often Karees felt bile rising in her throat.

Terus still marched beside her, but she feared him mad. He laughed like a child too often and spoke too little. She refused to abandon him to his fate and ensured she was always at his side, forcing him to eat and sleep when they could. He had saved her life too often for her to allow him to let his own life drain away so quickly.

They were almost at the wall. This was it. This was the end to whatever Chassius and Friarn had been planning.

The column came to a drowsy halt about half a mile from the wall. Chassius addressed them here. While the legionaries looked half-dead and wracked with guilt, he and Friarn looked as resplendent as ever. They even looked victorious.

"My friends. My glorious, tremendous friends!" Chassius began. Karees had never heard him so excited. In fact, she had never heard him express any emotion other than grim determination. It was jarring.

"On our great journey, we have all sacrificed much. We have sacrificed our place in Trima and possibly even in Urn. Some of you have sacrificed your humanity and your comrades. I tell you now simply that these sacrifices are nothing. Urn means nothing. We have a higher purpose, a more complete destiny. That destiny lies within the wall." He proclaimed excitedly. It all sounded like noise to Karees' weary mind, but some small snippets made their way to what still existed of her. Higher purpose? Within the wall?

"Fool." She muttered quietly. Terus echoed her and sniggered.

So, it was all for madness then. That seems right.

"Our friends have served us well. But we do not need them any longer."

As one the abominations dropped to the ground. Just corpses once again. The Legionaries nearest them flinched.

"You brought us here. Not them. Be proud of your achievements but prepare for ascension to a level of glory unheard of in Urn."

With that, he turned and continued. The column soon following him just as silently as before his nonsensical speech.

It didn't take them long to reach the wall. It was much as Karees remembered, tall and sheer-sided it was impassable for all in Urn. Any attempt to climb over or dig through it ended in tragedy. She very much doubted there was anything on the other side, or if there was then it was just as forsaken as Urn.

Here though there was an opening. It was small and would only admit one legionary at a time, but it was there.

It reeked of evil.

Chapter 17

Percy drank in the sunlight. There was not as much of it as he would have liked as it was filtered through the crumbling ceiling above him. They had emerged into a cavernous hall with the door to the Low Road at one end and a more conventional wooden door at the other. Thick, richly decorated columns marched in two lines down the length of the hall. The walls consisted mainly of stained-glass windows, each one depicting a different story of Triman greatness. The one closest to them showed, in exquisite detail the first Triman civil war which resulted in the rise of the first emperor. The colours were slightly faded, but otherwise, it was still a remarkable record of Trima's bloody past. Unfortunately, many of the other windows were damaged, missing some if not all of their stories.

"I take it this is Trima then?" Percy said, spinning to take in the glory of this hall.

"The city of Ureses." Marc said, locking the door behind them and slumping to the floor to pant.

"Ureses? The non-city?" Percy said. Marc didn't reply, he was resting his head back against the column with his eyes closed. He hadn't bothered to wash off the blood and dirt of the Low Road.

"Percy," Niv said, gesturing for him to follow her as she made her way down the long hall to the enormous door. The door opened effortlessly, and Percy was a little worried that it would break away from its hinges. Above them, the sun was a little less friendly than Percy had imagined, and the heat hit them immediately. Still, he did not believe he had ever seen a more beautiful orb of fire and heat before. Ureses was an ancient, abandoned city filled with buildings of classic Triman design. Extravagant stone structures with intricately carved facades surrounded them. They had stood the test of time well, but the signs of rot and degradation showed everywhere. Weeds had claimed the city-square, and most of the roofs had collapsed, prey to frequent wild storms.

"Percy, I think he's lying," Niv said quietly, however, in this dead city, a whisper became a scream.

"Lying about what? Can't we just be happy to be alive?"

Niv's expression was unreadable, it took Percy at least a full minute to realise exactly what he had just said. It all hit him at once, he had emerged from a dead tunnel into a dead city. Out of the twenty plus people who had entered the Low Road, three had left. He had lost Caitlin, Niv had lost everyone.

"The captain loved the others, but if they were lost, she wouldn't hesitate to leave them. They were dead, I am alive, and she would have come for me. He did something."

"He wouldn't. He's proud and between you and me, a little thick-skulled, but he's no murderer."

"You know who he is, don't you?"

"Well… Of course, I do. He's Marc, a stubborn adventurer."

Niv looked at Percy like he had spontaneously grown another head. "You live in a fantasy, don't you Percy?"

Percy didn't know how to respond. Marc emerged into the sunlight, blinking.

"We need to keep moving."

"Can't we rest here for a day? I mean, it's an abandoned city, I can't imagine a better place to rest right now." Percy said, his mind still reeling from Niv's words.

"Why was it abandoned?" Niv said, not looking at Marc, but at one of the buildings nearest them. It was one of the more significant structures and had a fancy seal carved into the stone.

"I've heard stories, one blamed the Low Road, saying that the monsters got loose. They sealed the Low Road and abandoned the city, saying that there was a taint on the city."

"Trima conquered most of Urn, they weren't afraid of anything that could come out of the Low Road. The truth is much less interesting. The Low Road has tunnels under the entirety of Ureses, and every now and then Ureses would sink into those tunnels. The governor's house was the last thing to disappear before they declared the city uninhabitable. The story of the monsters was told to keep looters and ne'er-do-wells away."

"Does it work?"

"No, hence why we have to leave, Ureses is the home base of most of Trima's mob-bosses."

Percy nodded slowly, resigning himself to a life of always moving, never being able to take a minute to rest.

"Where are we heading?"

"South. As far as south goes."

"The wall?" Niv said, frowning in confusion. "What exactly do you plan on finding at the wall? There's nothing."

Marc stared at her for a moment, his expression was blank. He rummaged in a pouch deep within his armour and produced a heavy coin-purse, it jingled exactly the way Percy imagined a coin-purse would. He wordlessly threw it to Niv who snatched it out of the air instinctively.

"Your services are no longer required. That's the payment promised, congratulations, you're now quite a wealthy woman, though you should keep that to yourself."

Niv stared at him defiantly before turning her gaze to Percy. Percy felt her eyes drill into him. Was she really going to leave?

"Percy, come with me."

"What?" Percy said in shock.

"You wanted to be a Woodcutter."

"The Woodcutters are dead. You're not taking Percy." Marc said, stepping forward and looming over Niv.

"While I survive, so too do the Woodcutters. Percy, he'll abandon you if it serves his purpose. Come with me."

Marc gritted his teeth, and his hand shot out, gripping Niv by the throat. Without a moment's hesitation, her hand reached for her sword, but Marc grabbed it, rendering her defenceless.

"I think you need to learn your place, mercenary!" Marc snarled. Percy stood dumb and useless as his master held Niv.

"You left them to die, didn't you?" Niv spat, her eyes were bloodshot, and her face was turning red.

"What would you care if I did? All that happened is you got a bigger cut of the payment."

"As good as a confession!"

"You're getting on my nerves, girl. You did your job, you have no more business with us, you can go and find a tavern to rot in, and there are enough of them in this kingdom."

"I'm taking Percy."

"Why? What benefit could he possibly bring you?"

"If he stays with you, he'll end up like the captain and my sisters."

"If he stays with me he will share in my glory before gaining his own!"

"Is that how you work? You sweep people up in romantic stories?"

"I don't think he needed any help with that. Percy is my apprentice, we have a contract, he will fulfil his end, and I will fulfil mine, it's incredibly simple."

"Please let her go," Percy said quietly. Marc turned his eyes on Percy, they were cold. "I'm not going with you Niv. I have to see this through."

Marc let go of Niv, she fell to her knees, gasping for breath. She looked up at Percy with open confusion on her face, there was also a hint of betrayal in her eyes. Percy immediately felt guilty though he was not sure why. He owed Niv nothing, he owed Marc his life.

"He'll leave you to die if he has to. I know exactly where you're going Marc, it's the only place more dangerous than the one we just left. You'll find nothing in the Caves of Infinity, nothing but your grave." Niv gasped.

"It's poetic, but you won't change anything. Leave." Marc said, stepping closer to Niv, she painfully forced herself up.

The name circled Percy's mind. The Caves of Infinity. That couldn't possibly be Marc's destination. It was a myth at best. An old Triman tale, nothing more. How can a myth be dangerous?

"Niv," Percy said, stepping forward and holding out a hand to hold back Marc who was turning increasingly red in the face. "I'm going to be fine. I'm not carrying on because of Marc, but because I have to."

Niv shook her head, not quite believing her ears. "How can you be so dense? You're so blind! I gave you your chance, now you're condemned to die with him, just like your warg friend!"

Percy's face fell before he felt anger rising, how could she blame Caitlin's death on him? Caitlin made her choice, now he was making his. "We all have our decisions to make, I've made mine," Percy said, immediately despising the pettiness he heard in his voice. He didn't sound like the proud, stable person he wanted to be. Instead, he resembled the petulant child that he suspected he actually was.

Niv took a moment to digest his words before nodding slowly. "I see." She turned away, her limp was worse. "There's a town just to the west. I'll rest there for a few days. After that... I don't know. Look after yourself, Percy. Marc, if you end up mangled at the bottom of a ravine, it wouldn't be a great loss." She said before she limped away, rounding a corner and disappearing.

"We'll finish this as we began," Marc said, striding past him, anger and drive overruling exhaustion.

"With just two of us?" Percy asked quietly. His mentor turned and looked him up and down before nodding confidently.

"Is that not all that's needed? We took on too much baggage."

"Caitlin was baggage?"

"Yes, she was."

Percy snarled. It was a primal reaction surely developed through overexposure to Caitlin. He liked to believe it was intimidating, it only elicited a raised eyebrow from Marc.

"She died so that we could run! She died to protect me."

"She was a monster. Don't think I'm stupid, I know what happened in the Landry house. I don't pretend to understand exactly what you are or what Caitlin owed you and I truly don't care. I saw what happened to the golem. I don't care if you're a sorcerer of pale magic. While you share a contract with me, you are my apprentice and nothing else. Do you understand?"

Percy couldn't speak, he couldn't move, so instead, he stood like a badly carved statue with his mouth hanging open. Marc knew everything. Percy was not as mysterious as he had hoped.

"Do you understand?" Marc said, the sternness in his voice shocking Percy into finding his words.

"Ah… Yes, I understand," Percy said. He wasn't sure he could have said anything else.

Marc did not utter anything else as he walked away, and Percy didn't dare.

Their money had left with Niv, so Percy and Marc were once again sleeping beneath the stars. Percy couldn't say he was disappointed, he wanted to see the moon and it obliged. It hung in the sky, swollen and bright. The moon and The Stranger. They were the same thing, but at the same time, they were separate. The moon has always existed, but The Stranger had not, The Stranger was new, and it brought Pale magic with it. It was what now played with Percy's life, what had decided he should be blessed with power and what still pushed him onwards. He was not the first, Mask had also been chosen, and he embarked on the same journey, though how it ended was a mystery.

'Is Mask truly Chassius?' Percy asked, not really expecting an answer.

His name is Chassius.

'Is he *the* Chassius."

I don't know who the Chassius is. His name is Chassius.

'You really can be quite useless.'

I'm not human, stop thinking of me as such.

'Then what are you?'

A magical parasite.

'No, what are you really?'

A tiny part of a bigger whole.

'Aren't we all?' Percy thought bitterly, the voice did not respond. Instead, a deep voice nearby spoke quietly.

"Percy, are you awake?" Marc said. His voice did not carry the same strength that Percy had become accustomed to. It sounded small and weak.

"Yes, I'm awake. I'm just enjoying being above ground."

"I can understand that. I know that the Low Road was hard, I know that regardless of what Caitlin was, you will miss her, though I cannot understand why."

Percy couldn't believe what he was hearing, was Marc apologising and relating? He pushed the thought aside, deciding it was ludicrous.

"She was a warg, that can't be denied. But she was also human. She was a young woman. A young woman died protecting me. It's shameful."

"Many women, young and old died defending us in there, their gender has no bearing. You're lying to me; I know you don't care about what shame it brings. You looked at her as a friend. Grieving is normal, but you cannot grieve yet. We are so close now, so close." Marc said, he almost sounded desperate. "Thirty miles from here is our goal, the end of our journey."

"The Caves of Infinity? It doesn't exist, or if it does, it's just an endless network of caves and caverns. I don't want to go into the dark again Marc, don't make me."

"We have no choice, so many have died so that we could get here, turning back now would be a betrayal. Do you want to betray Caitlin?" Marc said, a little louder and more forceful now. Percy didn't speak, he knew exactly what Marc was doing; he was manipulating him. It was working. He couldn't leave now, if not because of Marc, then because of The Stranger. Both had exploited a fundamental failing of Percy; his insatiable, undeniable, unending curiosity about things that he really should not be curious about.

Percy felt something land on his chest, he instantly reached up to wrestle with whatever it was and found it to be a small leather-bound book, the moonlight was bright, and he could just see an inscription in the spine of the book.

"Chassius. I'm getting a little sick of that name."

"That's the last journal of Legate Chassius, most see it as a collection of insane ramblings. All written in Old Triman."

"I have a copy of Chassius' last journal, this is nothing like it."

"Well, this one wasn't exactly made public."

Percy opened the journal, angling it so that the moon shone on the pages. It was covered in small, tight script with diagrams dotted throughout. This was the first time he had seen an entire book written in Old Triman.

"When we first met, you told me that you could translate Old Triman. It's time to back up that claim."

"Well… That's difficult."

The sudden silence was dangerous, Percy spoke again quickly to avoid the danger becoming more immediate. "Well, what I mean is, Old Triman wasn't actually so much of a language, as it was a code. It was invented by the first Triman Emperor to communicate securely with his generals. I would first have to decipher it from Old Triman into regular ol' boring Triman, then I need to translate it into our much more common tongue."

"How long?"

"My father could do it in a week, I would need at least a month."

"You have two days, that's when we will reach the caves."

"That's impossible!" Percy protested.

"You don't need to translate the entire thing, find where he details the layout of the caves and translate that into directions. We shall simply have to improvise from there on. Do a good job, and you can keep the journal."

"…I'll do my best," Percy said, the dejection from being given such a herculean task was fleeting, and the much more overwhelming excitement was more lasting. A secret journal written by Chassius, his mind exploded with questions. This excitement was tainted by the fact that he could not immediately indulge himself, he had a job to do.

Chapter 18

Percy wanted to travel. Percy wanted to see every country in Urn, every hidden place and every legendary location. Two countries topped his list, the northernmost territory of Jor and the southernmost, Trima. He was now in Trima, a country that spawned the greatest empire Urn had ever seen, an empire that was thought unstoppable. This was the land of heroes where every member of the population was required to undergo extensive military training so that they would be able to unleash hell if Trima was invaded.

It's slightly ironic that Trima's collapse involved no grand battles. Instead, it was merely a slow economic deterioration and mounting resistance within Trima's conquered domains. It was gradual at first, a slowing of campaigns in Bukkin and Civvo before the legions retreated to the Inner Kingdoms. The loss of Aellis and Perda spelt the end of the Triman Empire. The lack of agriculture and industry continued Trima's deterioration, and it was barely recovering decades later. On their journey from Ureses to the southern wall, they had passed no shortage of grand structures and ornate towns, each dilapidated. Each sun-ravaged Triman they passed dripped deprivation and poverty. This was a far cry from the glorious country filled with sprawling cities which were in turn infested with armour-plated warriors that Percy had envisioned.

Their destination was a triangular entrance to a cave, set into the titanic mountainous wall that surrounded Urn. There were few places in Urn where it was impossible to see the mountain-range, but this was the closest that he had ever been. It undoubtedly was incredible, the peaks stretching up and scraping the thin blanket of cloud that had moved in from the north.

"This is it," Marc said, approaching the hole.

"This is the entrance to the Caves of Infinity?" Percy asked sceptically.

"Percy, when are you going to learn that nothing is ever as grand as you expect it to be? That's just life."

"No, I know that. I'd just like to be pleasantly surprised once or twice."

"Well, in this case, the value is not the entrance. Do you have the directions?"

Percy nodded quickly, retrieving a folded sheet of paper, he opened it to show a comprehensive, if slightly cramped set of instructions with an intricate map drawn on the reverse. The map consisted of a web of thick black lines. He had found it challenging to represent inclines and declines on the map, so he ignored it entirely and opted for a representation that looked remarkably like a bowl of spaghetti.

"That doesn't look like progress, Percy," Marc said, his voice heavy with doubt.

"Trust me," Percy said, knowing full and well that he should not be trusted right now. He had done his very best to decipher the Old Triman, but it had been more difficult than he had expected. He had learned the basic rules from his father, but before this journal surfaced, he had had precious little material to practice on, and everything he had used had a correct answer. There were several instances where he had made an educated guess and would not find out if he was right or not until they reached an inevitable dead end. However, this wasn't what was scaring Percy, what was really terrifying him was the all-consuming blackness just beyond the entrance.

Marc strolled to the entrance as though he had forgotten the Low Road's horrors entirely, as though he had yet to grasp that nothing good had happened in the darkness and even less so when it was deep underground. He had little choice though, so he followed. As he reached the forbidding portal he looked back, up at the sky. The clouds obscured the sun, robbing Percy of his last glimpse of its splendour before he stepped into the gloom.

The tunnel was narrow and low, Marc grunted as he was forced to move like a crab, slowly shuffling sideways. The scrape of stone against his chest plate made Percy's teeth vibrate. This first tunnel continued for some time, snaking in all directions but always descending. The first intersection had three possible routes, one that winded to the left, a rather impractical shaft and a tunnel that would reduce them to crawling.

"Which way?" Marc said, holding out his lantern to illuminate the choices.

"Guess," Percy said.

Marc groaned and lowered himself, peering into the low tunnel. "Are you absolutely certain?" He asked, wanting to crawl through the tunnel about as much as he wanted to stub his toe on an irate troll. "Afraid so," Percy replied, keeping his voice as low as possible. He had found that few things unnerved him more than an echo in these caves. The voice that came back every time he spoke sounded alien, much too shrill and sharp.

Marc had always cursed, but he was really flexing his vocabulary as he squeezed through the small cylindrical crawlway. Percy was having a much easier time as he found his small, slight figure was suited to the tight spaces. Multiple smaller crevices led off from the shaft, each too tight to even imagine following. Percy froze to peer down one. Shadows danced in cracks and small, segmented bodies squirmed, he thought he even saw a bloodshot eye. He didn't investigate any of the faults after that.

Emerging from the hole was a liberating experience, and they found themselves in a much more reasonable grotto. Marc pulled himself to his full height and stretched as much of his body as possible. His joints cracked, and for once he groaned in relief instead of irritation.

"Percy." He said after he had assessed their options. There were dozens of paths, so many that they had to be careful not to disappear down a descending shaft.

"I know, Chassius had a hell of a time here."

"So which one is it?" Marc asked, a hint of warning in his voice. This was a delicate choice this early in their journey, if he were wrong, it would make every choice from this moment on an error, making them more and more lost until they were so far gone that they would never find the correct path again. This was also the riskiest choice as Chassius had almost been nonsensical when explaining the solution. Percy had hoped that seeing the options would clarify Chassius' rambling, but now that he stood before them, it was even more confusing.

"Percy, I don't have time for indecision," Marc said in a low voice, stressing each syllable and making sure that the full stop was heard.

"I know, I know. Give me a moment, this isn't as easy as it looks." Percy said as he inspected several of the entrances. On the fourth, he found what he was looking for. He traced the edges of the hole with his finger and felt the two vertical lines engraved into the stone, too perfect to be natural. "This is it." He said confidently. Chassius did not leave markers at every junction, but only at the most confusing ones to ensure that while someone with the journal could navigate the tunnels, any opportunists would run afoul of their own ambition.

After several more tunnels, Percy became more confident, calling out which turns to take in a firm voice, assured now that the echoes would do him no harm. The journey was arduous, it involved sliding down less that smooth tunnels, attempting to climb sheer-faced shafts and at one point they were forced onto their stomachs to pass under a low-hanging ceiling. They stopped to rest in a tight cavern. Marc refuelled the lantern as Percy panted, shoving something similar to salted beef into his mouth between each laborious breath. Time had become meaningless to Percy, he didn't know how long he had been in the Caves of Infinity, desperately hoping that their name was more romanticism than reality. It was useless guessing how long they had been in the caves when he didn't even know how long ago he had deceived his parents and followed Marc. They must have given him up for dead by now, it had been weeks. In these caves, it felt like Percy was already dead and cursed to shuffle through blackness forever.

"How far now?" Marc asked, uncorking his water flask and taking a swig. They had been able to refill in a small stream with water straight off the mountains, they had never tasted fresher water.

"I don't know. Chassius doesn't really deal in distances, but there are few directions left. Then there's what he only described as a 'wild ride'."

Marc shook his head. "Chassius was insane. What on Urn does 'wild ride' mean?"

"I have no idea, but I'm not looking forward to it."

"Lost your taste for danger, Percy?" Marc asked, the flickering light glinting off his clean white teeth. Marc could be hit in the face with a mace, spend months without any form of dental hygiene and would still have teeth whiter than milk. Percy had gone a few days without the use of blue-leaf paste and could feel a thick coat of grime covering every tooth. If this went on any longer, he would be tempted to cut his losses, remove his teeth and start over with a set of wooden dentures. The thought both terrified and amused Percy in equal amounts.

"I'm beginning to think I never had one," Percy admitted. "Perhaps this was a mistake. I would have made a grand accountant."

Marc spat into the dirt, the dry dust drank the liquid thirstily. "A fate worse than death, but I can't tell a man what to do with their life. If you want to live a life of tedium before dying as a nameless, faceless nobody without so much as a tale to tell then do it. But, if you can't tell a fantastical drunken tale to a stranger in a tavern, then what's the point?" Marc said before chuckling to himself. "If we survive this you can go home and live the life your father did before you. Do you think you could? After what you've seen? In the past few weeks, you've lived more than the last three generations of your family did combined."

"No… I mean, I don't know."

"Well, you should figure it out, this isn't a life you can drop in and out of when you please, and to be a legend requires your full commitment."

Percy was silent, he didn't know what to say because he didn't know what he wanted. As his systematic and well-organised mind tried to dissect the issue and formulate solutions, it became harder and harder. He still wanted his name to be sung and all of his exploits to be told and retold for centuries, but the fantasy had been soured. Would Caitlin feature in these songs? Would she be remembered for her sacrifice or would the warg be forgotten, or worse yet, would she be doomed to be the evil in the story, would the tale become so warped and twisted over time that her downfall would be the end of the story? Would it be better for her name to be forgotten entirely to spare her the pain or being made the villain of the story?

Just beyond the light of the lantern there was a passageway portal and for a moment Percy thought he could make out a faint silhouette. He blinked and the figure disappeared but as he blinked again he could see the image in the dance of random lights and colours that played across the inside of his eyelids. He had seen the silhouette before, long ago in a lonely forest clearing, just beyond the reach of the moonlight. Percy shook his head until the picture faded.

Marc stood, nodding to the nearest and tallest tunnel. "Please tell me that's the next one."

"Eh… Yes, actually. You're in luck." Percy said, half of his consciousness was there with Marc, and the other half was in the forest, the smell of fresh blood and forest flowers filling his nostrils.

He followed Marc, ducking under boulders and scrambling over mounds of dirt and rocks. He slowly regained his concentration and focus, there was still a job to be done. Whatever it was.

He could hear water, he looked at Marc nervously. In his opinion, drowning underground was not much worse than drowning above ground but still not ideal.

The water was pouring from an outcrop above them, they stood on a precipice that sloped away steeply. The torrent followed the slope into the darkness. There were no other routes open to them.

"I'm assuming this would be the 'wild ride' then," Marc said, his face had turned a deathly shade of white which Percy derived no small amount of amusement from. The big bad warrior that slew wargs and ghouls alike was afraid of a little water. Albeit water that flowed rapidly into an inky abyss. It was still funny though.

"This is it, if we go down there we cannot return, we'll never be able to get back up here." Marc continued, he held the lantern out over the edge, just short of the flowing water in an attempt to illuminate beneath them, the bottom was much too far.

"We're going to lose the lantern as well," Percy said helpfully. "And you might not like to hear this, but you certainly can't wear that armour. If this is what Chassius was referring to, then I think it's going to get deep. You'll drown with all that."

Marc nodded slowly, recognising the wisdom in Percy's words. He made no move to remove anything. Percy wasn't sure what Marc was expecting to face at the end of the 'wild ride', but he assumed that armour would be a requirement.

It took some time before Marc conceded and even longer to wholly remove the plate and chainmail armour that he wore. Percy was amazed by the layering and the number of hidden weapons present; two throwing-axes in the sleeves of his shirt, a dagger in each boot and what looked like a single-shot crossbow across his back, hidden under his cloak.

There were only two things that he refused to part with, the cylindrical package that he had acquired from the captain and his sword. He also produced a satchel made from waxed leather into which he insisted that they store Chassius' journal, Percy's own journal, writing materials and the hand-written instructions that Percy had produced as well as the rest of the food and water and other essentials such as matches. For his part, Percy had given up very little, figuring that it was better to have water-damaged belongings than have no belongings at all. He had no armour to lose and his shortsword, while still hefty would not pull him under the water.

Once they were prepared they stood on the edge, Mark sat the lantern on the rock next to them. They stood there, suddenly cold. Mark wore a thin cotton shirt with a deep red vest and fitted trousers, he didn't look much smaller than he did with his armour on. Percy had shoved the padded jerkin into his sack, deciding that while it had never fooled anyone, its added padding could at least act as a floatation device.

"What if this is all a cruel joke? What if there's nothing down there but sharp rocks and deep water. What if Chassius was a liar?" Percy said, he felt the coward in him rear its head, seeking to break his resolve. It wasn't too late, he was confident that he could find his way back to the entrance, he could leave and go home. He didn't have to be here, in this dark, cold place, he didn't need to traverse these places, places like Landry manor, or the Low Road where honest people have no business treading. He felt the cowardice grip his stomach, he felt it reach up his throat and seize his tongue. He very nearly felt the coward win.

"Percy. Look at me." Marc said in a commanding but almost compassionate voice. Percy couldn't resist, and he looked into his masters stern eyes. There was fear there.

"Right now we are only human, right now we fear, we fear death and the unknown. But I promise you, Percy, we are so close to no longer being humans, but instead being immortals. You and I will share glory not even Chassius or Bhoran, or Rykus saw. You see yourself as a coward, I know you do. But ever since the day I found you I have seen nothing but unbreakable courage. One more leap into the depths, young Percy. One more." Marc said, reaching out a closed fist and beating it softly twice against Percy's chest, the ultimate sign of respect between two Aelissean soldiers, something only comrades would share.

Percy only nodded dumbly, shocked and unnerved by the unexpected kindness.

"Are you ready?" Marc asked, all business again. Percy nodded and turned his eyes to the task.

Together they inhaled and stepped forward.

The stone was hard but smooth, worn by countless decades of continually flowing water. The water was cold but clean and fresh. The freezing temperature took Percy's breath away almost instantly. It didn't take long for them to travel beyond the lanterns glow and they continued to slide, gaining speed as the shaft sharply turned left and right. In the pitch blackness, Percy saw images, images that shifted and changed as he descended into the unseen. His

379

family, the Woodcutters, Mask, Marc… Caitlin. Caitlin lingered, her smile and her eyes, her silhouette as he lamented over his first kill.

The end of their journey consisted of a drop through nothing but air, culminating in the somewhat less than graceful entry into a freezing cold pool of water. Percy plummeted under the surface, managing to beat the back of his head against a rock as he did so. Percy ignored the pain and thrashed violently until he reached the surface. He gasped desperately, attempting to force the stale, still air into his lungs and only succeeding in coughing out half a lake's worth of water.

Something bumped against him, and a hand grasped his shoulder, steadying him in the water. He knew someone was talking, but they sounded far away and garbled until the words lost all meaning, as time passed the words became crisper, but just hearing them still managed to hurt his head.

"-Must be a ledge or something to climb onto. Percy. Percy!" Marc said, his voice commanding and annoyed.

"What? Yes, yes I'm fine. I just hit my head."

"Can you see anything?"

Percy slowly turned his head, attempting to see something in the absolute blackness. It was proving impossible, he could be staring at a wall inches from his face or a cavern bigger than Urn, and it would have been no different. As he was losing hope, he saw it. It was barely a pinprick of light, but it shone like someone had set fire to this canvas of black.

"There," Percy said, his own words sending lances of pain through his mind as the back of his skull throbbed. His head felt warm.

"Where?"

Percy reached out, turning Marc toward the light.

"There's nothing there Percy, how hard did you hit your head?" Marc said sceptically.

Percy scoffed and attempted to swim toward the light, guiding Marc behind him. It was surprisingly difficult, in his weakened state the water felt like honey and he spent the majority of his time just struggling to keep his nose above the surface. Eventually, Marc figured out the general direction Percy was leading them in and took over, moving him so he could cling onto Mark's shoulder. As they finally hit the edge of the pool, Percy scrabbled away from Marc and up the slope, lying on the wet rock and panting. He didn't see what Marc did, but he heard wet footsteps, moving away at first before returning.

"Percy?" Marc said, Percy responded with a tired sigh and Marc grabbed his arm, hauling him to his feet. "We don't have time to sleep, Percy. We have a job to do, we're almost there." Percy felt himself being dragged, he knew there were more words, but he couldn't make them out, it didn't take long for the splashing of the small waterfall behind them to dull into a constant hum. He stopped taking steps, allowing Marc to take all of his weight. Percy tried to speak but what came out was slurred and incomprehensible. If they weren't already in complete darkness, then he would be expecting his vision to start forsaking him. Instead, random colours and shapes danced across the black, taking solid form as people or places before fading again. The light still shone, and it was growing.

"What is this?" Marc said. Percy raised his head, he must have passed out because the light now stood about a foot in front of them. It wasn't a flame or anything natural. It was a flower, its petals giving off the ghostly light. It was beautiful, but there was nothing else. No passageway and no salvation.

"What is this?" Marc asked again, demanding an answer, though Percy wasn't sure if he wanted it from him or from the universe as a whole.

"A flower," Percy said in a small voice, in his half-conscious state he thought that Marc was being rather dim. Unusually so.

"A flower? We came here for a flower?" Marc said, his voice had lost its power.

It is awfully pretty though.

"It is," Percy said aloud. He laughed weakly. The flower turned slowly towards him and bloomed; its petals stretched wide into the shape of a sharp crescent.

"Oh so pretty." He said, stretching out his hand to the flower, silver ran in the veins of his hands and extended from his finger-tips in branching tendrils like lightning. In the flower Percy saw many things. Mostly he saw faces, flitting through his mind faster and faster until he brushed against the warm petal.

"Please." He said in barely more than a whisper. His hand dropped, and his body felt light. Marc didn't let him fall.

Percy didn't see the flower vanish into a cloud of light, nor did he see that light illuminate the way down a passage that had previously been sheer rock. He only had sweet dreams.

Chapter 19

The face that greeted Percy as he awoke was unlike any he had seen before. It was beautiful beyond compare, even his delirious mind could not have crafted a hallucination so other-worldly and perfect. No, this face must have been lovingly moulded by a god looking to create a masterpiece. She had eyes of deep green, more verdant than the deep forests of Bukkin, her dark hair looked soft, and her triman skin looked smooth and warm to the touch. She smiled, the smile alone could have owned Percy's heart.

That's when the owner of this angelic face slapped Percy. Hard.

"Ow! What the hell!" He exclaimed, raising his hand to his assaulted cheek. Her full lips moved, forming words. Gibberish.

No, not gibberish. It took a moment for the words to register as being spoken in triman. His mind quickly worked through the words. He was certainly not perfect when it came to triman, but after the more common tongue used by the majority of the inner kingdoms, it was the language he had worked at the most. This wasn't because he wanted to communicate with Trimans of course, it was because all of the best tales were in triman and something indescribable was lost in translation.

"You here!" The goddess said. A little dull perhaps, but he thought he could forgive anything for her.

Then the face retreated, and all he could see was a blinding light. He raised his hand to protect his eyes, after a moment he spread his fingers to study it. They seemed to be in a cavern that stretched in every direction for at least a mile, the ceiling was a large smooth dome and in the centre of it was the light. It hung in the air with no physical shape. It was not giving off the warm, yellow light of the sun, but instead the crisp white light of the moon. Despite this, the ground beneath him was still warm. He slowly and carefully raised himself until he was propping himself on his elbows.

The cavern was breath-taking, he had likened the Low Road and its maze of tunnels to an underground city, but this place had really taken the phrase and defined it. He appeared to be lying in the middle of a town square and beyond it were hundreds of simple stone structure that looked more like they had grown straight out of the rock rather than being built as they contained no straight lines or sharp edges and there was not a brick in sight. Their connection to the ground was seamless, and there was no glass in the windows with only a thin sheet of red cloth barring the entrance.

Gathered around him was a crowd of people, shocked, terrified and curious in equal measures. They were all dressed the same; a white cloth vest and baggy cotton trousers secured at the knees and ankle with lengths of string. They all wore very worn sandals.

"Uh…" Percy said. Though 'said' is probably not the correct word as Percy was really just making an assortment of random noises. The goddess stood a couple of feet away, still beaming down at him. Clearly, she was the only one pleased to see him.

"Where am I?" Percy asked, finding his big-boy words after a few moments of abject confusion.

"Cavorum Infinitatis." Someone in the crowd said, a rather tall individual with close-cut hair and the same dark skin as the rest.

"Well, yes, I know that. Wait, you speak the common tongue?"

"A little." The idol said before reaching down a hand to help him up. He took the hand gladly, it was much coarser than he had expected. She didn't let go of his hand.

"Karees," She said, nodding.

"Ah…" Percy said, his cheeks burning as he found himself lost in her eyes once again. Her smile turned to confusion and then sympathy.

"Percy. My name is Percy. It's a pleasure to meet you, Karees." Percy said, entirely forgetting the rest of the crowd that surrounded them. Karees nodded, then looked awkwardly at their conjoined hands as Percy refused to let go. It took another moment or two before Percy found the strength to let her go.

"So, eh, I think my earlier question is still valid… Where exactly am I?" Percy asked, forcing his eyes away from Karees to scan the cavern. There were no apparent entrances.

"Cavorum Infinitatis…" Karees said, stretching out the words and leaning forward as though that clarified the situation.

"No, I understand that. I guessed that we were still in the caves… But where, *exactly*." Percy stressed, looking around at the confused faces. Eventually, one shrugged and said simply "Home."

"Oh… I see. So… How are all you here then?" Percy asked. This should really have been his first question.

"Oh, we came long ago. Follow legate." Karees said, nodding sagely.

"Legate?"

"Legate Chassius."

"Chassius? You've been here for over a century?" Percy asked, disbelief plain on his face. "How do you survive down here? I mean, I don't see any crops." Another round of confused looks greeted him, the tall man approached and spoke quietly in Karees' ear.

"We think you should meet it now," Karees said after some deliberation.

"It?"

"The Stranger."

Percy couldn't speak.

'Is she serious or is this just another bad translation?' Percy thought.

Only one way to find out.

Karees and the man led the way with Percy and the rest of the crowd following. They walked through the winding streets of the city that didn't have any visible design to them, almost like the placing of the buildings was entirely random and unplanned. The city was not very large, mostly consisting of simple dwellings. Here and there it would open onto large spaces. They approached the edge of the cavern, set into which was a large stone door with the crescent symbol carved into it. Karees stopped at the door and knocked gently, surely such a timid knock would go unheard. The door opened instantly. Whatever lingered inside was anxious to meet him. Karees stepped out of the way, gesturing for Percy to enter, a reassuring smile on her face.

Beyond the opening, there was only shadow.

"Actually, I've walked blindly into very dark places several times in the past few weeks and on not one occasion has it worked out well for me. I might just give this one a miss." Percy said, smiling weakly at Karees.

"Trust me," Karees said, each word dripping with sincerity. He did trust her, even if she said the words and immediately burst into an evil maniacal laugh, he thought he would still trust her.

He summoned his courage, the majority being given by Karees' smile and stepped through the door which closed swiftly behind him. He had been wrong, there was some light, but it was weak, filtering through from cracks which cast broken lines of light across the floor, leaving the majority of the room a mass of sharp shadows.

In the centre of the room was a pale font which sprouted seamlessly from the ground. Percy approached the font. It was identical to the one that he had encountered in Aellis, yet here there were no mirrors and no moonlight to feed it. Inside was only water, no silvery worms ready to burrow its way into him and speak in riddles every now and then.

"I'm pleased you have arrived, my young friend." A voice said. It was a low rumbling sound that crackled like a campfire.

Percy span, the shadows congregated in the corner of the room, hiding whatever lurked there. He couldn't see it clearly, but it was big and had a wedge-shaped head.

"Who-… *What* are you?" Percy asked, putting the font between himself and the creature.

"You don't know? Have you not been looking for me? Shame, so few look for me." It said before laughing, a jolly sound turned sinister by the crackling voice.

"Are you… The Stranger?" Percy asked.

"No. But I expect I'm the closest you'll ever get."

"Why are you hiding in a corner?"

"I'm thinking."

"About what?"

"About how to best show myself."

"Well, at the risk of being a cliché, just being yourself is usually best."

It laughed again. It profoundly unnerved Percy, and he couldn't stop himself from flinching at the sound.

"As you wish, my friend."

What stepped out of the shadows was far from human. Percy gasped and stumbled backwards, falling onto his backside. The creature was huge, its scaly head nearly reaching the ceiling. It walked on all fours, each leg ending in a foot with talons like scimitars, it had a long, lean body covered in glittering silver scales, each larger than Percy's hands. Its head was long and angular, as it

392

opened its mouth to speak Percy saw teeth that would make the greatest heroes tremble.

"Are you satisfied?" It asked.

Percy couldn't speak, the beast was unlike anything he had ever hoped to see. It was colossal and mighty. It was a dragon.

"You're... You're a dragon?" Percy asked, his lip quivering and hindering his words.

"Sort of."

"Sort of? How can you sort of be a dragon? You have wings!"

"What have you always wanted to see Percy? What, in all the stories of might and magic did you find the most magnetic? What creature captured your imagination? I like dragons, they were the culmination of every ounce of wonder you humans contain... However, perhaps you're right. It can be difficult being confronted with the embodiment of legend itself. Perhaps something more subtle?"

The dragon vanished and in its place was a person. There was no gradual transformation like how a warg changed, there was a slight 'blip', and then it was something else. It was Niv.

Niv smiled.

"Is this better?" She asked, placing a hand in the water of the font and circling it to stand before Percy. She stood so close he could smell sweat and blood.

"Or this?" It asked as it changed again. Caitlin beamed at him, her face free from the wounds gained on their journey. She stood before him alive and well, full of all the innocence the monster should not have possessed.

"No, no... Please, not her."

"No? Why not?"

"Because I killed her."

"Monsters killed her."

"She died protecting me."

"As was her duty."

Percy couldn't bear to look into the innocent eyes.

"A shame. You were so similar, you know."

Percy shook his head, he couldn't imagine sharing any similarities with Caitlin.

"No? Boundless imagination and brilliant minds did not bind you two? You did not both contain a voracious appetite for tales of fancy? If not for her father's meddling where he shouldn't, she might have taken your place and arrived here a good deal sooner."

The being cycled through forms, faster and faster. There were so many. Percy recognised them all. Mask, Grey, Marc, the captain, Moira, Nica. A stranger.

Percy didn't recognise this person. They were short with fiery red hair, wearing a black robe with the red insignia of the Triman Empire painted onto the front.

"…Who's this?"

"His name was Friarn. It would seem you're not comfortable with the people you know, so this should do. Now, Percy, I think it's time we get down to business. I'm going to give you a rare gift. This gift is knowledge. You have a remarkable mind, Percy. You have an incredible attribute in your endless curiosity."

"You're just another fragment, aren't you?"

"I am, but I assure you I am much more potent and knowledgeable than the irritating voice that whispers in your ear."

Charming.

"Very well," Percy said, straightening his back. "What happened?"

"Elaborate."

"Urn isn't natural. It can't be."

Friarn smiled, nodding approvingly. He turned and began circling the room, unable to keep still.

"You're right. It's not."

Friarn waved a hand, and above the font, an image appeared. It was a sphere of light that took a definite physical form. It was a perfect ball with jagged shapes dotted across it. Percy recognised it as being identical to the maps he had seen in the Low Road.

"This is the world that your forebears knew," Friarn said, nodding to the sphere. He held out a hand and a circle recessed into one of the larger continents. "This is Urn. I created Urn."

"There's really an entire world beyond the mountains…" Percy said, circling the globe.

"This is an old world. At one point there were too many people to count. I loved this world, I watched it bloom, and its people flourish. You humans have something that I have never seen in any others. Your incredible love of stories. They were constantly envisioning new exciting worlds, never content with their own. Their imaginations created creatures and stories that fascinated me. Then they went and destroyed themselves." Friarn said. He shrugged. Across the face of the silver sphere, lights bloomed like flowers in spring. A few at first but then more and more until the entire globe had been covered twice over. "And that was that. I thought I would never hear another story. You can imagine how distraught I was." The fragment pulled an exaggerated sad face, like an actor in a play. Percy couldn't tell if it was joking or if it just hadn't quite figured out Friarn's features.

"But then I heard them, whispered tales from deep underground told by the old to the young. The stories were of a beautiful world. The first time that they told stories of their own world before they burned it. I couldn't leave them there, I couldn't leave children to live their lives in deep, dark places. So I began to build, like they had done. I took your stories and made Urn."

"In the Low Road, the monsters glowed with your power, but Niv didn't," Percy said.

"I created the monsters from the imaginations of the survivors, I did not create humans. In the Low Road, the fears congregated, as they do in all dark places."

"But why did you enclose us? Why did you create the mountains to contain us?"

"I'm not all-powerful, creating an entire world is too much for me. The mountains protect you from yourself."

"You didn't have enough power? I thought you were a god?"

"God? No. Gods don't exist. I'm just another being looking to be entertained, not all that dissimilar to your own kind, just a step ahead. You have one more question, my young friend."

"Where's Marc?" Percy asked. Friarn raised an eyebrow.

"Does it matter? He didn't show this much concern for you, why should you care for him?"

"You've known humans for so long, and you ask this?" Percy said, folding his arms, confident that he had outwitted the almost-deity.

"I just informed you that humans destroyed themselves. While I love your kind, you have an endless capacity for hate. Since I created Urn, you have constantly been at war. While I can't say this has ever really bothered me, you have to admit that my question is more than valid."

Percy didn't say anything, he resorted to staring down Friarn. Friarn sighed, the globe vanished, and in its place, Marc hung in the air, not created from light but flesh. He looked like he was immersed in water, his short hair ruffled, and the folds of his clothes constantly shifted. His eyes were closed.

"He's alive," Friarn said, nodding slowly. "He came here to kill me, following the words of Chassius. He wanted to kill a dragon. Oh, that reminds me. The dragons, I can imagine you want to know what happened to them."

Percy took a moment to digest Friarn's words. "Of course you do." Friarn continued. "Everyone always wants to know what happened to the dragons. It's much less of a mystery than it seems. Dragons were an incredibly old fictional creature that the humans believed was wise beyond compare. Unfortunately, a creature so wise discovered the truth of Urn rather quickly, and they became a nuisance. A few still live, the ones who chose to obey now live along the mountain range and eat prying adventurers. I dealt with the more resolute ones as peacefully as I could. I took away their ability to procreate."

Friarn seemed eager to share.

"Please release Marc," Percy said.

"Why? Like I said, he came here to kill me. To kill me and claim his glory."

"How could he possibly kill you? You created Urn, you're infinitely more powerful than he is."

"I am a fragment of what created Urn, human's hunted dragons, creatures that could turn towns to ash in the blink of an eye. You underestimated your own power and managed to destroy your world. I do not underestimate."

"If you're only a fragment of the Stranger then what would it matter if you did die? What would change if the Stranger is actually sitting on the moon?"

Friarn smiled before clapping his hands together.

"That's a good question. I have a proposal, young Percy. I will hold onto your friend here, just for a little while later. Worry not, on my honour he will not be harmed. I would like you to... Work through what I have told you, in a day or two you can return to me and tell me if you want me to release him or not. Do we have a deal?"

"This seems like one of those situations where I don't actually have a choice."

"It might be one of those situations," Friarn replied with a patient smile.

Percy looked up at Marc again, he didn't seem to be in pain, and he couldn't see anything harmful. However, he couldn't actually see if he was breathing either.

"Those people out there. Who are they?"

"Why don't you ask them yourself?" Friarn said. The door swung open, Karees was waiting just beyond it.

"I have another question," Percy said.

"You're out of questions."

"You want to answer this one. It's part of the story."

Friarn smiled.

"The golem. Why did you send it? It nearly killed me." Percy asked.

"You needed to understand what you had. You needed to embrace what you have been given. Otherwise, you would not understand what is to come." The fragment replied.

Friarn gestured to the door. Percy gave Marc one last glance before walking to the door, he looked back at Friarn.

"Percy, if you can't trust me, then I'm afraid you can't trust anyone. I will summon you when I think you're ready, friend." Friarn said. Marc vanished. Percy nodded and reluctantly left, taking comfort in the fact that Karees was waiting for him.

Chapter 20

The cavern was deceivingly large, the dome was huge by itself, but the Trimans who inhabited the cavern had found ways to amplify the space. They had carved into the walls of the dome for stone to add to the rudimentary buildings. While the original structures looked grown and seamless, these extensions and second floors were ugly blocky structures made from crude bricks.

Karees led him around the city, pointing to various buildings and points of interest. There were plenty of areas for leisure, including a large bathhouse, board-game rooms and a vast variety of sports arenas including stadiums for combat and a training yard. Percy asked Karees if every person living there was trained in combat and she just looked at him like he was stupid. Percy noticed the distinct lack of shops and restaurants, though there were several taverns serving drinks that were utterly foreign to Percy. After some insistence, Karees finally explained.

"No sun," Karees said, pointing up at the suspended ball of ethereal light that created a state of constant almost-day within the cavern. "Little grows here," Karees said, leading him to the outskirts of the town where they had built several small farms. These farms grew crops unlike any that Percy had ever seen. Hundreds of mushroom variations that varied wildly in size and shape, some even strayed from the bland grey that Percy was used to and had bright, vibrant colours and patterns. She led him further out to one of the recesses carved into the dome, here several Trimans milled around, shovelling a white substance from the ground into huge sacks which in turn were wheeled back into the town.

"What is this?" Percy asked, squatting and gathering a sample of the substance. He couldn't lie, he was largely attempting to look intelligent, sniffing the matter and grinding it between his fingers. He was about to lick the sample when he looked up at the ceiling of the small cave. Hundreds of eyes met his. Percy shook the excrement from his hand in disgust. When Karees was finished laughing she managed to speak. "Like small chicken, you see. Farm. We have others, insects, worms, deep-moles. Bats give most meat. Delicacy."

Percy nodded and backed away, wiping his hands on his trousers while his cheeks burned scarlet. Water cascaded from several openings in the dome of the cavern; the smaller ones would turn into a spray, creating constant rain in certain parts of the cavern while others ended in pools. Karees took Percy to one such pool in which many nude Trimans played and swam, even washing their limited amount of clothes.

"Here you can wash, do not drink. Others for drinking." Karees said, waving her finger at Percy like he had already taken a long, satisfying swig from the waters. As he walked with her through the cavern, he noticed two main things. The first of these was that while some of the Trimans were young, some even slightly younger than Percy, there were no young children anywhere in sight. There were also no old people. The oldest people he had seen were middle-aged. Where were the white-haired women with wispy beards that had seen in Aellis and Trima? The second thing he noticed was the way Karees' hips swayed as she walked. He shook his head and drew his mind back to what was going on around him. While many of the Trimans seemed happy in their lives, others were utterly hopeless. This portion of the population sat silently in the shadows and stared into frothy mugs of whatever unholy drink you can brew using mushrooms and bat droppings.

Something that he could not have failed to notice was the celebrity-like status he had gained on entrance. He and Marc were the first visitors this isolated community had received in quite some time, and as Marc was currently at the mercy of the Stranger, Percy was left as the only outsider in a homogenous society. This afforded him some fame. Wherever Karees led him the Trimans would flock, regarding him with excitement, curiosity and an ample dose of suspicion.

"How long has this society been here? You have survived underground so well... Because of that light." Percy asked, occasionally squinting at the light as he and Karees took a well-earned break from their adventuring.

"Mhm... You said hundred years... Not matter, I think. It has felt longer," Karees said, taking a sip from her drink. It was green and frothy; Percy had opted for water instead.

"So... Your ancestors were led here by Chassius?"

A flicker of anger and the cheerful smile returned. "Legate Chassius yes, and Friarn."

The Stranger's robed form flashed through his mind.

"Friarn… Who is Friarn?"

"Friarn Fire-finger, fieriest mage in Triman Empire, of course," Karees said, giving Percy the distinct impression that he was supposed to know that already.

"Oh, yes, right, that Friarn," Percy replied, nodding wisely. A fire-mage was mentioned a few times in Chassius' journals; however he was never described as particularly powerful, and he had not been mentioned in the vast array of literature Percy owned on Triman heroes.

"Why did they come here?" Percy asked.

"Why did you?" Karees replied.

"I didn't have a choice. My mentor brought me here."

"Why did he?"

"Well… I know now that he came to do exactly what I thought. He came to slay a great beast and make his name, he came to create his legend. The same reason I followed him."

"Same as Chassius and Friarn," Karees said, shrugging.

"I met a man who wears a mask. He claims to be Legate Chassius."

Karees features became dark, she stood and turned away from him.

"Where?" She asked.

"The last place I saw him was in the Low Road. Could it have actually been him? How could he have survived this long?"

"He is cursed. Cursed with immortality." Karees spat, her friendly demeanour had vanished, leading Percy to wonder if it had ever been genuine.

"I'm not sure I'd consider immortality a curse," Percy replied, immediately regretting it.

Karees chuckled darkly, shaking her head slowly. "That's what you came for."

"Of a kind, yes. Immortality as a legend, living on through word and song... As a hero."

"Heroes not exist."

"Of course they do. Bhoran the Berserker."

"Bhoran killed innocents and burned villages. Not hero."

"Well... Perhaps not to a Triman... Rikkan Roran defeated a colossal troll that was going to destroy half of Bukt!"

"Rikkan lied. Someone else kill troll and die in the process. Rikkan takes credit. The troll was dormant, it only wanted to sleep."

Percy frowned. "How do you know these things? That was only forty years ago, how do you know about it here?"

Karees smiled and pointed at the door to The Strangers sanctuary, turning back toward Percy. "The Stranger like stories, like to tell them to us. the Stranger see everything, you know. No lies for the Stranger, no false heroes. Stranger see all evils. Dark not help. Dark not hide."

"Why does it like stories? It's practically a god, surely such things should be beneath it."

"Perhaps such things should be beneath you also, no?"

"I'm only human."

"They are only the Stranger." Karees shrugged and grinned, anger forgotten. "Soon they will call for you again. There is one more thing I should show you. It will help you."

Karees led Percy away from the town to a small opening in the caverns furthermost wall. Percy was hesitant to enter as tunnels had not been overly kind to him. Unfortunately, he found it quite impossible to deny Karees. He would have volunteered for another stroll through the Low Road, a week-long vacation in the Landry estate and even dance in the courtyard of the Yellow Fort if she had asked. The tunnel ended in a small circular room, there was a shaft in the ceiling through which warm daylight poured. Percy stepped forward, looked up the shaft and imagined he could see the sky. The hole was a perfect cylinder cut out of the rock.

"The Stranger make this. Give us a way out if we want," Karees said, walking around the light, careful not to touch it.

"A way out?" Percy asked.

Footsteps came from down the tunnel, an adventurers reflexes made Percy spin and back off. The tall man present at Percy's awakening stepped into the room, looking at the two with a blank expression. He nodded to Karees. Karees held up a hand, partly in greeting and partly asking him to wait. She turned to Percy and smiled sadly.

"Percy. That sword you carry is his."

Percy shook his head with a laugh. "My sword? It's an antique, they don't make this style anymore."

"Honour Lost." The man said in a strong, clear voice. His voice carried little of the triman accent. "I scratched those words into the pommel when Chassius abandoned his duty and led us back to Trima. I left my blade there, and my heart with a girl named Charlotte Landry. I spent longer in Aellis than most."

"When Chassius led you back? You'd have to be a century old!" Percy said, shaking his head at the insanity. "You're Chassius' legion? You were given immortality as well?"

The man laughed long and hard, not exactly disputing Percy's belief that he was insane. When he finally finished he straightened his back and wiped a rogue tear from his eye. "Hold onto that sword, it served me well, and I expect it must have been bored all these years." He said, he looked at Karees and said a few words in triman. She smiled and nodded, a tear welling in the corner of her eye.

The man stepped forward to the edge of the light. He took a deep breath before stepping into it. Percy gazed in horror at what happened. First, the skin stripped away from him, then the muscle, then his bones turned to dust. It was over in an instant. Percy couldn't speak. Karees chose not to.

410

"You're all dead. Every one of you is dead."

"The Stranger killed us after Friarn tried to kill it."

"Then how can you be here?"

"The Stranger… Is lonely, I think. Likes telling stories, you see. Some can't take it, come here to fade away."

"I think I would like to see the Stranger now."

"They haven't summoned you."

"I don't care," Percy said as he walked away, through the beam of light. For a moment he felt the suns warmth. It didn't touch the coldness in his core.

Percy stormed through the town of dead men and women in a fit of rage. He felt anger like he had never felt before. It threatened to overwhelm him and use his body to do terrible things. Exactly what he could do to a being that transformed into dragons just for fun he didn't know. He would find out.

When he reached the door he didn't knock gently, instead opting for the more assertive 'slamming both of your fists against the door technique'. It was a full five minutes before the doors swung open at the speed of a snail recovering from a horrific racing-related injury.

The Stranger stood in front of the font, smiling at him with the mouth of a dead man. "Hello my young friend, I wonder if you don't understand that I am the one who summons people."

"They're all dead," Percy said. He hadn't planned the words; they were just the ones that came out.

"Karees informed you then?"

"The Stranger sees all, no?"

"Almost all."

"The light, it's the only thing keeping them living. You killed them and then created these cruel after-images just so you have someone to tell your senseless little stories to?"

"Little stories? Your entire world is built on stories, without stories Urn would be a smoking wasteland and you would either be dead or doomed to live as a rat stuck in a hole. Don't underestimate the power of stories."

"You took away their lives so you could cage them! Urn is just a bigger version of the cage you built down here! Did you destroy our world just so you could cage us like animals and watch us tear each other apart? In the Low Road are you certain they weren't just hiding from you?" Percy was breathless and wasn't sure what he was saying, the words just spilt out. He was terrified and exhilarated at the same time, he found an insane joy in the danger.

The room vanished, fading away in a silver haze. Percy stood in the street of what he assumed was a city of sorts. All around him, buildings of mirrored glass stretched to the sky. People hustled this way and that all around him, they wore odd clothes and held blocks of stone or crystal to their ears. As one they all stopped moving and looked to the sky. In the distance a speck of light was approaching at an incredible speed, leaving a streak of smoke in its wake. He craned his neck to watch it. When it was directly over his head, everything died. The fire that bloomed from it obliterated everything, the people were stripped of flesh, and their bones made into ash. The force blew the mountainous structures away, leaving only the barest hint of their previous magnificence.

The devastation was total, and it stretched as far as Percy could see. A cloud hung over the city, and the sky was a dirty brown colour. Percy gawked in horror. This could not be real, why had all this occurred, and he remained untouched?

The scene vanished, and he was in the chamber again with the Stranger.

"Man-made weapons caused that carnage, many billions of them stripped the life from the surface. Petty squabbles. Ideologies. Fighting over resources when

413

cooperation would have ensured enough for everyone. I didn't do that, I couldn't have."

"But... The Trimans."

"Friarn. He hit me with everything he had, it was not enough, but it was enough to destroy his legion. Chassius, who I had chosen, who embodied the powers you now hold turned and ran, too afraid to do what had to be done to save his legion. Friarn saw what he had done and fell to his knees, begging me to put it right. That light out there is Friarn's sacrifice."

"Friarn... But Friarn had none of your power."

"Oh, I'd say you humans have something just as powerful. Despite your suicidal tendencies, collectively you have an incredible will to live. Ironic, given what I just showed you. I feed the light, but Friarn sparked it."

"Without you..."

"The light goes out. My greater part sitting on the moon is much too busy to care about a few Trimans in a mountain."

"Sacrifice... What sacrifice was Chassius meant to make?" Percy asked, suddenly afraid of the answer. Friarn smiled. Marc appeared above the font once more, no more conscious than when Percy had last seen him. "I think it's time I give you back your mentor."

Marc fell to the ground, gravity finally having its way. Percy rushed to his side, kneeling and lifting his head. He proceeded to violently shake Marc.

"Marc... Marc!" Percy yelled as he continued shaking the warrior. He begged the man's forgiveness before administering the least restrained and most enjoyed slap in history. Marc's eyes snapped open, bloodshot and panicked.

"Marc, it's me, it's fine. The Stranger let you go. We can leave."

"Leave?" Marc said. Percy saw something else in his eyes, something mad. Percy felt a familiar fear rear its head once again. "Without what I came here for?" Marc pushed Percy away and clambered to his feet. He swayed, and Percy rushed to steady him.

"I know what you came here for. You will leave disappointed." The Stranger said.

Marc shook his head, the cylindrical package appeared in his left hand, a match in the other. With his teeth, he tore off the leather and revealed the metal object underneath.

"No, I won't," Marc said, using his thumb to flip off the endcap of the cylinder. A thin fuse unwound from it. Percy gasped, immediately raising an arm to try and stop

Marc, his efforts were rebuked with a fist to the cheek. As Percy sprawled across the ground, Marc lit the match against the side of the cylinder and held it to the end of the fuse. It sparked and began stuttering, the sparks moving steadily closer to the tube. Percy wondered briefly why he had bothered arguing against the use of the armouries weapons if similar weapons could already be made in Urn.

Friarn vanished, the great silver dragon taking his place. Percy felt his heart seize with fright at the sight of it, he was sure it was even greater than before. The dragon took a deep breath before roaring, a sound so deep and powerful the cavern shook, shaking off some dust and rocks from the ceiling high above, through the door, Percy could just see the destruction it caused.

Marc froze for a moment, the fuse getting dangerously short. He returned his own roar at the dragon, not quite as impressive but not bad for a human. He threw the cylinder. Percy prayed for it to swerve away from the dragon, to be deflected at the last moment. The explosive flew straight and true, detonating inches from the dragon's head.

The explosion rocked the room, and Percy threw himself behind the font at the last moment. It launched Marc backwards, slamming him against the stone wall.

After the initial blast the room filled with smoke. The explosive was rough and unrefined, and the smoke was thick and choking, it took a long time to clear enough for Percy to see the dragon itself. The tremendous hulking beast was gone, a small figure lay in its place.

As he drew closer, he saw that the figure was female, with long black hair. Percy stopped, his feet frozen to the spot.

"Caitlin?" He asked tentatively. No, not Caitlin. Another of The Stranger's images.

Caitlin looked up at Percy weakly, a thin smile on her face. "Well… That was unexpected." She said before laughing painfully.

"You won't die surely? You're almost a god, a little thing like that… You can just brush it off, right?" Percy asked, kneeling at its side.

"Afraid not. It's not so important, I'm just a piece, and the rest will live on."

"If you die, then everyone out there will die… They'll degrade and disappear."

"They're already dead, what does it matter?"

"It does matter."

"Are you sure?"

"I am."

417

"Then perhaps you can help."

"What do you mean?"

"Your power could feed the light," Caitlin said, gasping as a spike of pain shot through her body.

"Then... I could give up my powers?" Percy's mind flashed back to the Low Road, to the terrible, hallucination-inducing worm that dwelled there, he saw the tendrils wrap its body again, he had known there that ripping the magic from the worm would tear it apart.

"I would die?" Percy asked quietly.

"You would die, yes. But they would live."

"They wouldn't live, Percy. They're already dead, they died a hundred years ago. It's time to let them fade." Marc said from his slumped position against the wall. "You can let them go. You need to live."

"Why? Why do I need to live?"

"Because you need to write my story, you need to be the one to write my legend. I need you, Percy."

"That's all you've ever needed? You didn't intend to teach me, did you? You just wanted a witness."

"At first... You became something more than that." Marc said, coughing and growing silent. Percy ignored him.

Percy laughed. It was a deep laugh that he felt in his toes.

"Of course… Of course. Of course, it would happen this way. I wanted to be the hero, and I became one." He looked at Caitlin. "But this is one of your stories, isn't it? It's not mine. I've gotten everything I wanted, haven't I? I'm just going to have to make the 'heroes sacrifice' a little sooner than I hoped."

"No matter who wrote the story, it's still very much real Percy. You have a choice, and that choice matters." The Stranger said.

"I have a condition."

"It's already done."

Percy looked up at the door where another stood. A familiar smile, a familiar face. Caitlin, as alive as The Stranger could make her. "She will live as long as the light does."

Percy took a moment to consider the choice he was about the make. He tried not to think too hard on it, fearing that if he did he would change his mind.

"Just do it."

The Stranger smiled and took his hand. At once Percy felt it, he felt himself being drained. It didn't hurt so much, it only felt like falling asleep. Before his vision turned black, he saw his family, his mother and father. Would they be proud of his sacrifice? Would they be ashamed that their son gave his life so that ghosts could go on living in a cage in a mountain? The last thing he saw was Caitlin standing in the doorway. She said something but his hearing had already gone. It looked like 'Goodbye.'

Forgive us Percy. I beg of you.

Chapter 21

Everything was dark, no light penetrated wherever he was. A scratch and a hiss and fire bloomed into life, illuminating Marc's face.

"You're dead too?" Percy asked. "Rough day, eh?"

"We're not dead, Percy. The Stranger lied to you." Marc said, his voice was still weak, and the impact had clearly taken its toll. "The light went out regardless. I expect it really just wanted to see if you were actually foolish enough to give up your life for the dead."

"But... Caitlin... Karees..." Percy stuttered.

"You saw Caitlin die. You knew that those things weren't real, just images." Marc snarled. "You were going to give your life for absolutely nothing, who would have believed my story if you were dead? I would just be another lunatic claiming that they had slain a dragon!"

"Your legend is more important than them?" Percy asked in disgust.

"Yes!" Marc yelled as though he was speaking to a simpleton.

Percy stood up and backed away from Marc.

"Just go back to Aellis, Marc. You've done what you came here to do."

"You will write the story, Percy. You will."

Two doorways had appeared in the wall of the sanctum, one bland and mundane, made from wood. The other was similar to the stone door to the sanctum with a raised crescent on one door and a flower on the other.

"I think this door is for me. I'll see you around, Marc." Percy stepped towards the stone door, and it swung open.

"Percy!" Marc called, but he already sounded far away. The door slammed shut behind him.

Percy kept walking, the tunnel was long and straight, perfectly cut and though there were no braziers or lanterns it was lit with white light. As he walked, he tried not to think about the events of the last few hours. Karees was dead. Caitlin was dead. Nothing would bring them back. He had met the previous owner of his sword, a century-old ghost.

'Are you there?' He asked, looking for some indication that he wasn't alone. His mind was silent, no strange voice replied.

Before he knew it he was sobbing as he walked, the tears streamed down his face freely and alone in the tunnel he didn't feel the need to stop himself. He wasn't entirely sure why he was crying, perhaps it was the sudden crushing feeling of loneliness, the realisation that he had left his home to find something that didn't exist and it had only killed or dehumanised everyone around him. There was no happy ending to his quest if it could even be called that. It ended with a lot of death, a madman chasing dragons and a boy crying under a mountain.

There was a light at the end of the tunnel, not the unnatural cold light of The Stranger, but the warm light of day. He let the tears dry on his cheeks as he emerged from the tunnel. The light blinded him for a moment, and when he could see again, he stood somewhere that his mind couldn't make sense of. There was a strip of ground covered in pebbles of all sizes and colours, beyond that was more water than Percy had ever seen.

The water stretched toward the horizon. There was so much water that it tried to stride onto the land, continuously washing against the rocks.

"It is beautiful," a voice said.

Percy turned, sneering at the familiar mask.

"Oh, do not be like that," Mask said. He reached up and removed the mask. The man underneath was dark and handsome with nearly black eyes. Chassius smiled.

"I thought you might vanish with the rest of them. I had hoped."

"Well... No, I am a little different. I never died. I just ran like a coward."

Percy shrugged and looked back to the vast ocean before him.

"We're beyond the mountains."

"Yes."

"How did you get here?"

"The second tunnel in the Low Road. No longer a dead-end. Monsters are gone, worm dead."

"The way is open then," Percy said, taking a seat on a flat, wet stone, looking out across the water, attempting to understand what he saw, the closest comparison was the Great Lake in the centre of Urn which was merely a puddle compared to this.

"It is going to cause war."

"Well, firstly, it's not my problem. Secondly, it won't if they don't know about it. No one uses the Low Road."

Chassius shook his head.

"I am afraid that your friend Marc will soon be travelling it again."

"Well, there's his proof I suppose. War it is…"

"What will you do now?"

"A big question. You know, I might just go home. Not really sure I'm cut out for this whole 'hero' thing. I'm not even sure it exists, really."

"Well… You tried to save the dead… Instead, you uncaged the living. I think perhaps you should try and redefine what a hero is."

"What does that mean?"

"Your story is not over young Percy. There is a whole world out there, and you should be the one to explore it."

"The Stranger lied to me. It said that my death would ensure their existence. They disappeared, and I lived."

"I know… It made sure I saw. A torment I suppose… I am sorry Percy, it should not have been you."

Percy was silent for a long time, he felt his face grow warm, and his eyes became blurry again. "But why?" He mumbled. "I was ready, I was willing. One life for so many. It seemed so simple."

"I shall not pretend to know The Stranger's mind. I'm not sure it knows its own. It's split into so many parts that insanity was always inevitable."

"No," Percy said resolutely. "I can't accept that. I can't accept that I went through everything because of a maddened god. It has meaning. It must."

Chassius reached down and plucked a pebble from the ground. With a practised flick of his wrist, he sent it skipping across the water until a wave devoured it. He shrugged wearily.

"I have spent so long pondering the Stranger and its intentions. So long wandering Urn and swearing vengeance upon it. I believe that until now I never saw my own weakness. I took my legion into its lair and failed its test."

"Test…" Percy echoed.

"Someone worthy would fight for others even when a victory is impossible. But that force of will does not make it any less impossible. Friarn and my legion died long ago. The Stranger used them. It used your warg friend. I do not know how many fools like me had to fail and doom our kin before you finally ended the cycle."

Chassius suddenly turned to Percy, there was a kind of passion in his eyes.

"Forget it." He said, waving a hand to illustrate his point. "Forget the Stranger. Forget Urn. There is so much more. More land, more Low Roads. More people waiting for the saviour that the Stranger couldn't be. Or chose not to be. Perhaps there are people still living in the darkness of their burrows."

A long time seemed to pass. The wind stung Percy's eyes and chilled him, forcing him to hug himself for warmth. Eventually, he rubbed his eyes.

"Perhaps," Percy said, standing again. "But I don't think I should do so alone."

"I am flattered, but I have my own places to be. I might be centuries old, but now that the Stranger has no hold on me I can return to Trima and rebuild."

"With all due respect Chassius, I wasn't referring to you. If I never see you again, then I will be eternally grateful."

"Good luck," Chassius said with a small smile.

Chassius left, striding along the strip of the beach before disappearing, Percy hoped it was the last time that he saw the ancient. Percy sat for a long time, watching the waves as they charged the pebbles only to be dashed against them, the gentle breeze licked his cheeks with salt, and somewhere he thought he could hear the song of a bird. What would he find if he did go forth and explore this new world, a world that had not been filled with the fancies of a bored deity? Was the world dead like it had claimed? Was Urn the only place where life still existed?

Soon these lands would be flooded with Urnians and Urn itself would erupt into war over the rights to the new world, if he wanted to see things that no one else had, he would need to be quick. He had no resources, no coin, little experience and only a modicum of bravery. It could very well be suicide, diving head-first into a dead world. He could end his journey early on at the bottom of a ravine or in the stomach of some horribly mutated beast. Madness, surely it would be madness. Percy sighed and forced himself up, off the rock. He brushed himself down. Percy was going against the odds, so he decided to even them a little.

"Sounds like I need a mercenary." He said to no one, turning and starting back towards the tunnel.

Being a hero is a tricky, sticky and sometimes dirty business that you should not wish on your worst enemy.

But someone's got to do it.

ABOUT THE AUTHOR

Alex Rollings is a teacher, a writer, and self-proclaimed master of sarcasm. He has nothing else to say on the matter.

Printed in Great Britain
by Amazon